Red Lips & White Lies

Breathtaking

USA TODAY BESTSELLING AUTHOR
BELLA MATTHEWS

BREATHTAKING

A KROYDON HILLS LEGACY NOVEL

RED LIPS & WHITE LIES
BOOK SIX

BELLA MATTHEWS

Copyright © 2025

Bella Matthews

All rights reserved. No part of this publication may be reproduced or transmitted by any means, electronic, mechanical, photocopying, recording or otherwise, without the prior permission of the publisher, except in the case of brief quotation embodied in the critical reviews and certain other noncommercial uses permitted by copyright law.

Without in any way limiting the author's exclusive rights under copyright, any use of this publication to "train" generative artificial intelligence (AI) technologies to generate text is expressly prohibited. The author reserves all rights to license uses of this work for generative AI training and development of machine learning language models.

This is a work of fiction, created without use of AI technology. Resemblance to actual persons, things, living or dead, locales or events is entirely coincidental. The author acknowledges the trademark status and trademark owners of various products referenced in this work of fiction, which have been used without permission. The publication/use of these trademarks is not authorized, associated with, or sponsored by the trademark owners.

This book contains mature themes and is only suitable for 18+ readers.

Editor: Dena Mastrogiovanni, Red Pen Editing

Proofreader: Emma Cook | Booktastic Blonde LLC

Cover Designer: Val, Books and Moods

Interior Formatting: Brianna Cooper

SENSITIVE CONTENT

This book contains sensitive content that could be triggering.
Please see my website for a full list.

WWW.AUTHORBELLAMATTHEWS.COM

To the boy who made me a mommy.
I'm in constant awe of the young man you've become.

This one is for you.

Few things in the world can settle your heart like a kiss on the forehead from the man that you love.

— BELLA'S SECRET THOUGHTS

CAST OF CHARACTERS

The Kings Of Kroydon Hills Family

- **Declan & Annabelle Sinclair**
    - Everly Sinclair - 29
    - Grace Sinclair - 29
    - Nixon Sinclair - 28
    - Leo Sinclair - 27
    - Hendrix Sinclair - 24

- **Brady & Nattie Ryan**
    - Noah Ryan - 26
    - Lilah Ryan - 26
    - Dillan Ryan - 23
    - Asher Ryan - 17

- **Aiden & Sabrina Murphy**
    - Jameson Murphy - 26
    - Finn Murphy - 23

- **Bash & Lenny Beneventi**
    - Maverick Beneventi - 26
    - Ryker Beneventi - 24

- **Cooper & Carys Sinclair**
    - Lincoln Sinclair - 19
    - Lochlan Sinclair - 19
    - Lexie Sinclair - 19

- **Coach Joe & Katherine Sinclair**
    - Callen Sinclair - 29

The Kingston Family

- **Ashlyn & Brandon Dixon**
    - Madeline Kingston - 30
    - Raven Dixon - 14

- **Max & Daphne Kingston**
    - Serena Kingston - 23

- **Scarlet & Cade St. James**
    - Brynlee St. James - 29
    - Killian St. James - 27
    - Olivia St. James - 25

- **Becket & Juliette Kingston**
    - Easton Hayes - 34
    - Kenzie Hayes - 28
    - Blaise Kingston - 18

- **Sawyer & Wren Kingston**
    - Knox Kingston - 22
    - Crew Kingston - 19

- **Hudson & Maddie Kingston**
    - Teagan Kingston - 23
    - Aurora Kingston - 20
    - Brooklyn Kingston - 15

- **Amelia & Sam Beneventi**
    - Maddox Beneventi - 28
    - Caitlin Beneventi - 25
    - Roman Beneventi - 23

- Lucky Beneventi - 21

- **Lenny & Bash Beneventi**
  - Maverick Beneventi - 26
  - Ryker Beneventi - 24

- **Jace & India Kingston**
  - Cohen Kingston - 22
  - Saylor Kingston - 21
  - Atlas Kingston - 14
  - Asher Kingston - 14

For family trees, please visit my website
www.authorbellamatthews.com

Part One

Lennon

Chapter 1

Umm . . . If I have to put on pants with actual buttons and a zipper, the answer is no.

—Lennon's Secret Thoughts

Okay . . . I get it. Sometimes a good cry is called for. Cathartic, almost.

I'm as happy as the next girl to have my heart ripped out and stomped on, but I need to be ready for it. Preparations need to be made. Like when I'm reading a great book. I'd go as far as to say there are few ways I'd rather spend a night off than curled up on my couch with some rocky road ice cream and a beautiful love story that will make me laugh and cry and kick my feet all in one book. I mean, really . . . does it get better than a sexy, swoony man who falls deliciously in love with some sassy heroine and sweeps her off her feet, broken parts and all? Add in some really great sex and absolutely gut-wrenching drama, and I'm all in. The chocolate, marshmallowy goodness doesn't hurt either.

And now I'm nostalgic for a good book and a good cry.

But that's not what I got tonight.

No . . . I'm sitting here, sobbing over the end of an *Avengers* movie.

Who does that?

Apparently, I do.

And I'm doing it with bad ice cream. Well, not bad, really. But not rocky road because the store didn't have any today. Can I send one of my security detail out for better ice cream? I mean, that would probably cement me firmly into the diva category, so I'm going to say no, but I bet it would make me feel better.

Instead, I dig a frozen peanut butter cup out of the pint I had to settle for, more than slightly annoyed with the less than top-tier candy. And yes, I do realize I sound like a spoiled brat . . . or maybe a serial killer.

I can imagine the headline now—*Princess Set Fire to the Store When They Didn't Carry her Favorite Ice Cream.*

A ridiculous laugh bubbles up my throat until I snort the most unladylike sound I may have ever made. My mother would be ashamed of me if she were here now. She'd also be a ghost since she's been dead for three years. So there's that.

And that thought has laughter mixing with big, fat, crocodile tears streaming down my face.

What the hell is wrong with me?

The door to my flat opens with a flourish only my brother Atticus is capable of, and I look up over my spoon and confirm my assumption. My older brother looks horrifically mortified by the sight of me. "What the fuck is wrong with you?"

I shrug, wipe my nose on my sleeve, and lick the melting chocolate from my spoon.

Atticus, the asshole, slams the door shut behind him and throws a paper sack at my face. Reflexes demand that I swat it down with my spoon and watch innocently as chocolate ice cream splatters across the room, causing another sob to catch in my throat.

There's never a reason to waste chocolate . . . even bad chocolate.

"Okay." He points at me from where he's standing in all six foot two of his judgmental glory. "That's enough." I sniffle, and the big bully tries to take my ice cream from me, but I hang onto it for dear life.

Who knows what I'm capable of doing in the name of chocolate?

After quite the glare-off, I eventually give in and let him wrestle it away. Mainly because Atticus's resting bitch face is way scarier than mine, and I've been told mine is pretty bad. But also because it's not like it was rocky road. "You . . ." He picks up the paper sack from the pharmacy down the street and holds it out in front of me. "Take this. Get your little ass up and go into the bathroom."

"My ass is not little. I'll have you know I have a great ass." Years of dancing has given me that. It's also given me ugly feet, but you take the good with the bad.

The asshole shakes the sack in my face until I snatch it out of his hand. "Do as I say, Lennon."

"What are you talking about?" I peek inside the sack, and my jaw drops. "I'm sorry . . . What in the fucking hell is that?"

Does my brother shrink back when I scream like I've just seen my first penis and don't have a clue what to do with it?

No.

He shakes his head like I'm daft.

"Retract the claws, little sister. I'm here to help, and apparently, the first step in helping is yanking you out of the denial you've planted your *perfect* ass in. I mean, that ass could actually be my first point. It *is* getting bigger."

"Atticus—" He's right. I want to claw his eyes out. But that's before my next tear falls. "My ass is not getting bigger." I kinda wish it would. I mean, who wouldn't want to look like J.Lo in jeans? Mine is great, but hers is perfection.

"Umm . . . hello, mood swings. It's like you're making my argument for me. You're moody as hell. Crying over everything. You look like shit, and you've put on weight for the first time ever in your skinny bitch life. And my God, woman. Your tits are huge."

"Eww. You're my brother, and we're not those kind of royals, you dick." I finally stand up and smack his chest.

"Listen, the blind guy who lives beneath you can see your tits have grown. There's no missing them. They're massive. That's not normal, Lennon. Take the bag into the bathroom and pee on a goddamned stick, so we can figure out how to tell Dad and Grandfather you're going to have to move the wedding up to this year."

Pee. On. The. Stick.

Oh, bloody hell.

All the blood rushes from my head, and I grab Atticus for balance.

I can't be pregnant.

No. *No.* No.

"Whoa there." His strong hands hold me steady as I sway on shaky legs. "Come on, little sister." Before I realize what we're doing, he's walked me to the bathroom and opened the door. "In you go."

The air whooshes in my ears like I'm holding my breath under water while I stand—staring at the bag in my hands. "I can't be pregnant," I whisper more to myself than to him.

"Listen. I'm not sure what bullshit Monty is feeding you, but condoms aren't 100 percent effective. Now take the test, and we'll figure the rest out." He pulls the bathroom door shut, and I drop the bag on the marble vanity and stare at my reflection in the mirror.

Suddenly, the one staring back at me isn't one I'm familiar with.

Flushed cheeks and gaunt, tired eyes stare back.

I pull my sweater over my head and cup my boobs in my hands.

Holy shit. He's right.

They're bigger.

It's like I've lost all the weight in my face, and it's gone right to my tits.

I turn and want to sob again. The fucker is right. The weight is evenly distributed between my ass and my tits. Thank God we're between shows. I'm not sure who'd be more pissed . . . the costume designers or my dance partner. As a principal dancer with the London Ballet, we get weighed weekly, and there's no way they wouldn't notice this.

What the hell?

I yank the box from the sack and manage to wave off the impending panic attack and the bile building in my stomach.

Am I really going to pee on a stick? As I open the pink and white box and dump out the tests, I'm pretty sure that's exactly what I'm about to do.

This is so bad.

Unfathomably bad.

A minute later, when three tests, the instruction sheet, and a pair of ridiculous plastic gloves are all scattered across the counter, it becomes a little too real, and that panic attack is starting to look like a solid plan.

Plastic gloves . . . really?

I stare at the offending objects and decide I might as well get this over with. Maybe I'm wrong. Maybe I'm just extra hormonal and need to lay off the ice cream . . .

Because the other option is far worse than going on a diet.

I stare at the three sticks and wonder why three.

Do I need to use all of them?

What if they don't all agree?

What then?

Apparently, what I should have been wondering was how to do this without making a mess. *Guess I should have used the gloves.* I lay each test flat on the counter and wash my hands while I wait the required seven minutes for three stupid sticks to decide my future.

There are so many reasons why this can't be happening.

Good reasons.

Valid reasons.

Frightening reasons.

Number one—my family is going to kill me. An unmarried, pregnant Windsor princess would not be acceptable. Not even a little bit. Not to my father or my grandfather. My late mother was the daughter of the king of Mornea, and my father is a royal prince of Elwyn. Appearances have always mattered.

Once my mother died, my oldest brother Rhys became the heir apparent to the throne of Mornea. And that spotlight shines bright and wide on our entire family. What I do reflects on them as much as me.

Number two—Montgomery Hastings V, Duke of Mornea. My fiancé . . . On paper if not in any other way. I don't even like the man, but that didn't seem to matter to either of our families when our marriage was arranged.

Number three—ballet. My career. My escape. I can't dance if I'm pregnant. I hang my head and close my eyes, hoping this is all a bad dream. Maybe the ice cream was spoiled and this is some kind of reaction to food poisoning.

Atticus bangs on the door, reminding me this is very much real life.

"It's been nearly fifteen minutes, Lennon. Either you come out or I'm coming in."

Terrified and spiraling out, I crack the door open and step back, allowing my overprotective big brother to push inside and grip my shoulders in his hands. "Did you do the deed?"

Apparently, I'm already too stressed to try to decipher his question.

When Atticus was little, he used to try to make Rhys and me learn whatever made-up language he'd come up with that day. Rhys, being the oldest and most serious of the three of us, wanted no part of Atticus's nonsense, but I'd always try. Half the time, I'd fail miserably, but I was never as smart as Atticus. Pretty sure I'm still not. My brother is a genius. "Which deed?"

"Don't play daft." He looks around, stopping on the counter. "Uhhh . . . Lennon."

"Don't," I warn him and close my eyes, not ready to face this reality he just force-fed me. "This is your fault."

"Nope. Sorry. I'm not taking the blame this time. Like you said, we're not those kind of royals."

I slide down to the floor as the walls close in around me, pulling my knees protectively up to my chest as shock sets in. "I don't know how this happened."

I try to count back in my head, but it's a struggle. I'm going to blame that on the way the room is pirouetting like it's opening night of *Swan Lake*.

"Pretty sure you know exactly how it happened. The bigger question is when? I didn't think you were actually screwing the douchey duke. Or should I say I thought you might have been the only one in the entire country *not* screwing him, because I'm pretty sure he's worked his way through every other titled woman in Europe."

My eyes bug out of my head. Yes. My future husband is a fuckboy. Not like I had anything to do with picking him out. Our marriage was arranged when we were children, and the news was broken to me when I turned eighteen. Lucky for me, according to the contract, we didn't have to get married until I turned twenty-five. Even luckier, he decided he wanted to go to law school and pushed the wedding back another year.

Not that any of that even matters at the moment.

"I'm not sleeping with Monty, you asshat," I snap. "I never have."

Confusion settles in my brother's kind green eyes.

He may be the smartest guy in nearly every room he walks into, but this has him stumped. Serves him right for assuming. He slides down next to me and plants his ass on the radiantly heated tile floor beside mine. "Oh . . . Now *that's* a problem."

I drop my head to his shoulder. "You can say that again."

I have to marry Monty. It might as well be written in unbreakable stone.

Mornea needs this marriage.

Monty's family is the most politically influential in the country, and with the way the anti-monarchists have been growing in strength lately, this is one of the best ways to strengthen our family birthright.

No pressure or anything.

"So . . . do you know *who* the daddy is?" I throw my elbow into Atticus's gut so hard, he doubles over. "Sorry. Geez. I guess I could see how that sounds bad," he wheezes.

"You think?" I bite back and drop my head back against the wall so hard, it reverberates down my entire body.

"Is he—does he . . . fuck, Lennon. How the hell am I supposed to ask this?"

With my eyes closed, I picture the only man who could be the father. "No . . . he doesn't know. I didn't even know."

Atticus leans his head against mine. "Is he from London or Mornea?"

I can see why he'd only consider those two countries. The one I work in and the one I've spent my life living for. But the world is so much bigger than Mornea and London.

"He's from Kroydon Hills," I whisper softly. *Hesitantly.* Atticus knows what that means.

"You didn't," he gasps like every gossipy ballerina I've ever worked with. "You dirty little dancer."

"Shut up." I sit up and turn toward him. "Seriously, what am I going to do?"

I'm not sure what scares me more.

Telling my parents.

Telling Monty.

Or telling *him.*

"Well . . ." Atticus grins, and I brace for whatever the hell he's about to say, because I know it's going to be outrageous. "Exactly how long has this buttery little croissant been baking in the oven?"

I rub my temples. "My brain hurts. Could you try to reel the crazy in for just a few minutes . . . *please?*"

His eye rolls should have their own translation guide, he has so many. "Exactly how pregnant are you, kid?" When I wince, he groans. "Like mid-summer night's sex pregnant?"

I look him in the eyes and fight back the tears that are back and dying for their chance to drown me. "More like snowstorm pregnant."

"It's the middle of fucking August, Lennon. What the hell?"

"Don't yell at me. I don't get regular periods. I never have. The doctors always said with my rigorous dance schedule and the way I couldn't gain weight, it was normal. They weren't worried about it. And it wasn't like I was having sex, so I wasn't worried about it either," I yell back at him as my tears burst free. "I haven't even seen him since that night. How am I supposed to call him and tell him I'm what . . . ?" I try to do the math. "Four . . . maybe five months pregnant?"

"Oh, sweetie . . . this isn't a call kind of thing. This is a your ass on a plane, heading to America kind of thing."

I think back to that night and wonder why I'm even surprised.

Of course I'm fucking pregnant.

Leave it to Maddox Beneventi to have super sperm.

Chapter 2

Five Months Ago

Some days, I think about running away. Then I remember how much I hate running, and I book that ticket faster than you can say first-class.

—Lennon's Secret Thoughts

*I*n hindsight, maybe flying across the Atlantic Ocean without my royal protection detail wasn't the best move. But in my defense, they'd have never let me come on such short notice, and I wasn't in the mood to be told no.

I mean, I was thinking it was better to ask for forgiveness than permission.

I'm fairly certain that train of thought has officially gone off the tracks and wrapped itself around a big, old tree. RIP.

The steam melting the snow from my now possibly totaled rental car would definitely be Exhibit A in that argument. I guess you could consider the tree the front of the car is basically wrapped around Exhibit B.

Who am I kidding?

My attempt at freedom with a splash of independence definitely screams epic fail.

My head throbs, but I'm pretty sure that's from the culmination of everything. The accident. The past week. My entire future. It's all just a damn headache. Most of which I was trying to escape.

Escape . . . Well, that's a joke.

There's no escaping my world.

Powerful people would never let that happen.

Those same people who silently pull the strings behind closed doors will never allow my strings to be cut. Who am I kidding? I'm lucky if I'm not summoned home the minute they get wind of me ghosting my protection detail and, God forbid, hopping on a commercial flight to America.

I'm not sure why I thought this weekend would be different. I flew halfway across the world to surprise my friend, managing to do so without my security team or any help from anyone else, *thank you very much,* only to have my plan thwarted by a snowstorm and a damn deer in the middle of the road.

I wasn't expecting the brakes to lock when I tried to avoid hitting the deer.

If you choose to look on the bright side, I didn't hit the deer. The tree, however, didn't fare so well. Bambi stares back at me from outside the car for a hot second before looking at the tree and the steaming car. She probably realizes just how screwed I am and doesn't want to be here to witness my impending breakdown—and that sucker is barreling down on me right now, so it's happening soon. Naturally, she prances rather contently right off the road and into the woods without a backward glance.

At least one of us is walking away from this with their dignity intact.

Mine is questionable at best at this very moment.

My phone rings again, and Maria's name flashes across the screen.

Oh hell. She's got to be having a cow.

Royal protection officers don't generally like it when you leave the country without them. Especially ones who have been with you for a decade. But really . . . it's not like she's ever had to pull her gun on anyone. How much can my safety be in question if no one even knows I'm here?

And it's just one weekend.

I'm fine.

This is fine.

We're all going to be fine.

Maybe if I keep telling myself that, I'll believe it.

Maybe not, but it's worth a try.

As far as pep talks go, definitely not my best.

Okay . . . I can do this . . . Time to think.

I send Maria to voicemail and power off my phone. I can't think with her blowing it up, and that phone hasn't stopped since the pilot announced we could turn them back on after the flight.

After a few measured breaths and a little finger and toe wiggling to test out my limbs that are numb with shock, I'm pretty sure I'm okay. The car . . . not so much. And who knows—maybe I'm overreacting. Maybe this isn't so bad . . . maybe it's just a little fender bender that my overly dramatic brain is blowing way out of proportion.

Wouldn't be the first time.

Doubt it will be the last.

Only one way to find out.

The snow gently falls around me as I step out into the freezing street and immediately regret the beautiful blue

Louboutin's that make my ass look incredible and my legs look longer than your average eleven-year-old's. What can I say? I'm short and love heels. It's not like I dressed for a snowstorm, a spooked Bambi, and an irresponsibly placed tree.

Fuck my life.

I wobble on the slippery asphalt as I slowly make my way to the front of the car, with absolutely no clue what I'm looking at but feeling like I should at least look—*right?* The giant tree-shaped dent and the actual tree still there confirms my fears. I'm screwed. "Bloody hell. I broke it."

Can this night get worse?

I should know better than to ask. Headlights approach and slow as a sleek, black SUV drives by . . . because why wouldn't they?

The first time I've slipped my security in years and I'm going to be murdered on the side of the road in Kroydon Hills, Pennsylvania, like the focus of some bad true-crime podcast.

I can see the headlines now—*Her Royal Highness, Princess Lennon Allison Windsor Dead at Twenty-five. The Cause—Her Own Stupidity*. My father will be so proud.

Backup lights flash in front of me, and I cringe.

Umm . . . the only thing worse than a car driving by me on a dark, snowy road in the dead of the night is one stopping and backing up because they think I look like easy prey.

Damn it.

I'm going to die.

I will never ditch Maria again if I survive this.

Never.

I take a hesitant step toward the driver's side of the rental, hoping I can make it to my purse and my phone before this crazy person pulls out a gun.

How's the crime rate in Kroydon Hills?

Big boots crunch in the snow, and I look over my shoulder to find a man in a dark coat and black boots having gotten out of the SUV.

This is not happening.

Time to move... I open the door.

"Lennon?" That voice... It stops me dead in my tracks.

Oh, you have got to be kidding me.

I might actually prefer a murderer to the man that voice belongs to. The one I would recognize from an ocean away. The same one I could go a lifetime without seeing again and it would still be too soon.

"Maddox?" I'm not sure why I bother asking when I know deep down in the depths of my soul, it's him. He seared himself there years ago when he stole a little piece for himself. "What are you doing here?"

I turn back and slide on black ice... because everything about this night isn't already humiliating enough. And of course, Maddox's fast hands catch me before I'm ass first in the snow like a real-life prince charming.

Only this man is no prince.

More like a rake.

"Careful now, *piccola principessa*. Pretty sure *I* belong here. You, however, last I heard, were in London. Or was it Elwyn?" His brilliant blue eyes harden, watching for a reaction.

Typical Maddox.

Always watching and waiting.

After a moment, his stare softens, and he gently pushes the hair from my face. "What happened, Lennon?"

As his thumb brushes the bruise no doubt blooming on my cheek, I pull back, already overwhelmed by his touch before remembering he's the only thing keeping me steady on this damn ice.

Seriously, universe... It couldn't be anyone else?

"Come on." He tugs me closer, and my body heats and freezes simultaneously. "You need a hospital."

"No," I snap. If one more person tells me what to do, the last string of the single fraying thread of sanity I have left will snap, and I won't be held responsible for the chaos that ensues. "No hospital. I'm fine. Just a little shaken up. If I go to the hospital, this is news. And it can't be news."

He looks around, piecing it all together with his brilliant blue eyes. "Where's Maria?"

"Still in London." My cheeks flush, knowing she'd never have let this happen.

His beautifully crooked smile tugs at his wicked lips. "Ditched the bodyguard, huh? I'm impressed."

"Don't be. If she were here, I doubt my rental would be wrapped around a tree." I shake my head, then whimper when it hurts. "If I'm lucky, she hasn't already told my family I left without her."

Maddox's smile fades as his gaze sharpens, and his hold on me tightens. No doubt, he feels the adrenaline leaving my body. Years of dancing, of honing my craft and developing long, lean, strong leg muscles, mean nothing when you stand on shaky feet after an accident. And right now, I think this man might be the only thing keeping me upright. "What are you doing here, Lennon?"

"I wanted to surprise Gracie," I softly admit.

Grace Sinclair Wilder is one of the few things Maddox and I have in common. We're nearly opposites in every way, but my sweet best friend loves us both. She had her triplets earlier this year, and I've been trying to find time in my ridiculous schedule to get here since.

A pang of longing hits me when I think about how it's taken me nearly three months, but with my schedule, earlier wasn't an option. Lucky for me, Grace understands. Few people in the world truly get the rigorous schedule of a professional ballerina unless you've lived it. Grace and I lived it. We met as flat mates her first and only year dancing with the London Ballet. But that was before she went and got herself a hot hockey-god husband and five ridiculously stunning kids. Twins, then triplets. Apparently, everything in America really is bigger, including pregnancies.

I was with her the first time she went into labor, but this time, I was onstage an ocean away.

"Pretty sure Gracie's asleep by now." He looks over at my car and shakes his head, while I take the unguarded moment to really take him in. *My God*. It's been years, and if it's possible, he's even more mouthwatering today than he was back then. Older. More distinguished. He was a sexy young man, but now . . . now he's a devastatingly gorgeous man. Dark hair a touch too long frames his face and brilliant blue eyes. Chiseled cheekbones and a jaw that could be cut from granite are covered by a dusting of day-old dark stubble. Stubble that looks so damn sexy, my panties dampen, thinking about what it would feel like against my skin. And those eyes . . . The only thing more beautiful than Maddox Beneventi's eyes is his smile, and that's like finding a pot of gold at the end of a rainbow. If you see one, count yourself lucky because he gives them out sparingly. "Come on. Let's get you out of the cold."

He slips out of his leather jacket and slides it over my shoulders, and that scent. The clean, crisp scent of sandalwood and bergamot mixed with something else. Something entirely Maddox—dark and cool and delicious. It wraps around me, soothing me like a weighted blanket. "I can't just leave . . ."

"Do you trust me, Lennon?"

Trust? This man may as well be a complete stranger for how long it's been since I last saw him. Last touched him or talked to him. The memory of the night still hurts worse than the time I tore my ACL. Physical pain heals. Mental pain lasts much longer.

But yet . . . he's no stranger. He never could be. In some ways, I let him know pieces of me no one else ever has. I trusted him in ways I've trusted very few people. *Son of a bitch.*

"I'm not sure . . ." I murmur, regretting every choice I've ever made that's led me here.

Maddox cocks a dark, full brow as if he's daring me to say more, but he doesn't loosen his hold. *Nope.* This fucker just waits me out, holding me close and keeping me safe.

I might question my decisions, but I'm not sure he's ever questioned a single thing he's done. He oozes confidence and charm in a way most men exude stupidity.

"Fine . . ." Damn him. "In this particular instance . . . on this particular night . . . I guess I trust you."

A smirk slides into place on his handsome face.

Yup. He's a full-blown wanker.

"Such a ringing endorsement, *principessa*." My breath leaves me in a whoosh as I'm lifted in his arms, and said wanker carries me to the car like he'd carry his bride over the threshold.

Only I can never be his bride.

"What the hell are you doing?" I yelp as I throw my arms around his neck and hang on for dear life.

"Getting you out of here before this turns into an international incident." Carefully, he sits me on the leather passenger seat of the Escalade, then reaches across and buckles my seat belt as I fight to ignore the way the brush of his fingers against my body still sends just as many goosebumps racing across my skin as they did the very first time I met him a million lifetimes ago. "Do you need anything out of the car?"

I nod, unable to speak.

Scared of what I'll say.

Or what I won't.

Maddox doesn't look impressed, but he doesn't call me out on it either. Just shakes his dark head and shuts my door.

This man . . . He's so utterly different from the perfectly posh prep schoolboys I've known. The ones whose mummies and daddies sent them to Eton so they could learn to manage the family fortune. The ones who've never gotten their hands dirty or worked their muscles in any place other than the polo field. The ones who would never dream of manhandling a princess. The safe, boring, socially acceptable ones.

The ones I've never wanted.

A few moments later, he tosses my suitcase in the backseat and hands me my purse before he fires off a text and throws his vehicle into drive.

"What about the car?" I look back at the cute little red sports car and the tree nearly ripping it in half. Guess I should have gone with an SUV.

"I'll take care of it. Let me get you out of here and get a doctor to the house to check you out—"

"Maddox—"

"I didn't ask a question, *piccola principessa*."

I find bossy obnoxiously annoying on most people.

Why does it have to be so damn hot on this man?

Maddox
Chapter 3

Five Months Ago

I stand off to the side of my living room with my arms crossed, watching as Doc checks Lennon over with my fat, lazy bulldog sitting guard at her feet. Doc has worked for my dad for years and understands the need for discretion. And for the right amount of money, he doesn't hesitate to make a house call in the middle of the night, snowstorm be damned. The two speak in hushed tones I can't quite hear while her eyes keep straying to mine. It's as if she's making sure I'm still here. Like she's scared I'll leave. Or maybe just scared.

And that right there . . . the thought of her scared.

Fuck. I hate that.

Hate that I wasn't there to protect her.

Hate that even after years of not seeing this woman, that's still where my mind goes. And now she's sitting in my condo an entire continent away from where I last saw her. From where she's supposed to be happy with her preppy douchebag of a duke.

Lennon fucking Windsor in my condo.

Not where I thought my night was gonna go.

Everything about this woman is delicate and utterly feminine. From the long lean lines of her body to the way her waist nips in and her hips flare out . . . She's the face of every fucking wet dream I've had for five years, and her creamy skin would turn a flaming shade of red darker than even her hair if she knew. She's beautiful, and she knows it . . . She owns it. And since the day we met, there was something about her that's brought out every single protective instinct I've ever had.

She used to be full of fire and light, burning brightly for the world to see. So fucking magnetic, you couldn't look away. Lord knows I never could. But now . . . now that light has somehow dimmed, and I fucking hate it.

I shouldn't give a shit. It's been years since the last time we were together, but that doesn't matter one bit. She's always been the one who got away. The one thing I've regretted not going after. The only thing I didn't fight for. But she's also always been the one person who pissed me off like no one else ever could—because she's the one who walked away. The one who begged me not to chase. Not to follow. The one who asked me to forget.

Like that was ever going to happen.

But for her, I'd try.

Maybe one day it'll work.

I watch the way she clings to the dark-blue blanket wrapped around her delicate shoulders and want to shake her. Who wears a silk dress and heels in the middle of a snowstorm? And who ditches her security when she does it?

Lennon Windsor, that's who.

After a few more minutes, Doc picks up the cup of hot tea from the end table and hands it to her. Lennon's hands shake as she accepts it, but she sips it like a good girl.

Doc looks satisfied before he catches my eye and nods his head toward the door so I'll follow.

I rest my hand on the door, making sure he understands

he's not leaving until he fills me in. Pretty sure he already knew that though. "Is she okay?"

Doc's glasses slide down his nose as he looks back at the couch and grins.

Yeah . . . Lennon has that effect on people.

She pulls you in and charms the hell out of you without even realizing she's doing it.

"The princess is shaken up, but she's fine. I'd feel better if she'd let us get a scan, just to be safe, but that's just my old age wanting to make sure a young woman is fine. Do I think it's really needed—no, I don't. My professional opinion is that poor girl has had a hell of a night and a hell of a scare. Just watch her tonight, and if anything changes, call me."

The knot in my chest loosens with his words, and I offer him my hand. "Thanks for coming out in the snow."

The old man smiles. "I wondered what it would look like when the Beneventi *principe* finally fell. Guess I've seen it now."

"Whatever, old man. Don't fall on the ice and keep this between us, got it?" I pull his hand in and squeeze a little harder than necessary, and that fucking grin grows.

"No one but your dad will know, Maddox."

I drop his hand and open the door. "Understood."

My father's already aware. I learned a long fucking time ago it was better to clue Sam Beneventi in before he found things out from other sources. And when your dad runs one of the most powerful crime families in the country, there're always other sources trying to use your information to get on his good side. He may not have raised my brothers and me to take over the family business, but he raised us to respect *it* and its ways.

I lock and bolt the door behind Doc once he's gone, then cross the room until I'm in front of Lennon and Meatball, who's now curled up next to her with his brown and white bowling ball of a head resting in her lap, sleeping peacefully. Lucky fucker. "How are you feeling, *piccolo principessa*?"

Long black lashes kiss her cheeks as she blinks up at me with wide eyes that would put the greenest emerald to shame. "I feel like I've told you about a hundred times I hate when you call me that."

She has . . . but she lies. She loves it. Always has.

I ignore the taunt and sit next to her, careful not to get too close, even if I want to. A part of me wants to do more than that, but I beat that motherfucker back and lock it away in a basement. She's probably scared and tired, and somewhere packed away in my cold, dead heart, I know that. "So you wanna tell me why you're really in Kroydon Hills?"

"I already told you—"

"Yeah, I heard you. You're here to see Gracie. I call bullshit. If you were just here to see Gracie, your trip would have been planned. Maria would have been with you, and Grace's husband would have picked you up from the airport. Do they even know you were coming?" I stretch my arms along the back of the couch until my fingers hover over her soft, red hair. "What's got you running, Lennon?"

"Who says I'm running, Maddox?" She sips her tea, and my jaw clenches as her engagement ring catches in the light.

"I didn't hear a denial . . ." Fuck, this would be easier if I wasn't focused on another man's ring on her fucking finger. If a diamond can cut glass, I wonder if it could slit another man's throat . . .

"Whatever." She rolls those pretty eyes and turns her body to face me, leaning more into my hold than she probably meant to. And a years'-old spark of electricity hums to life between us. One that's spent half a decade lying latent. "I needed to get away for a little bit, and I haven't met the babies yet, so I thought I'd come surprise Grace. There. I admit it. I'm a shitty friend." She throws her hands in the air and blows out a breath of frustration and maybe guilt. "Happy now?"

"You're not a shitty friend. You could have flown to a private island and hidden out with a margarita in your hand and no tan lines for a few days." *Now that's a pretty picture I'd like to see.* "And there wouldn't have been snow or deer either. But you didn't. You came to see Grace." I give in to the urge and wrap a lock of soft hair around my finger, tugging gently. "What had you running, princess?"

"A lot of people call me that, but the only time it sounds like a sneer is when it's falling from your lips," she counters. "And I wasn't running. I just didn't feel like dealing with everyone for a few days." She holds up her phone, and her lips tilt up, and the power behind her pretty smile nearly takes my breath away. "And I just convinced Maria to give me three days without saying a word to my family, so there's that."

"She's probably scared she'll lose her job."

Lennon's fingers dig into Meatball's fur as she scratches behind his ears, and I swear the dog smiles between snores. "Maybe. But I wouldn't let that happen."

I watch as she rubs her hand over my lazy dog's head, and that damn ring might as well be bathed in a neon fucking light. "You're still wearing his ring."

Her beautiful face flames a crimson red as she looks at her hand with devastation locked behind her eyes, and fuck if that doesn't do some serious damage. I can handle tired Lennon and annoyed Lennon. I can even handle scared Lennon. But broken . . . I haven't left her alone for years to see her broken. Not when I would have done anything in my power to have kept her whole. "I don't have a choice."

She's a goddamn broken record. I've heard that same sentence so many times.

"When's the wedding?" I ask like a masochist who likes

the fucking pain. And maybe I do. Why else would I still care?

I'm not sure she even realizes she's doing it, but she spins her ring round and round on her finger. Like it's a foreign object . . . *still*. After all these years. "We'll announce next month that it will be the following May."

Damn.

I've taken punches from MMA champions that have done less damage.

"Does he treat you right?"

"I hardly ever see him outside of events we're required to attend together. I live my life in London and have no idea what he's doing back home." Lennon bristles, looking as regal as I've ever seen her look before she drops the front with a sad smile. "Is this really what you want to talk about?" She brings her bare feet up onto the couch and tucks her pink polished toes under my legs. Guess she's still sensitive about her dancer's feet.

Like any man would care if her feet are pretty or not.

"How about you tell me what you've been up to? Like where are your roommates? Do you live here alone now?"

I look at the penthouse through her eyes and wonder what she sees. At one point, five of us lived here. But not now. "Nah. Not yet. I have one roommate left, but they're gone for the weekend."

"Did you ever finish designing your dream house? The one you were working on . . . Maybe put that architecture degree of yours to good use?"

"I did." Pride settles in my chest, remembering the first time she and I talked about my plans. Lennon was the only person I'd told back then. "I bought the land a few years ago and broke ground last fall. It's under construction now. Should be done mid-summer." I pull her feet into my lap and dig my thumb into her arch until she moans.

Fuck, that sound . . .

At this rate, there's no way this ends well.

It can't.

"That's not fair," she murmurs and rests her head on my other arm on the back of the couch. "I can't think when you're doing that."

"Whoever told you I fight fair lied, Lennon." I only ever fought fair for her because she begged me to, but telling this woman no wasn't something I could ever do.

Lennon leans forward, resting her elbows on her knees, bringing her so fucking close, I can smell the mint in her shampoo as her long hair falls in pretty waves over her shoulders. "How's your family?"

Damn, she smells good.

I feel like we're moving pieces across a chess board with the strategic way we're feeling each other out. Both protecting our queen.

Strategic.

"Good. Caitlyn's pregnant." I watch as her eyes double in size.

"Your little sister? Oh my . . . How did *your* dad handle that?"

"Yeah. He didn't handle it well." Pop doesn't ever handle something being out of his control well. Sure as shit not his baby girl getting pregnant before she got married. I think about the fucking chaos my family's been through this year and all the ways I made that shit worse. "Callen's the father."

"Your best friend?" she gasps, and there goes my mind, right back to all the other ways I'd like to make her gasp for breath.

I should have taken her to her hotel.

This was a bad idea.

"Dad wasn't the only one who struggled with the news."

"I guess so. Callen and you were thick as thieves. How did that go?"

"Not great at first, but we're working on it," I admit.

She nods as she takes that bomb-drop in. "Wow. When's she due?"

"Next month." I switch my fingers to her other foot and watch her eyes close again. This woman is so damn responsive. She's also dangerous, and there aren't many things I consider dangerous. "How about you? How are Atticus and Rhys?"

Lennon's shoulders relax at the mention of her brothers. "Well . . . after Mom's death, Rhys had a bit of a reckoning. Being next in line to the throne is very different from being second in line. The weight is different. But he's holding it well. He doesn't smile as much as he used to, but then again, we all have our parts to play for the crown, and this is his. And Atticus . . . well, he's doing his thing. I'm not sure exactly what that is, but it makes him happy, so I don't question it. I'm pretty sure he's putting his brain power to good use as one of Rhys's top advisers, much to Grandfather's dismay. He doesn't really take Atticus seriously. Which I think is part of my brother's evil plan. The less people expect of you, the less you have to do. When Mornea gets to be too much for Atticus, he'll come stay with me for a few days and fuck his way through the dancers in my company. The girls and the guys. He's not picky."

My proper little princess loves to surprise me with her dirty mouth.

"And how about you, Lennon? Are you happy?" My chest tightens as the words hang heavy between us. In all my adult life, I've cared about exactly one woman, and she's sitting here on my couch, with another man's ring on her fucking finger. Let her at least be happy.

"I'm happy right now." She reaches out and grabs my face,

and I'm not sure if she's trying to convince herself or me. Either way, that fucking ring might as well be burning my fucking skin.

"Don't." I grab her wrists and hold her there. Not sure if I'm pulling her closer or pushing her away.

Lennon ignores the warning in my voice and traces the lines of my face with her thumbs. I know I *need* her to stop, but fuck if I *want* her to. "It was always so easy between us, Maddox," she sighs softly.

"It was never easy, princess. You were always his," I remind her, but I'm lying. To her and myself.

"I've never been his . . ." she whispers, and there's the lie.

I know she means it. I know she thinks that's true. And in some ways, it is. But that fucking ring on her finger is still there. And that goddamned wedding date still looms. "I hate him. I hate my life. I don't even like ballet anymore. It's just a means to an end. As long as I'm performing in London, I can live there and have some semblance of freedom . . . from my family. From the crown. From Monty."

Red blurs my vision at the mention of his name.

"Don't, Lennon—"

She ignores my sharp words and climbs into my lap, framing my face with her hands. "I've missed you, Madman."

Fuck . . .

"What are you doing, Lennon?" I groan but pull her closer instead of pushing her away.

She drops her forehead to mine. "What I should have been doing all along."

"You said no. You turned me down. You fucking begged me to walk away, Lennon. Walking away from you once was the hardest thing I've ever done. Don't ask me to do this." Christ. I've never been able to say no to this beautiful girl.

"My memories of those nights with you are what have gotten me through the past five years. But we . . ." She nibbles her lip, and I know what she's thinking. I can read her mind and her body better than I can read myself. Time and distance haven't faded a fucking thing between us. "Maybe this is why I'm here. The universe's way of putting me where I need to be. I know the hell I'm going home to after this weekend. Give me one more memory to take with me. Give me this weekend, Maddox. Give me memories to last me the rest of my life. Memories I can have for when that's all I'm left with."

She pulls back and rubs her soft thumb under my eye. "Please."

Lennon
Chapter 4

Five Months Ago

"Please," I beg softly . . . so softly, it's barely an echo of a whisper caught in the night. It hangs there between us, beaten and battered by the years and distance I asked him to give me. And now, I'm asking for more. "Maddox . . ."

No sooner does his name fall like a plea from my lips before he seals his mouth over mine. Strong, warm hands cup the back of my neck and angle my head as he steals my breath from my lungs and swallows the whimper that's ripped from my throat with the first delicious taste.

God. I've waited a million lifetimes for this.

I dig my fingers into his hair, and Maddox pulls back. A fire behind his eyes burns brighter than a towering inferno as he seems to hold himself back. Every muscle locked like it's taking all his strength.

"The ring comes off," he growls, and *ohmygod* . . . It's like those angry words have a direct line to the hypersensitive nerve endings in my body. My pussy clenches, and my nipples peak, and my mind goes dark.

What ring?

I'm not sure I know my own name right now, I'm so tied up in him.

"Lennon . . ." he warns, and it snaps me out of my sex-starved stupor.

I rip the diamond from my finger and drop it to the table, not caring where it falls.

Not now.

Not here.

Not with him.

Maddox's brilliant blue eyes deepen and darken, full of a lust I know is matched in mine, and that's it. That's the only warning I get before his mouth is back on mine. Demanding and dominating. Controlling me in a way no one ever has. And I let him. I give in and give myself over to him.

His tongue pushes into my mouth, and he swallows my desperate moan, meeting it with his own guttural growl. Fuck. This is happening. It's not a dream I'm going to wake from *alone* in a cold sweat.

My body tenses, and Maddox drags his teeth over my earlobe. "Relax, Lennon. You're safe. I've got you."

His voice, deep and dark, calms my suddenly frantic nerves, and I momentarily forget . . . Who we are. Why we can't happen. A strong arm wraps around me, lifting me from his lap and lies me down on the couch beneath him. Maddox towers over me before sliding to the floor on his knees. "I'm gonna need you to relax, baby."

"How am I supposed to relax when you're looking at me like that?"

"How am I looking at you?" I'm not sure if it's the wicked grin on his beautiful face or the devil in his dark eyes or the unspoken promise in his words, but my God, it's intoxicating, and I want him more than I've ever wanted anything before.

His big hands possessively slide up my legs until confident fingers find their way between the silk of my dress and my bare skin. His rough touch against my thighs stoke the already burning fire, and my breath catches in my throat with each new touch until I'm positive I'll hyperventilate before the night's over.

Maddox licks and sucks every inch of my neck as his hands continue their exploration. My body doesn't know whether it's coming or going as anticipation courses along every inch of my hypersensitive skin, and I forget how to breathe.

I'm suddenly blissfully ignorant of every reason this shouldn't happen, and there are many . . . Instead, I focus on him. On his hot breath and warm fingers. On his weight and his body. On the way I've always felt with him.

Safe.

Protected.

Wanted.

It's a heady sensation and not something I've experienced before.

"Tell me you want this." One hand slides possessively around my throat, and his thumb presses down on my thrumming pulse as he tilts my face to his. "I need your words, *picolla principessa*." He kisses the corner of my mouth before dragging my lip between his teeth and biting down.

And holy hell . . . that earlier spark of electricity fires and crackles between us, lighting my body up in ways I didn't know possible.

"Please, Maddox. Yes. I want this." I wrap my fingers around his wrist and hold him there. I hold his eyes for what feels like a lifetime . . . one of many I'm positive I've had with this man, but in reality, it's one single second frozen in time. Over before it started. Kind of like us.

But this moment . . . It's one of those moments I know, with unquestionable certainty, I'll never recover from. But

I'd rather spend one night in his arms and live a lifetime broken than spend that same lifetime never feeling this . . . with him.

I lean over and wrap my arms around his neck as I press my lips to his and suck his tongue into my mouth. "I want you. Right here. Right now. I want this. Us. No regrets."

His pupils blow wide with need, and a delicious, guttural groan works its way up his throat.

"Do those words work for you?" I whisper against his lips.

We both know this is it.

This is all we get.

This night.

This weekend.

The question is will he take it.

Maddox's eyes shudder closed, and I worry I'm losing him.

Damn it . . . My next words are going to either win me the battle or lose me the war.

"Maddox . . ." I sit up so we're face-to-face and pull my dress over my head. The white and blue silk falls to the floor, and I watch his chest shake from the strain of holding back as he gets his very first look at me without my clothes. Yay for my expensive lingerie addiction. Thank you, La Perla. "I can't give you forever. But I can give you what no man has ever had. I can give you me. Please take it. I want it to be you."

His face shifts as he tries to decipher my words before I watch delicious possessiveness wash over him when he finally understands their meaning.

"How?" he growls.

I flatten my palms under his old West End t-shirt and drag my nails over his abs. "If it couldn't be you, I didn't want it to be anyone else."

"Fuck, Lennon. You can't tell me that," he rasps and grips my face in his hand.

My body shakes under his touch. So utterly desperate for him, I'm ready to explode when his fingers slide along the edge of my panties. He teases me over the silk as he trails warm, wet kisses down my neck.

A needy moan spills past my lips.

I need more.

"Your skin is so fucking soft, *principessa*." His words . . . his voice . . . the feel of his hands on me, they're all too much. Heat pools in my belly with frantic anticipation. "Eyes on me, Lennon. Watch me. Stay with me."

I hadn't even realized I closed my eyes, but my God, when I open them, the look in his does me in. He pushes his fingers under the silk of my panties and hisses when they slide along the bare lips of my pussy.

"So fucking wet. Tell me this is for me."

I nod and whimper and tremble as his thumb slides around my clit without making direct contact.

My legs shake as he teases me. So close but not enough.

"Maddox . . ."

"Shh . . ." he coos and finally presses a finger inside me.

Stretching me. Playing me until my body clenches around him and practically purrs from the overwhelming intense sensation.

"Fucking drenched for me, Lennon." He pushes me back against the couch and drapes my legs over his shoulders, and I don't have time to hesitate. Don't have time to overthink. I'm immediately overwhelmed with a million sparks coming to life as I curl my fingers in the dark hair curling at the back of his neck and moan, long and without a care as he presses his face against the expensive silk of my panties. His tongue licks a long line up along the silk, and chills break out over my heated skin.

"Maddox," I plead and beg, no longer sure what I'm asking for.

Just knowing whatever it is, he'll give it to me.

"I've got you." He inhales me one last time, then pushes the silk aside and flattens his tongue.

Oh. My. God.

"Please, please, please," I beg, knowing exactly what I want now. I rock my hips against his face, knowing I'm going to have beard burn tomorrow to remind me that tonight is real. This is real. *He* . . . is real. "I *need* . . . I need more."

Maddox growls against my sex as he does it again. *And again.* Tasting me. Teasing me. Soothing the ache and creating a whole new one until I'm writhing under him. Unsure of anything other than I want more.

More time. More of this. More Maddox.

Just more.

The orgasm teases in the distance, building powerful and beautiful.

A storm just out of reach but threatening destruction.

"For years, I've dreamed of you. The taste of your cunt. The feel of your body. What you'd sound like the first time you come on my tongue. My cock. Gonna need you to come for me, *picolla principessa*. Give me what no one's ever had."

I tremble and moan and drag his face back to my throbbing clit.

"That's my girl," he growls, and that's it.

The sparks explode, raining down around us in a beautiful kaleidoscope of destruction.

His words . . .

The power of it all.

Threatening to burn the world around us until I can no longer think or speak.

I can only feel, and *my God*, I feel fucking everything.

I may only have tonight with Maddox Beneventi, but

that's all he's going to need to eviscerate me. He fucks me with his fingers and his tongue and his words.

His brilliant blue eyes stay locked on mine as my juices coat his face.

And I have no doubt this image will stay with me forever.

He sucks my clit between his lips as I chase my orgasm, edging closer with each tease of his teeth. With every touch of his thick fingers inside me.

My knees shake, and my heels dig into his back.

Scoring his skin.

I tremble with each new stroke.

My body lighting up like it was made for his pleasure, and he plays it like he's done so a thousand times. Teasing me, over *and over*. Stealing my breath and maybe another piece of my soul.

"Maddox . . . please," I moan, desperate for more.

"Patience, Lennon. I've waited forever for this . . ."

He edges me. Teasing me over and over and over again. Each high closer than the one before but not close enough. Until my vision darkens around the edges, and I'm not sure I can take it anymore.

"Please . . . *please* . . . *please*," I plead and thrash, and damn if his eyes don't light up, loving it.

"Please what?" His wicked grin is dark and delicious, and I want to lick myself off his face . . . so I do. I grab his face and lick his lips, then let him devour me. "Please make me come, my dark prince."

Maddox pulls back, satisfied, then slaps my pussy, and I cry out, throbbing, practically crying, but not from pain . . . No . . . from pleasure. I'm on the edge of ecstasy.

So close but not enough.

Until . . . *oh God*, he finally scrapes his teeth over my throbbing clit, and the shower of sparks from earlier is nothing compared to now.

Color explodes behind my eyes.

Firing everywhere while I shatter and scream as he works me through my orgasm, refusing to stop until he's wrung every last drop from my trembling body.

And when he stands like a golden fucking god and pulls his shirt over his head, with his wicked grin firmly in place on his handsome face, I know I've made a mistake. One night will never be enough to soothe the heartbreak standing in front of me. But I'll be damned if that's going to stop me from wringing every single second of happiness I can from what little time I have.

Maddox Beneventi is going to save my life or ruin it.

And I'm not sure I care which it is, so long as it's him.

Maddox
Chapter 5

Five Months Ago

I carefully tug my t-shirt over Lennon's naked body and hold my hand out for her to take while I hold my breath. This woman has no fucking clue the power she has over me. A power I've never given anyone.

Thank fucking God, she takes my hand in hers and lets me guide her up the stairs in silence. It's not that either of us is uncomfortable, more like we're both hanging on by a quickly fraying thread.

Her hand is in mine, her taste on my tongue, and her expensive, spicy, flowery perfume is clinging to the air. Basically, I'm ready to attack her like a dog in heat if I don't manage to keep myself under control, and that's not gonna happen. She deserves better than that.

I swear to God, I eye the marble staircase with each step we take, weighing the discomfort with the instant gratification I'd get from fucking her right here, right now. But I've waited too long to be with this woman, and it's her first time. I can't just screw her against a wall.

A virgin.

How the hell is this beautiful, intelligent, sexy woman a goddamn virgin?

Back in the day, everyone assumed we were fucking, and call me an asshole, but I let them.

It was easier that way. No one blinked twice at the thought of me fucking a princess. But if they'd known we were just hanging out, they all would have questioned it. They'd have known it was more.

I wasn't ready for that then, and by the time I was, we were through.

But five years is a long time ... And she's never ...

We stop outside my bedroom door, and I slide her long hair over her bare shoulder, her body so small, my shirt's fallen down on one side. Lennon leans back against the wall and digs her hands into my hips just above my jeans as she pulls me to her. "What's behind the door, Beneventi?"

I drag my lips down her neck, hunger and need fighting for equal dominance. "A bed, *principessa*. A big one I plan on worshipping you on in so many ways."

Lennon's gaze sharpens, and her nails dig into my skin. "How many women have you worshipped on that bed, Maddox?"

"You jealous?"

She drops her head back against the door and pulls me closer until I'm crowding her. "Of them having you while I couldn't? You're fucking right, I'm jealous."

I drag my lips over hers and wrap a hand around her throat. Not cutting off her oxygen but holding her tight enough for her to feel it. To feel the honesty in my next words. "I don't bring women here. I never have. This is my home. It's my safe space, and I've never let anyone in it before tonight."

Her lips form the cutest fucking O. I slide my hand under my t-shirt covering her incredibly toned legs, then cup her sex, swallowing her moan before dragging my finger along the soft lips of her bare pussy.

"I like seeing you jealous. Like seeing you feel a little of what I've felt whenever I've had to think of you with him." I lick up her neck and along her jaw, loving the way she squirms and gasps. Loving how fucking responsive she is. I tap my finger against her still-drenched sex, then drag it through her wetness and circle her clit. "Now that I've had a taste of your sweet cunt, I might not ever let you go." We both know it's a lie. There's no way for us to work. But right here, right now . . . she's all I see. "I need you laid out on my bed, soaking my sheets, while I learn every fucking inch of your body." I push my finger inside her swollen pussy, and she trembles. "I need to take my time if I'm going to learn exactly how to make you scream my name. I want to know what you feel like strangling my cock when you think you can't take another second. When you're begging for release. I want to know what you taste like coming on my cock. I want it seared into your brain, so you never forget I'm the first man who ever got you there."

"Ohmygod," she moans, and I slide a second finger deep inside her perfect pussy and curl them until I hit that perfect spot that makes her legs give out and her arms grasp for purchase.

"Open the door, Lennon, or I'm going to stop being a nice guy and fuck you up against it." I pull my fingers out and trace the lines of her lips. "And trust me, princess, you're going to take every fucking inch of me and beg for more. So the question is do you want it out here." I press my fingers down on her tongue, and she sucks like it's the most delicious thing she's ever tasted, and goddamn, does my dick like that. "Or do you want it in there? Because either way, you're taking my cock, aren't you, Lennon?"

She nods silently and reaches behind us to open the door.

The second it swings open, I lift her from her feet, and she wraps her legs around my waist as I spin us around and press her back flat against the bedroom door. Lennon grinds down against my hard cock, and I'm pretty sure I could come just like this with her just like that.

I've wanted this woman for so fucking long.

I cup the most perfect ass that ever existed, and Lennon melts into me. Her delicate curves press against me. All the soft curves of her body against the hard planes of mine.

"Last chance to change your mind," I warn, and she takes my lips with hers and bites down.

"Don't you dare offer me that again, Maddox Beneventi."

I smack her bare ass, then squeeze it, my finger sliding down until I find her wet sex, and she moans into my mouth. Something about it is different. Something about that sound breaks the control I hold so fucking tightly.

"Fuck, Lennon . . ." I wrap a hand around her throat, and those emerald eyes fly frantically to mine, glittering excitement staring back at me.

She swivels her hips slowly in time to a rhythm only she can hear and tugs my hair until we're so close, we're sharing our breaths.

"I want to feel you inside me. Filling me. Stretching me. Branding me," she pleads.

Fuck, do I want that too.

"You're gonna feel me for fucking days, princess. Every time you move, you're going to feel me." And just that thought has my cock hard as steel. I don't just need to be inside her. It's more. It's visceral. I need to lay claim to her fucking body and her fucking soul.

"Good," she pants. "I need it to last a lifetime."

Fuck . . . Does she even realize what she's asking?

I adjust my hold on the goddess in my arms and cross the room in two long strides before I lay my princess out on my bed. My shirt rides up her thighs until it's barely hiding her from me. Her long, red hair pools around her beautiful face, and her pale, creamy skin lies in stark contrast to my black comforter, leaving her nearly glowing in the silvery moonlight.

She's incredible.

A storm brews behind her lust-filled eyes as they stare back at me, and I claim her mouth, needing to silence the noise in my head.

Slowly, I drag my tongue along her soft lips and take her mouth, swallowing each sweet, sexy little sigh.

I'm drunk on her taste. Her sounds. The way she feels in my arms. The way I always knew she'd feel.

I don't have one single delusion that one night will ever be enough.

Fuck, one lifetime wouldn't be enough.

But I know better than anyone that family comes first.

And Lennon will never go against her family.

This is all we get. One night. So we better make it last.

I stand from the bed and pull my shirt over her head and love watching the way a pretty pink flush works its way all the way down her chest. Her pale nipples peak, and my mouth waters to taste them.

"Do you like what you see, Mr. Beneventi?" she smiles, and I'm a fucking goner.

This woman's happiness has always mattered to me.

It's why I've stayed away.

I'd burn cities to the ground for her happiness, and she'll never fucking know it.

Lennon sits up and stares at my chest. "Looks like you're overdressed."

My cock presses against the metal zipper of my jeans, trying to force free of its confinement. "Then how about you do something about it, princess?"

She crawls on her knees to the edge of the bed and presses her lips to the base of my jaw, while her nails trace the ink on my skin. "You are a beautiful man." Her fingers trace my family crest that's inked on my chest, then lower to a scripted font in Italian.

"What does it mean?" she asks as she unbuckles my belt and jeans.

If we were in daylight and Lennon was thinking straight, I have no doubt she'd be able to translate my tattoo. And maybe I like that she's so sex drunk, she can't, because a smile tugs at my lips. "*È meglio vivere un giorno da leone, che mille giorni da agnello.*"

"It's better to live one day as a lion than a thousand as a lamb?" she questions back as she slides off the bed.

"I'd rather be feared than protected."

Her long lashes flutter as my words sink in.

I want to tell her I can protect her. But I don't.

I'm already holding tightly to the last frayed threads of sanity I've got left tonight.

And when Lennon tries to wrap her fist around my cock, all the blood in my body rushes right to my dick before she licks the fucking tip and smiles.

Fucking smiles as she looks up at me.

Her tongue swirls around the head, hesitantly at first, getting a feel for it, and I'm going to fucking hell because this woman on her knees is going to be what I see every time I get myself off for the rest of my miserable fucking life.

"You gonna be a good girl and suck my cock, baby?"

If I thought there was a chance Lennon wouldn't like my words, I had nothing to worry about because those green eyes sparkle as she takes me into the back of her throat and gags. Fucking gags but keeps going.

A white-hot, scorching shock of need builds at the base of my spine and threatens to take me down. "You look so fucking pretty on your knees for me, *picolla principessa*."

I gather her silken hair in my hand and wrap it around

my fist, tugging as her pouty pink lips stretch around my cock. Tears build in her eyes, and she moans, stroking my shaft and working me up and down.

She's a vision like this.

On her knees in front of me.

Her beautiful body completely bared to me, wanting and wet and so fucking ready.

"Fuuuuck . . ." I growl when she swallows me down and slides her hand between her own legs, already needing relief I refuse to let her give herself.

"No fucking way are you playing with that pussy tonight." I pull back, and she whimpers with frustration. "Your orgasms are mine for as long as you're here. You don't come unless I say you come and unless I'm making you come."

"But . . . what if I can't come from sex?" she whispers.

I cup her face in my hand. "Then whoever you're having sex with should be fucking shot."

I pick her up and toss her onto the bed, then fist my cock as Lennon laughs. It's the sexiest sound I've ever heard. And when she brings her knees up and leans up on her arms, staring right into my eyes and smiling, I know I'm fucking screwed.

Five Months Ago

Maddox hovers over me like a dark and dangerous god. His black ink stretches over stacked, corded muscles I want to trace with my tongue. And suddenly, I can't think of anything but this man's weight on me.

At least not until he rolls a condom down his enormous cock with a deliciously filthy look in his eyes. Because why would this man be blessed with anything less than a monster cock? Sweet Jesus. He was always going to ruin me, but I'm a little concerned he might actually break me.

He drags his dick through my soaked pussy, teasing me until I'm trembling and aching and pleading for him. "Maddox... Please..."

His lips tip up into a sexy, crooked smile, completely pleased with my frustration, and I whimper desperately. "I gotta make sure you're ready for me."

That velvety voice grows raspy with each wicked word, and my pussy pulses with the need to be filled. "I'm ready," I pant and drop my legs open. "Please, *please*, please."

He leans down and drags his tongue up the length of my pussy, and I shake and scream until he crawls up my body and covers my mouth with his. Our tongues dance a wicked dance. Each stroke intensifies my need until I'm teetering on the sharp edge of a sword disguised as my sanity. Unsure how much more I can take but more than willing to follow him to the ends of the earth to push my limits.

Maddox wraps strong, thick, deliciously calloused fingers around my neck and presses down the tiniest fraction. Not cutting off my airway but slowing it, leaving me at his mercy. Lost in the moment. *Lost* in him.

"Eyes on me, *principessa*. I'll try to be gentle."

I drape my arms around his strong shoulders and stare into his eyes. "Don't be."

As if something snaps inside my dark prince, a deep, visceral sound works its way up his chest as he pushes the head of his cock deep inside me, and what little breath I have left leaves me in a whoosh.

Pain sears, threatening to split me in half as Maddox dominates my mouth, whispering words of worship between every taste. Every touch. Until the pain subsides and the pleasure warms me. Until I can't think of anything but us, but this, but how much more I want. "So fucking beautiful, baby. Breathe, Lennon."

Only then does he finally move. Slowly pulling out, dragging his cock along every inch of my sensitive sex until he's pushing back in again even slower.

Until I'm gasping and moaning.

Until agony battles ecstasy for control.

Ecstasy wins.

Maddox owns my body, bending it to his will.

Grinding into me.

Slowly. Sensually.

Until my tense muscles relax and the painful stretch turns to scorching-hot pleasure.

With each new inch, I melt against him, begging for more.

Soothingly sexy words kiss my lips as I dig my nails into his shoulders.

Dying to get him deeper.

Clawing to get him closer.

Because I still need more ... I want it all ... Everything.

What I wouldn't give if it meant I could keep him.

"Stay with me, Lennon," he growls, sensing my warring thoughts. His hand tightens on my throat and lights up my soul as he finally seats himself fully inside me, and we both suck in a breath with the absolute perfection of the moment. Of us.

He releases my throat and moves his hold to my face. To my jaw. Holding me hostage while our tongues dance a savage duet. His hips snap against mine, and I moan, loud and long, dragging my nails down his muscled back until I'm gripping the strong, powerful globes of his ass. Urging him on. Needing him impossibly deeper.

"Maddox..."

"Fuck, Lennon." His lips pepper my jaw. My neck. My collarbones. Until he dips down and licks a lazy circle around my nipple, and my back bows off the bed.

Electricity courses through me, and I pull him closer—*deeper*—as he sets a punishing rhythm. With every strong thrust of his hips, his incredible body owns mine. Fucking me harder and harder until I'm not sure where he stops and I start. Until I'm not sure I can take any more. Until I'm chasing a high I've never felt.

Only then do his hands slide under me and grip my ass. Lifting me. Holding me. Changing the angle and driving into me again and again until my vision dims, and all I see is him.

"Tell me you're mine, Lennon." Maddox's brilliant blue eyes burn like an electric flame as they lock on mine.

I crash my mouth to his, giving him all of me and the only answer I have to give.

"Yours," I whisper, both of us knowing it's the truth wrapped in a vicious, cruel lie.

Intense and overwhelming and threatening to destroy us both.

I'm back on that sword's edge, balancing.

"Yours," I whisper again as he fucks into me over and over.

It's heaven and hell.

Purity doused in lies.

But even if only for tonight, I'm his . . .

"*Mia principessa* . . ." he whispers, and a beautiful flame erupts, burning blue in his eyes.

I gasp his name on a silent scream as my body tenses, and my orgasm washes over me, warm and heavy, drowning me as I cling to him.

Giving me life and taking it away in one moment frozen in time.

My dark prince tenses as he follows me over the cliff with my name falling from his lips, a sacred benediction. One I know I'll hear every time I close my eyes in my daydreams and nightmares.

We fall to the bed, a tangle of limbs, heavy breaths, and heavier thoughts. No space between us until Maddox climbs out of bed and gets rid of the condom. He comes back with a warm washcloth, bringing a silent tear to my eye. No one would ever believe how kind and gentle this man can be, but with me . . . he's never shown me any other side.

And once he climbs back into bed, I pull him down to me, needing to feel his weight again. I run my nails through his thick, dark hair and hum until he relaxes and eventually begins to doze off. "Don't leave, Lennon."

His words are whispered. Barely spoken. But they're there. And they break my heart.

Because I can't give him that.

Even if he's given me this.

"I'll be here when you wake up, my prince," I whisper back.

I keep my promise.

I'm still here when Maddox wakes up, and we *woke up* a lot last night.

I mean . . . technically, we *woke up* a few times this morning too.

I laugh at my own joke as I walk into his closet to grab myself a shirt. I'm not sure what time he got out of bed, but he kissed me and told me he had to take Meatball for a walk. That was exactly one red-hot shower ago, and my heavens, did it feel good. I considered waiting for him, but honestly, I'm a professional ballerina at the peak of my profession, and somehow, muscles I didn't know I had hurt. Not necessarily in a bad way, but in a *I need a little break* way. I search through his closet until I find a pile of neatly folded West End t-shirts and slide one on before I make my way to the kitchen in search of a cup of tea and maybe a slice of toast. I don't remember the last time I ate. Oops.

Each step I take reminds me of exactly how many times we *woke up* last night, and I smile as I step into the kitchen, then scream.

"Fuck!" one of two huge men yells back at me while the other smiles.

I scream again, and the fucker glares. "Christ, woman. Shut up."

My eyes dart around the kitchen, searching for a knife or

a phone before the door slams open, and Maddox and Meatball rush in.

He glares at the men and cups my face, looking completely unfazed. "You okay?"

I try to focus on him but can't tear my eyes away from the laughing twat leaning against the counter with a cup of coffee in his hand. They're both tall, dark, and almost as handsome as the man currently holding me. That's when I see it. The resemblance. "Let me guess . . . these must be your brothers?"

"Ohh," the shorter of the two mocks me. "She's British."

I growl.

Yes, I may have spent the last decade in London, but I also spent the majority of my early childhood in a boarding school in Switzerland. My accent is weak at best, and I am neither British nor Swiss. I consider myself a citizen of Mornea or possibly Elwyn. Maybe both. But calling me British is like calling Americans Canadians or vice versa. We don't appreciate it. But I don't bother arguing because something tells me it would simply fall on deaf ears.

I shake my head and slide further behind Maddox, hoping to block the shorter one's view of my legs, because he's leering, and I won't be held responsible for kneeing him in the nuts if he looks any harder.

First, he calls me British, then he acts like a lech.

That's two strikes against him already.

"What the fuck are you doing here?" Maddox groans.

The tall one smiles. "Seeing if you want to go a few rounds at Crucible." He bounces on his toes like an excited child. "Got a couple of inches of snow last night, so the gym should be almost empty."

"Looks like you're busy though. You gonna introduce us?" He lifts his chin toward Maddox, and I pull at the hem of my t-shirt, wishing I'd put my dress back on.

Maddox turns and looks at me, as if to ask permission.

Well, okay then. I step around him and enjoy the way Maddox keeps his grip possessively on my hip as I offer the tall one my hand and force a smile. "Lennon."

He takes my hand in his and grins back at me. "Rome. Nice to meet you, Lennon."

"Ahh . . . the middle brother," I muse, thinking of the stories I've been told.

"Wait," snaps the one I'm assuming is the baby of the family, Lucky. "Lennon. Like Gracie's roommate, Lennon? The princess?"

Lovely. So much for staying under the radar.

"Yes. But I'd appreciate it if you could keep that quiet, please."

"Don't tell anyone she's here, or I swear to God, I'll rip your arm from its socket and beat you to death with the bloody end," Maddox threatens in disgustingly graphic detail.

"What the fuck is up with you banging princesses, brother?" Lucky asks, and Rome coughs and looks away while I tilt my head and study the youngest Beneventi, attempting to decipher his words.

"I'm sorry." I step out of Maddox's hold. "What?"

"Fuck," Rome mutters, and Lucky's smile grows.

"First the Elwyn princess and now you." He shrugs like he didn't just blindside me, and I have an overwhelming urge to wrap my hands around the collar of his shirt and shake him, size be damned. I've got adrenaline on my side because right now, I feel murderous. "I am the Elwyn princess."

Rome shakes his head slowly, and bile fills my throat.

"Nah . . . the other one."

The room spins as I close my eyes.

No.

This is not happening.

I have two girl cousins in Elwyn. The heir to the throne and—

"Lennon—" Maddox reaches for me, but I sidestep him.

"Please tell me you didn't," I plead with quiet fury, but the answer is right there in front of me. It's in his eyes. "My cousin?"

"Lennon—" He grabs my shoulder, but I shake him off before I realize I didn't *just* shake him off. My entire body is shaking with rage.

"You slept with my cousin?" I repeat, begging him to lie to me. "Oh my God. I'm going to be sick."

"*Principessa*," he murmurs as I walk past him, and the two clowns behind me suck in simultaneous breaths.

"Don't," I warn him. "Don't call me that."

The doorbell rings, and I take the chance to slip into the powder room and lock the door before I scream like a maniac in front of all three of them.

I stare at the reflection in the mirror and don't recognize the person staring back at me.

There was no way this weekend was going to have a fairytale ending. But this . . . ?

This is like a Brothers Grimm fairytale.

And I played my part, like a fool.

Present day

"And then what?" Atticus asks from next to me on the floor.

I think back to that day . . . to everything we said and everything we didn't.

To the hurt in Maddox's eyes and the heartbreak that had to be reflected in mine.

And I look at my brother, no longer lost in the memory. Just drained from it.

"I left. The doorbell was Maria. She'd agreed not to tell Mom and Dad because she knew she was hopping on a plane to get to me. Maddox may have saved me the night before, but Maria saved me that day. In twenty-four hours, I was saved more than I ever had been in twenty-five years." I drop my head to my hands, more nauseated than I was finding out Maddox had slept with my cousin. "Who's going to save me now, Atticus?"

"Oh, there's no saving you from this, little sister. You've screwed the pooch this time. And that dirty dog is a mob prince. Definitely not the kind of royal you're allowed to marry." He stretches his legs out in front of us and crosses one over the other, then pushes up to his feet and holds his hands out for me. "Come on. Up you go."

"Tell me something I don't know," I whine but take his hands and let him pull me up. "Dad and Rhys are going to kill me." My chest tightens, and anxiety clogs my throat. "And oh my God . . . Grandfather. What is Grandfather going to say?"

"The king is going to lose his shit," Atticus announces excitedly, like he's watching some ridiculous soap opera and not talking about my life. "Oh, please let me be there when you tell him."

"Oh my God, I hate you." I drop his hand and storm into my kitchen, slamming cabinets as I search for the chocolate bar I hid a few weeks ago. "This is serious. I'm supposed to marry Monty in what—nine months?"

Atticus laughs, and I throw an apple at his head.

"What?" he asks as he ducks. "Come on. Nine months? Kind of poetic, if you think about it."

I open the fridge and yank out the produce drawer, and

there, under a questionably old bag of celery, is my chocolate bar.

I found you, you little wanker.

When I slam the door shut, Atticus is looking at me with a worried gaze. "We'll figure it out, okay? No need to go commando on the apple. I don't need one of your guards rushing in here to save you and accidentally shooting me. This face was not meant for scars, little sister."

I break off a piece of dark-chocolate goodness and close my eyes.

Pregnant.

There's not enough chocolate in the world to make this okay.

Part Two

Lennon
Chapter 7

The obnoxious ringtone Atticus programmed in my phone for Monty as a joke wakes me a week later. For a hot moment, I consider throwing it across the room and watching it shatter. What do I really need a phone for anyway? I can order food online now. It's not like we have to call anymore.

I've barely slept a wink since Atticus forced me out of denial, and last night was the worst by far. How could I, knowing today is the day? *D-Day.* Also known as the day I see my doctor and either confirm or deny the grand total of twelve pregnancy tests I've taken since Atticus threw a sack at my face. My hope was that one of them would come back negative and give me a smidgeon of hope. News flash—none did. But I'm still trying to stay optimistic. I wouldn't go so far as to say it's working, but I'm trying . . . I guess that's something.

Even now, the weight of the world—or at the very least, the crown—is crushing me.

I sit up and grab my literal to-do list from my bedside table and cringe.

I like to write things down. I always have. There's something about physically checking things I've accomplished off an actual list that gives me a much-needed serotonin boost.

Hell, I've been known to add tasks to my list after I've completed them, just so I can drag a line through the words. Don't judge me.

This week's is a mile long and an ocean wide.

And is singularly focused on one thing.

Preventing an international scandal.

Talk to my father—Not yet.

Advise the king—Umm . . . Also not happening. Not yet. Not ever, if I can help it.

Tell my fiancé—hell no. I'd rather walk naked through a hill of rabid fire ants. Okay, so maybe it's time to lay off the Nature channel.

Break the news to the father—I mean . . . is this one negotiable? Do I have to tell him?

The phone rings again. Only this time, it's Maria.

MARIA
> Confirming our itinerary for the day. You have an appointment at eleven, after which we're driving to Mornea. Is there anything else I should be aware of?

LENNON
> The appointment is confirmed. I'm not sure if we're going to Mornea. I'll let you know later.

MARIA
> Copy.

Monty's name flashes as soon as Maria messages, and I stuff the phone under my pillow. I'll answer him once I've showered. That sounds good . . . a long shower. Can I shower for the entire weekend? Then I could avoid the appointment and avoid the event I know I'm supposed to be attending with the douchebag duke.

Avoidance—any proper royal's favorite way of dealing with conflict.

And I'm here for it.

One hour, one piping-hot shower, and three different outfit changes later, I'm as ready to face what's likely going to be the worst day I've had since the day we laid my mother to rest as I'm going to get. My makeup is on point because let's face it, good makeup is a shield for the world to see and for me to hide behind. My hair looks as good as it's going to get, and every inch of my body is semi-recently waxed, buffed, and lotioned.

I flip my head upside down and fluff my hair, only to look at the woman staring back at me with pity. The one whose breasts are overfilling her bra cups. Whose normally nearly concave stomach has the slightest softness. Like she ate one too many fish tacos last night, when in reality, she hasn't had an appetite in days.

I remind myself of something my mother used to say often.

Chin up, darling, or the crown slips.

What would she think of this?

Pretty sure the crown is about to be seriously tarnished, but there's not much I can do about it now. When Monty's muffled ringtone chimes again from under the pillow, I force myself up. Time to face the music.

His name flashes on my phone as I slide my thumb across the screen to answer.

I can do this.

"Hello, Montgomery." His name tastes like acid on my lips.

"Why aren't you here?"

Right to the point.

No hellos or niceties. No *how was your day*. Just *why aren't you where I want you*.

Montgomery Hastings gives douches a bad name.

Here goes nothing. "I'm leaving for a doctor's appointment in a few minutes. I think I'm coming down with something. I don't want to get anyone sick, so I'm not coming home this weekend."

Not like they can catch what I've got, but he doesn't need to know that.

"Don't be ridiculous, Lennon. Of course you're coming home. Pack your bag, get your bony ass in a car, and tell them to have you here this afternoon. Pre-dinner cocktails are at five, and dinner is being served at seven."

My ass is not bony, and I'm getting tired of people commenting on it.

Fucking wanker.

"I thought the party wasn't until Sunday evening." I'm not sure why I even bother arguing, but I do it anyway because he's pissing me off.

His annoyance bleeds through the phone, and I should probably consider ending the call.

Whoops.

Poor cell reception.

But I'm a bigger person. *Bony ass* and all.

Fucker.

"Father's birthday reception is Sunday. There's a dinner tonight, hunting tomorrow, and another dinner tomorrow night. I've been told your grandfather will even be in attendance Sunday."

Of course he will. Because why wouldn't we make this even more complicated?

"Montgomery . . ." I pull the only card I can think of. "I think I have the flu. Could you even imagine if I come and infect all your parents' friends? The scandal. Not only that everyone got sick at their party, but that the king could get sick as well. I mean, that's social suicide."

A disgusted noise gurgles thick in his throat.

Gross.

"Fine," he grunts and disconnects the call.

Such an asshole.

The entire ride to my doctor's office, I replayed that miserable conversation over in my head. I wish I could say it's out of the ordinary for Monty and me, but it's not. We've known each other for most of our lives, and my brothers and I have disliked him for just as long. But I guess that wasn't enough to make my parents think twice about our arrangement.

It's not like they were bad people.

They were just people who relied on tradition to guide their lives.

Unfortunately for Atticus, Rhys, and me, they relied on it to guide ours as well.

My life has rarely ever been mine to live as much as it's been a tool for the crown to use in some way. It's why I pushed so hard for ballet. I knew if I was good enough, it would be my golden ticket to freedom. I'd hoped at the time it was all I'd need. I had no idea about the contract or the plan my parents had for my future.

I'm not sure which was harder . . . finding out who my fiancé was or realizing that my family essentially sold me for political gain.

Now, here I sit after peeing in a cup, chilled to the bone in an itchy paper gown on a table in my ob-gyn's office. Waiting for someone I see once a year to come in and essentially either disarm the impending bomb I've created in my head or press the button that's going to blow up my life.

"Knock, knock," I hear from a sweet voice on the other side of the door before my doctor comes in. "Hello, Your Royal Highness." Her smile is riddled with anxiety, causing uncontrollable laughter to bubble up in my throat.

"I'm sorry," I try to tell her through my laugh. "It's just . . . you look so scared. Aren't you supposed to be the one calming me down?"

She looks down at the tablet in her hands, then back at me. "There's nothing to be concerned about." She moves next to the table and smiles. "How are you feeling, Lennon?"

"I'm about as good as I'm going to get. My nerves are shot, and I'm hoping you're about to tell me the many pregnancy tests I took at home were all wrong and instead maybe I have some incurable disease or something." Okay . . . Maybe Atticus is right, and I am a teeny, tiny drama queen.

Her face tenses, and my stomach drops.

I can't do this. I need to know.

She closes her tablet and places it on the counter, then looks back at me with a soft smile and grabs a pair of gloves. "It appears those were correct, Lennon. According to our test, you are pregnant." She moves next to me and grabs a squeeze bottle. "How about you open your gown and we'll see just how far along you are?"

It's crazy how much one hour can change things.

I walked into that office convinced—well, at least trying to convince myself—there was no way I was pregnant. Of course I was wrong. But that's not why I'm shocked.

No . . . What's shocking me isn't the fear. And there's plenty of that pulsing through me. It's the other emotion balancing that out. The one I can't quite name. The one making my heart speed up and slow at the same time.

Maria clears her throat from the front of the car. "Are we going to Mornea this weekend?"

I run my thumb over the ultrasound picture, still reeling. "No," I murmur without looking up. "We're going to Kroydon Hills."

Maddox
Chapter 8

"Hey, man." My brother Rome walks into il leone and looks around like he always does. It might not look like much yet, but the restaurant is getting there. It's the biggest undertaking I've had since I started opening businesses a few years ago, but it's also the one I'm most excited for.

"Dude, when is this place supposed to open?" He drags his finger over a stack of boxes, then blows the dust off like he's a drill sergeant and this is a white-glove test.

"Fuck off, asshole. It's right on track." We're looking at a November soft launch, even if it's hard to see right now.

"Still don't know why you'd want to put the place in an old bank," he taunts.

"Look around. They don't make buildings like this anymore." This place was built in the early 1900s. The marble columns, stairs, and floors are all original. The massive ceilings and sheer magnitude of the place is a sight to be seen. Hell, the wrought-iron gate that closes over the doors is so heavy, it needs something like eight men to open and close it. It's only been pulled down twice in the last hundred years. Once during the Great Depression, when people flooded the streets and the original bank in a panic, trying to get to their money, and once, when the Kings won the Superbowl. I guess you could say Philadelphia is a *special* city.

Rome doesn't look impressed. "I heard everyone is heading to Kingdom tonight. You going?"

"I promised Lilah I would," I mutter, wishing I hadn't. But when our cousin's wife bats her eyelashes and pouts as she asks you to do something, she's hard to say no to. Luckily, she doesn't pull out the big guns often. But she did for tonight.

A friend of Lilah's is singing at the bar our uncle owns, and Lilah and her husband invited us all to go.

"You think her sister is gonna be there?" Rome asks, trying for nonchalant like a fucking tool.

"Dillan? Probably." The dumbass looks excited, and I shove him away. "Why don't you just fuck already? The two of you have been circling each other for years." I roll up the plans I was looking at and shove them in my bag, then grab my phone and keys. I've got to get the hell out of here.

"Ehh . . . I don't know. The chase is kinda fun. How about you? You been chasing anything good lately, Madman?"

I shake my head. "Fuck off, brother."

The dumbass laughs. "You might want to fix that soon before it becomes a permanent issue."

I smack the back of his head as I follow him out.

It's not like I've been trying to avoid women the past few months.

It's just none of them are her.

Fuck.

*K*ingdom is packed to capacity when I show up, but the bouncer spots me and points me upstairs where the rest of my cousins are. Even two years ago, this would have been my scene, but not now. Not anymore.

Jesus Christ, I sound like a whiney little bitch, even to myself. *Fuck this.* I make my way to the bar and smile at the hot little bartender. "Macallan, neat."

Her bright eyes glitter with interest, and I have no doubt I could take her home if I wanted to. "Yes, sir. Can I get you anything else?"

She's hot, in short black shorts and a black silk tuxedo vest with a white bow tie. Her tits are pushed up under her chin, and she's definitely looking the part tonight.

But yet . . . nothing.

My cock doesn't even jump.

Fucking great.

I spot my cousin Maverick across the private VIP bar area above the stage and dance floor and decide he's as good an excuse as any to ignore the hot bartender. "What's with the whole moody, emo, bastard thing you've got going on?"

He turns his head and arches his brow. "Emo? Seriously?"

Seriously?

Has he looked in the mirror?

I tap my glass to his bottle of beer. "I mean, to each his own, man. But why the hell are you off in a corner, sulking?"

"Thought you were *the all-knowing*," he calls me out, looking down at the floor below us filled with our family and friends. Everyone having a good time. Care-fucking-free.

"I know you're a fucking idiot," I laugh. Maverick and I are two years apart, but we've been tight our whole lives. Our moms are sisters, and our dads are brothers. This whole damn town is a little incestuous, and sometimes our family is a prime example.

Mav grins. "You're unsurprisingly not the first person to tell me that today. Might want to ask Jamie how it went for him."

I ignore the comparison since Mav's roommate is as big a dumbass as my brothers. "Want to talk about it?"

He lifts his bottle to his mouth, stalling. "Not even a little bit."

Rumor has it there's something going on with his neighbor. Might as well go on the offensive before he starts asking me questions I don't feel like answering. "So it's a woman, huh?"

"You heard me say I didn't want to talk, right?" The crowd below us screams as the band pulls Lilah onstage to sing with them, and Mav acts like it's the most riveting thing he's ever seen so he can ignore me.

I get not wanting to talk about something, but there's no way I'm letting him off that easily. "Get your shit together, or don't. That's on you."

"Thanks, Yoda," he grumbles.

I've been called worse.

"You ever want something you know you shouldn't have?" he asks.

Damn. Talk about a direct hit.

"Every day for almost a year," I answer honestly. I can pinpoint just about the exact date. "But I want something I *can't* have. Pretty sure you're torturing yourself over something you *can* have. There's a massive difference."

"Has anybody ever told you the way you have of knowing everything is unsettling? Because it is."

My chest shakes with silent laughter.

Touché, cousin.

"I watch. It's what I do. You've always acted. It's what you do. Or it sounds like what you used to do." I look out over the crowd and shrug. Everyone underestimates the power of observation. "You've always been the first one to jump into shit, Mav. You got me in so much trouble growing up because you had to do everything I was doing, like a little dickhead. It didn't matter that you were younger. You were fearless. Act first, think later. How many times did our moms get on us about that shit?"

We both laugh because it's true.

I got in more trouble than he ever did because Mom and Aunt Lenny always said I was older and should know better.

They didn't care that we told him not to do it.

They just cared that he did it and I let him.

"Wanna tell me what's changed?" I push as the band transitions, and the beat of one of Lilah's biggest hits starts bouncing off the rafters.

I think about that question.

What's changed?

I know what's changed for me.

Pretty sure I know what's changed for him too.

"Rosie." His kid . . . yeah, that's what I thought he'd say. But that's not the right answer. "She changed it all. My life. My priorities. Rosie changed everything. Her happiness and her safety trump everything else."

"Bullshit," I call him out. "I've watched you hook up with plenty of people since Rosie was born. You didn't stop because of her, you just became more discreet. But rumor has it the new nanny has you tied in knots."

"Since when do you believe everything you hear?"

Awfully defensive for someone with nothing to hide, little cousin.

And just as quickly as I think that, I realize I've become a fucking hypocrite.

Damn . . .

"Answer one question and I'll leave you alone," I taunt him and lift my glass to my mouth. "Better yet, answer me one question, and I'll get everyone to leave you alone."

"Cite your source, and I'll answer," he counters.

"Dude." I shake my head. "My mom mentioned it. Pretty sure she's been talking to your mom." The two of them together are bad news, but they're not the only ones talking. "Jamie may have said something the other night when he stopped by the bar for dinner. And Ryker mentioned the hot nanny last week at the poker night you skipped out on. Even Killian—"

"I never said a word to Killian," he argues, but he's already lost this fight, and he knows it.

My grin grows as I hammer the final nail in his coffin. "You didn't need to. Lilah was at your house when some dude showed up at the nanny's house, and she said you went ballistic."

"I didn't go ballistic," he grumbles. "And she has a name." As soon as the words are out of his mouth, he knows he just proved my point. "What's your question?"

Maverick has no clue how easy it is to read him.

This girl isn't just some girl.

If she was, he wouldn't be defensive.

This wouldn't be driving him to drink alone in a bar full of people who care about him. We don't stress over ass. We don't worry about who said what over women who don't matter. I should know.

This girl matters to him, and she's here, in Kroydon Hills, living next door and helping with his kid. She's standing in front of him with nothing in the way . . . nothing holding him back but himself. And he's going to miss his chance. "What's holding you back? What are you scared of?"

Right for the jugular.

What can I say? I don't pull my punches.

"That was two questions."

I hold up two fingers. "Two questions—one answer. Same goal. You've hooked up since Rosie. But you haven't dated since Denae showed up at your doorstep pregnant. You didn't love her. I'm not even sure you liked her. But you haven't dated since her either, and I'm pretty sure you want to date this girl."

Maverick looks away, clearly frustrated, when all he has to do is take a look at himself.

"So what's holding you back? Because the Mav I know isn't scared of anything." I swallow my whiskey in one gulp and signal for a waiter. "You've always been fearless, and I've always respected that."

"It's easy to be fearless when you're only worried about yourself. But it's not just me. It hasn't been for a long damn time. I've got Rosie to think about. To worry about. How am I supposed to date and bring someone around Rosie when I know it will devastate my kid when they leave? How am I supposed to trust someone with her heart. This girl is young. I doubt she's looking for an instant family."

"Don't put words in other people's mouths, Mav. Don't assume you know. It never ends well." I signal the waiter and order another drink.

The waiter points at Mav's beer, but he shakes his head. "Sounds like you're talking from experience, cousin."

You could say that.

I think back to the first time Lennon asked me to walk away.

To the fear in her eyes.

The way her voice trembled.

The way she pleaded with me to do it for her because she wasn't strong enough to do it herself, even if she had to. I could have stayed. I could have fought. But it would have just made things harder on her, and it wouldn't have changed the outcome. "Maybe . . . I don't want to see you make my mistakes." I tilt the ice still in my empty glass, eyes locked on the cubes as I lean over the railing.

Mistakes are a cruel fucking bitch that come back to haunt you when you least expect them to.

Especially mistakes you know you had to make because, for someone else, they were the only choice.

Mav mirrors my stance and stares down at the people below. "I don't know . . . I've just got this feeling . . ." He leaves his words hanging in the air. Like there's more he wants to say but can't. Won't.

"Take the chance or don't, Maverick. You're the one that has to live with the consequences. But take it from me, consequences fucking suck when they're permanent, and age doesn't matter. Fuck, your parents met when they were twenty-two, and they were making out on the dance floor at Killian and Lilah's wedding a few weeks ago. They're still happy, and you know it. It can happen. We're surrounded by examples of what it looks like when it works out."

And he's standing next to a man who's a prime example of what happens when it doesn't.

There's a flicker of something in his eyes as he turns his back on the crowd. "Why do you care so much?"

"Because I always did the things first and you followed, and I don't want you to follow my mistakes this time." The waiter drops off a fresh drink, and I drop a fifty on his tray and add my empty glass. "Regret sucks, man."

Maverick thinks about that before he cracks his neck and drops his empty bottle next to mine. "You're like a broken record."

"What do you have to lose?" I challenge, wanting him to make the choice I couldn't.

His situation may be complicated, but I doubt it's got

anything on the royally fucked up shit Lennon has to deal with.

"Rosie's nanny," he answers, clipped.

"Sounds like the possible good outweighs the bad. If this girl is all sweetness and light like the guys are saying, she'll stick around until you find someone else, even if you turn into a giant dick and fuck her over. Hell . . . maybe her brother could set her up with someone else on the team to ease the pain."

Mav's gaze goes fucking feral.

And my work here is done.

"I fucking hate you," he tells me as he grabs his keys from his pocket.

I watch the motions kicking into gear and fucking smile. "I'm okay with that. Go get the girl, Mav."

"Dumbass," he groans as he walks away.

At least one of us has a chance at going home to his woman tonight.

I swallow my Macallen in one gulp and drop it to the table.

Looks like Meatball and I have another night alone coming at us.

Chapter 9

**My pride warned me it was going to be hard.
My nerves warned me it was going to be scary.
But my heart . . . my heart whispered it was going to be worth it.**

—Lennon's Secret Thoughts

ATTICUS

Dad just asked if you're coming home for Monty's father's party. What do you want me to tell him?

LENNON

Maybe don't tell him I'm in Kroydon Hills.

ATTICUS

Acca-scuse me?

LENNON

Grown men don't quote Pitch Perfect, Atticus.

ATTICUS

Grown men don't know what they're missing out on. It's fabulous, and I'd bend that uptight little blonde over until she was singing my name.

LENNON

Eww. I just threw up in my mouth a little.

ATTICUS

Morning sickness?

LENNON

No. Brother sickness, you twat.

ATTICUS

Okay, you're in Kroydon Hills. Have you seen the mafia prince yet? Does he know he has super sperm?

LENNON

Remind me why I put up with you.

ATTICUS

Because if you kill me, you're one step closer to the throne, and none of us want that.

LENNON

Point taken. Fine. You may live.

ATTICUS

There's my evil queen. Okay. You're in Kroydon Hills. What's the plan, Stan?

I shake my head. I swear, having a conversation with my brother can be utterly exhausting sometimes. Our parents had him tested for ADD once, and to all our surprise, he doesn't have it. Keeping this man on track is hard. Matching his level of energy is even harder.

> **LENNON**
> I don't exactly have a plan.

I walk into the living room of the penthouse suite I'm renting and find Maria already sitting on my couch instead of the room I rented for her, one door down. We got in late last night, and she and I went to our own rooms, but Maria always has a key to my room. I guess she let herself in while I was showering.

I may have overslept a bit. But in my defense, I'm not sure I've ever been as physically and mentally drained as I am right now.

She looks up from her laptop, nods, then goes back to work.

A woman of few words.

> **ATTICUS**
> Okay. How about this? Tell the baby daddy he's about to be a daddy. Then go for round two, and let him be your DADDY before you have to come home and marry the douchey duke.

I stare at the message, with ice coating my veins, reading it and rereading it.

I may not have planned anything about this pregnancy or even thought I wanted this, but all it took was hearing that galloping little heartbeat for me to fall in love. And the thought of still marrying Monty and letting him anywhere near my baby scares me to the core.

> **LENNON**
> I don't know, Atticus. I just . . . I don't think I can.

ATTICUS

Pretty sure you don't have a choice, princess bride.

> **LENNON**
> OMG. Stop with the pop culture and be serious. And while you're at it, try reading a book for a change.

ATTICUS

Blasphemy.

> **LENNON**
> Proud you could spell that.

ATTICUS

Thanks. Me too.

Grandfather will never let you break this engagement. Monty's family is too important to the crown. He forced his own daughter into an arranged marriage. Do you really think he's above doing it to you?

> **LENNON**
> . . . .

It takes me so long to respond, my phone actually falls asleep.

> **LENNON**
> I don't know what I'm going to do, but I know what I don't think I can do.

ATTICUS

Seems to be a theme. You flew halfway across the world. Pretty sure it's time to figure it out, don't you?

LENNON

I think I need to talk to Maddox before I make any decisions. He might not even want any ties to the baby.

ATTICUS

Denial isn't just a river in Mexico.

LENNON

It's Africa, you moron.

ATTICUS

I thought it was in Egypt.

LENNON

Which is on the continent of Africa.

How did you pass your secondary school exams?

ATTICUS

I blew a professor or two.

LENNON

Sounds about right.

ATTICUS

Maybe try blowing the mafia prince. Maybe you could get him to put a hit on Monty.

LENNON

Please tell me you're not serious.

ATTICUS

Nope. If I thought that would work, I'd put the hit out myself. But he's like a cat with nine lives. He'd probably come back a bigger asshole than he already is.

LENNON

Truth.

ATTICUS

Hope you're wearing something that shows off your tits. He may take the news better if he can see the fun bags.

LENNON

I hate you.

ATTICUS

You don't.

LENNON

Fine. I don't. But you're a pain in my ass.

ATTICUS

I accept that. Call me later and let me know how he takes it.

LENNON

Love you.

ATTICUS

You too.

I sit down next to Maria and drop my head back against the cushion, wondering how I ended up here. Absolutely furious with myself for feeling so helpless. For allowing myself to even be in a position where everyone else has more say over my life than I do. But completely unable to see an answer through the maze laid out before me. "Any chance you can use your super-secret spy skills to find me a needle in a haystack?"

Maria cocks her eyebrow and turns her computer my way.

A website for West End Bar & Grill stares back.

"The easiest thing to do would be to call him. But if that's not an option, I'd start here."

I pull her computer onto my lap and run a finger over the screen.

Looks like I'm finally going to West End.

Walking into the bar is like walking into one of Maddox's stories. He talked about this place so often and in such detail, I feel like I've been here a hundred times before. Edison bulbs are strung from the ceiling, and beautiful old, repurposed wood gives the place a chic, warm vibe. It's cool without trying, and I love it. It's also packed for barely noon. Even if my body hasn't acclimated to the time and thinks it should be closer to dinner than lunch.

Waitresses walk by, busy with trays of food that smell phenomenal, and my stomach growls. Shoot. When was the last time I ate?

A plate of fries passes by, and my mouth waters.

Ohh . . . I need some of them.

Shoot.

Focus, Lennon.

Maria hangs back, giving me space and the small semblance of privacy I asked for as I make my way to the bar and an unfortunately familiar face.

"Well, well, well," the youngest Beneventi brother grins when he sees me. "Look who decided to grace the common folk with her royal presence."

I cross my arms over my chest and glare. "I'm sorry . . . Have I done something to offend you or are you just naturally an asshole?"

He blows me off and fills two pints of beer while I wait

for an answer, with my frustration growing incrementally by the minute until he turns my way again. "Did you want a drink, princess?"

I shake my head. "Is Maddox here?"

"Nope." The jerk seems really happy about that answer too, and I don't have the energy to overanalyze that little nugget.

"Could you please tell me where I can find him?" I ask as sweetly as possible, but Lucky Beneventi isn't impressed, and I'm losing my patience.

"Why should I? The last time he saw you, you bailed. In our world, that makes you worthless."

Well hell.

Little Beneventi just called me worthless.

I've been called quite a few things in my life, but that's a new one.

I narrow my eyes, attempting to hold my temper at bay. "If I remember correctly, you'd just informed me that your brother had slept with my cousin."

Even hearing myself say those words still stings.

"Were you two dating?"

"Excuse me?" I bristle, and I immediately see Lucky perk up.

He likes the fight.

Of course he does. He's Maddox's brother.

Ugh . . .

"You and Maddox. Were you dating? Exclusive? In a relationship?" he rattles his questions in quick succession. "Did he break a promise by fucking your cousin?"

"Maybe you should ask your brother that if you really want to know," I counter. "In the meantime, how about you tell me how to find him."

"Do I look like I'm my brother's keeper?" he argues.

My frustrations mount, but years of social graces being

drilled into me refuse to let me make the scene I wish I could. "You look like you're enjoying this."

He completely ignores me and grabs a rag from the back of his jeans and starts wiping down the bar until I slap my hand down on top of it, stopping him. "Listen, I'm asking nicely, and I'm using small words, so I'm fairly certain you can understand me."

Lucky tries to pull away, but I grab his wrist and lean in conspiratorially against the bar, then motion for him before looking over my shoulder. "Do you see that woman behind me? The one in the blue suit?"

I follow Lucky's eyes as they search for Maria. She's not hard to find. She sticks out like a sore thumb in the bar full of low-key patrons here to enjoy lunch and drinks. My royal protection officer looks like she's about to murder someone. Something I may be able to use to my advantage.

When he brings his eyes back to mine, unimpressed, I smile. "She knows 150 ways to kill a man and has diplomatic immunity."

"Looks more like a glorified nanny to me," he huffs.

She doesn't.

He's bluffing.

"Would you like to find out?" I push harder.

I really don't want to call Maddox.

This is a conversation that needs to happen in person, even if it would be so much easier if I didn't have to stand in front of him and tell him this.

"Lucky . . . please," I ask as nicely as I can. "I'm not here to hurt him."

Shockingly, little Beneventi softens for a split second before he grinds his teeth. "He's probably at il leone."

"Could you please tell me where that is?" I ask with a smile and have a pretty good idea of what il leone is.

He did it.

He talked about it for ages.

He's opening his restaurant.

This beautiful man is putting all his plans in motion.

And at this rate, I won't be here to see any of them.

How can I when I'll be a continent away, raising his child?

Lucky looks over my shoulder again before grabbing a cocktail napkin and jotting something down. "Don't fuck over my brother, princess. You might think your girl back there is a good shot, but my mom's better." He pushes the napkin my way but doesn't lift his hand yet. "That being said, I may have underestimated you."

I tug the paper away and tuck it in my purse. "You're not the first person."

**It's okay to be scared.
Fear is natural, and hesitation is healthy.
But strength in the face of both is one of the great
wonders of the world.**

—Lennon's Secret Thoughts

I've never considered myself a particularly strong woman. I wouldn't say I was weak either. I just know my place in the world, which is basically to smile and look pretty. I'm a trophy to be had. Even in ballet, we're used as tools to get benefactors to donate to the company. It's archaic, but it is what it is. And I've played that part well for twenty-five years.

I've smiled.

I've curtseyed.

I've learned languages and customs.

Observed traditions.

Been told what to wear, what to eat, and how to style my hair.

I've been contracted to marry a man I loathe.

And I've followed every order down to each minute detail.

I know my place.

I'm the granddaughter of the king.

I was the daughter of the future queen before she died and have been the sister of the future king since the loss of my mother four years ago. There's a weight far heavier than any tiara that comes with those titles. One it takes a lifetime to learn to balance. One I'm fairly certain is crushing me as I stare at my phone while we navigate the busy streets of Philadelphia.

> RHYS
>
> Where are you and why do you only have Maria with you?
>
> Lennon . . .

My brother isn't used to being ignored.

The entire world has kissed his royal ass since the day he was born.

The heir to the throne of Mornea and currently fifth in line to the throne of Elwyn.

His life was set for him the minute his heart beat in utero.

He'd never even taken his first breath, and his choices were nonexistent.

I rest my hand over my still-flat stomach and wonder if I can do that to my child.

God willing, Rhys will marry and have plenty of heirs himself. My child won't ever be put in that position. And even if for some reason, he doesn't, Atticus is still before me. But still. Every breath we've taken has been watched . . . curated for the benefit of the crown. It may be hard to believe, but I never thought about bringing a child into this life before now. Especially once I was informed I'd be marrying Monty.

My mother once told me having children would bring me joy, even if marrying Monty didn't. She thought I'd find new meaning in life with my children. And I can clearly remember thinking I'd never have children with a man I didn't love.

But as my driver pulls up in front of a gloriously old building—not old by Mornea standards but old by American standards—I realize I've refused to have children with one man who doesn't love me, only to turn around and do so with another.

I'd love to know what I must have done in a previous life for this kind of sick karma.

"We're here, ma'am."

I meet the driver's eyes through the rearview and nod. "Thank you. I just need a minute."

I don't tell him or Maria that the next few minutes could determine the rest of my life.

I'm sure Maria knows. But we haven't discussed it. Not yet.

Some days, I'm positive she doesn't even like me.

Today, I'm certain she's disappointed at the very least.

But that's okay because so am I.

We're all fed a fairytale growing up, royal or not.

We're told we'll live beautiful lives where we'll be loved and cherished and have beautiful weddings, loving marriages, and happy babies. We're told we'll be happy.

But the truth is far less shiny and much less enjoyable.

RHYS

Lennon – I'm worried about you.

LENNON

> Don't be. I'm taking care of something. Maria is with me. I'm safe. But maybe don't mention that to Grandfather. If anyone asks, I'm sick and not coming home this weekend.

RHYS

> Are you sick?

LENNON

> Don't ask me questions you don't want answers to. I'm sick. That's all you need to know to answer anyone who asks. This way, you're not lying.

RHYS

> Should I be concerned?

LENNON

> No. I love you. I'll be home soon enough.

RHYS

> You know it would take me one phone call to find you.

LENNON

> But you won't because I'm asking you not to.

RHYS

> Do you need help?

Oh, big brother, I need so much more than you can give me.

LENNON

> No. I'm fine.

RHYS

> Fine. I'll cover for you this weekend. But come see me when you get home.

> **LENNON**
> Is that a command?

> **RHYS**
> No. It's a request.

> **LENNON**
> Good answer.

> **RHYS**
> Be safe.

> **LENNON**
> Always.

I take a cleansing breath and tuck my phone in my purse before looking at my driver. "I'm not sure how long I'll be. I'll call when I'm ready for the car."

"Yes, ma'am."

Maria holds the door for me, and I stop. "I need to do this alone. Could you please stay out here?"

"No."

One word. Two letters. All the conviction in the world.

I need to learn how to do that.

People pass us on the street, rushing by, having no clue whatsoever who I am or why I'm here. I want to scream that no one knows me. There's no threat here. But I think back to the night that got me into this mess and bite my tongue. I'd love to regret that night, and maybe I do. . . but maybe I can't. "Fine. But stay by the door please."

"I'll do my best," she agrees. Or at least humors me as much as she's capable of as I walk past her and inside the restaurant, which appears to be under construction.

It's stunning.

Even with tarps covering half the surfaces, it's a beautiful work in progress, and I can easily imagine how much

Maddox has loved taking this lovely piece of century-old architecture and giving it a whole new life.

"You can't be here," a rough voice calls out, and I turn and catch a man in a hard hat heading my way. "Are you lost, ma'am?"

Maria moves fast until I raise my hand, stopping her.

"No, sir. I'm here to see Maddox Beneventi. Could you please point me to him?" My words are sweet and sugary, laced in honey in hopes of not being thrown out before I get what I want. Now here's hoping they work.

"The boss?" The man looks at me, untrusting, and I think I'm about to get tossed out before he smiles. "I think he's downstairs in the vault room." He motions behind him to a wide set of marble stairs, and I swallow down my fears and push forward before he can change his mind. And maybe before I can too.

It's now or never.

Well, that sounded ominous.

And now I'm having a conversation with myself.

My goodness . . . Okay, I've got this.

"Thank you." I smile and move past him, careful not to trip on the soft tarp protecting the floor. I grasp the brass railing and carefully take the stairs down to what appears to have been the original vault but at the moment is open with tables covered in building plans and paper coffee cups. Maddox is discussing something with a handsome older gentleman, and maybe had I not met both of his brothers already, I wouldn't notice the family resemblance. But there's little doubt this man is Maddox's father.

The resemblance to the Beneventi boys is too strong.

Dark salt-and-pepper hair. Chiseled cheek bones. A beautifully strong jaw.

And those shoulders. The ones I loved being wrapped around.

Maddox is the spitting image of his father.

And suddenly I wonder who our baby will look like.

Will he be the next generation of Beneventi boy?

Or maybe a little girl with my mother's eyes?

"Lennon?" Maddox's voice pulls me from my momentary loss of focus.

I step carefully into the vault, my eyes darting between him and his father, but I don't miss it. That moment of longing in his brilliant blues before his gaze hardens. Sharpens. Before anger fills his eyes. "What are you doing here?"

Those words bring me back to the last night.

To the snowy street.

To my throbbing head.

The brush of his fingers.

The safety in his touch.

Everything that came after.

Including the next morning.

His brothers. My cousin.

This raging storm I seem to be standing in the eye of.

And he's no longer the only one angry.

"Hi, Maddox . . ."

Maddox

*A*nd there she is.

The one thing I can't have.

My biggest fucking regret.

Looking like a wet fucking royal dream in another prim and proper little blue-and-white dress with a sexy slit up her thigh. Her heels are just as high today as they were last spring, and if it's possible, she's even prettier.

Shame she's—

"Are you going to introduce me, son?" My father interrupts my walk down memory lane, but it's for show. I have no doubt he knows exactly who this woman is. He makes it his business to know everything. If it happens in his city or affects his family, he knows. And right now, this woman is doing both.

What I want to say is *see yourself out, old man*, so I can deal with this without an audience. But I respect him more than that. "Right. Sam Beneventi, meet Lennon . . . Windsor."

I look over at her and wonder if this is the most informal introduction of her life.

Dad offers his hand. "Princess."

There we go.

He knows exactly who she is.

Lennon sucks in a quiet breath, and I'd give anything to know what she's thinking.

She's the hardest person I've ever tried to read.

Most people broadcast their motives and their next moves long before they ever make them. But not Lennon. She keeps everything close to the vest. She keeps it locked down like no one I've ever met.

I'd be impressed if it didn't drive me fucking crazy.

"Nice to meet you, Mr. Beneventi." She blushes as he takes her hand in both of his.

"What brings you to our beautiful city, princess?"

I clear my throat, and the old man grins. "Any chance you'll give us a few minutes?"

He drops Lennon's hand with a smirk and a dip of his head. "I've got to be going anyway. Your mother is expecting me soon. Maybe I'll get to see you again before you leave. I know my wife would love to meet you as well."

Christ. Could he lay it on any thicker?

I'm surprised the fucker didn't just bow to her.

She smiles, but it's forced and doesn't meet her eyes, and as he walks away, those green eyes narrow on me.

"I wasn't expecting to see you here," I tell her honestly as I move around the table and stop in front of her. The urge to touch her is strong and warring with the urge to ask her what the fuck she's doing here. Because every time this woman steps into my life, she leaves a fucking path of destruction in her wake.

"Well, let's see." Her cheeks flame red, and my cock immediately hardens in response. Damn, she's sexy when she's pissed. "I flew halfway around the world because I thought it might be fun to fuck up your life the way you're constantly fucking up mine."

"That's rich, coming from you, *princess*. Pretty sure I've ever only done what you wanted me to." I move closer until mere inches separate us. "Which is ironic, considering I've never done a goddamned thing I was told to do a day in my whole fucking life. I do what I want. When I want. But with you—fuck, Lennon. Everything I've done since the day I met you was what you wanted from me. So you feel like telling me just how I'm fucking up your life? Because I'm pretty sure it's the other way around."

This woman is infuriating.

And beautiful.

Her pale skin flushes, and the delicate freckles dusting her collarbones rise and fall with each deep breath as she fights to maintain control.

Even if she's so much hotter when she loses that tightly held control.

"Oh, that's funny. How exactly have I fucked up your life? Obviously, being with me or without me didn't stop you from fucking other people or having other relationships. I asked you to walk away so you could have a life. Not so you could fuck my cousin." She doesn't even realize she's taken another step closer until our breath is mingling between us. "But you know... Can't have one princess, let's replace her with another. We're all the same, right? Interchangeable? Pretty little redheads with tiaras and titles. And now..."

Her chest heaves as she shakes her head, putting words and thoughts in my mouth that I've never had. Never said. Never wanted.

"And now what? Did you think you'd come back and what, we'd pick up where we left off? You yelling at me about something I did when we weren't together? You pushed me away, Lennon. And I didn't know she was your cousin."

There're other things I could say to defuse the situation.

But I don't.

I harness the anger because it's easier than the other emotions I feel when I see this woman. So many fucked up emotions.

She steps back and reaches into her clutch, then smacks something against my chest.

Fury radiates off her, but neither of us move.

As if held in place by an electric shock that's reached around us, holding us frozen in place... Locked in the pain, refusing to let go.

I don't know whether to kiss her or kill her.

But living in a world without Lennox Windsor isn't an option.

I cup her face in my hands while she still holds her own flat against my chest.

My thumb grazes her cheek, and fuck, I don't want to kill her.

"Tell me no, Lennon. Tell me to stop," I groan.

Her eyes soften, and she removes one of my hands and

lays it over the paper against my chest, then slips away. "No, Maddox."

I crumple the paper in my hands, never taking my eyes from her.

"You might not want to do that," she warns.

"Why are you here, princess?" I ask as I open my palm and flatten the paper.

I stare at it, confused.

What the hell?

"I'm here to tell you I'm pregnant." Her green eyes burn with anger. "I'm here to tell you, you ruined my life. My career. My marriage. I've only ever been good for one thing in this life, and I'm supposed to walk down the aisle in less than a year to fulfill that stupid fucking destiny. And one night with you ruined that." Tears fill her eyes. "You've ruined me," she whispers, which is so much worse than her screams. "And you're going to be a father. Congratulations."

Well, hell. I've heard people say they could be knocked over by a feather, but I've never experienced it . . . until now.

I stare at Lennon, not sure I heard her right.

I couldn't have . . . could I?

I open my mouth to say something, but for the first time in my life, I'm speechless.

The weight of the paper in my hand suddenly becomes unbearable.

I smooth it out and realize the long strip is a series of sonogram pictures.

Holy shit.

I stare at the pictures, expecting them to change.

To not be a baby.

And when I feel like I can finally move again, I look up at Lennon, who's crying.

"A baby?" I whisper as a tear tracks down her cheek.

She nods. "Yes, you jerk. Your big, fat, stupid super sperm managed to get past the condoms."

"Are you sure?" I ask, knowing I shouldn't. But... *Fuck*.

"Am I sure what?" she snaps back slowly, hatred fortifying each word. "Sure that it's yours?"

"No. I didn't—"

"You dick. Yes, I'm sure it's yours. I was a virgin before you, and I haven't been with anyone since. Which ought to make this fun to tell my fiancé."

That word is all it takes for me to see fucking red.

She's still engaged.

To another man.

My vision swims as the hits keep coming, but I cling to what I just sussed out of that statement. "He doesn't know?"

She throws her hands up in the air, exasperated. "Are you even listening to me? No. Monty doesn't know. I haven't told him. I thought you should know first."

"Who knows?" I growl as my mind flies in a million directions.

"You, me, and Atticus." She rolls her pretty eyes. "I mean, Maria probably knows, but she's discreet by nature and kind enough not to ask. So I'm not 100 percent sure."

I look past her for the first time and see Maria in the distance at the bottom of the stairs. At least she brought her this time.

"Don't worry, Maddox. I don't want anything from you. I just wanted you to know and thought I owed it to you to do it in person and not over the phone. But apparently, that was a mistake." She pulls her phone from her purse, and her fingers fly across the screen before I can even register what she's doing. "This doesn't have to change anything."

She turns to leave, and I see fucking stars.

"This changes everything, Lennon." My words are slow and steady and strong. There's no hesitation. "You can't throw something like this at me and then be pissed when I don't react the way you wanted. Give me a fucking minute."

This beautifully infuriating woman looks over her shoulder and purses those pretty lips I've been obsessed with for fucking years. "That might be the only thing I'm not pissed about, Maddox. I didn't handle it well when I found out either. Which, by the way, was only last week. I literally caught a flight hours after my doctor confirmed it, because unlike you, I respect you enough to be honest. You should try it. See how it feels. Either way, I'll be at the hotel in Kroydon Hills for a few days if you want to talk."

She takes a step before she stops again.

"I'm fine, by the way. So is the baby."

Shit.

I watch her cross the tarp-covered floors and walk up the steps like the Princess Royal she was raised to be. Her shoulders back and her head held high. And then I see the way Maria looks at me before following Lennon. Like I'm a bug she'd like to squash.

Get in line.

Chapter 11

MADDOX
Hey, man. You home?

CALLEN
Wanna tell me why the fuck you're texting me from my driveway?

MADDOX
Didn't want to wake the baby.

CALLEN
Don't worry about it. She's on a sleep strike.

Stop stalking like a little creep and come inside. You've got a key.

I open my best friend's door, and immediately, he puts my beautiful niece in my arms. Anastasia is four months old and the spitting image of my sister. Shocking jet-black hair, big beautiful blue eyes, and the palest, prettiest skin covering all the fat rolls on her chubby body. "Hey, *piccolina*." I hold her above my head and blow a raspberry on her belly and smile as she giggles.

Man, that's a great sound.

"Who's your favorite uncle?" I cradle her in my arms and

let her wrap her fist around my finger and bring it to her mouth. "Uncle Maddox. Not the other boneheads, right? Just Uncle Maddox."

"Dude. Get your finger out of her mouth until you wash your hands. Who the fuck knows where it's been?" Callen groans, and I hand Anastasia back to him and walk into the kitchen to wash my hands.

"Did Callen yell at you?" my sister asks as she pulls breaded chicken cutlets from the oven and lays them over a bed of arugula and tomatoes.

"Yeah. I did," Callen answers as he walks in behind me. "Wash your hands so you can hold her. I'm hungry, and you've been slacking on your godfatherly duties, dickhead."

Caitlin kisses my cheek and sets the dish on the kitchen table before she pulls out an extra plate. "You hungry? I made plenty."

"No thanks, Cait."

I wash and dry my hands, then hold them in front of Callen like a doctor waiting to glove up until he passes the baby back to me, grumbling something about hot water and thirty seconds, like it's the first time I've ever held my niece.

"Suit yourself." She sits down and makes herself a plate. "So what's going on, big brother?"

I look from her to Callen. "Kind of wanted to borrow your husband for a bit."

Caitlin points her fork at me. "I actually went all domestic and made Mom's cutlets tonight. Let the man eat while it's still hot."

Callen kisses Caitlin's temple and whispers something, and I gag. "Seriously, married or not, it's still weird as hell, man."

"I knocked her up and married her, asshole. Pretty sure I can kiss her," Callen laughs, and Caitlin points her fork at him. In anyone else's hands, it might not be a weapon, but Cait could probably do some serious damage with it.

"Fine. But you owe me." She picks up her plate and walks into the other room.

"Dude. She's gonna gut you while you sleep," I warn him, half joking.

You never really know with Caitlin.

"Then this better be good, Madman. Because you look like you just saw a ghost, and my wife is apparently going to gut me because of you. I won't tell you what she's actually gonna make me do because you know . . . the whole sister thing."

"Fucking stop, man," I grumble and kiss Anastasia's forehead. "Your daddy's a dick when he wants to be, *piccolina*."

Callen smiles like a fat, dumb, and happy little shit, and if it weren't for the fact he's with my sister, I might be jealous of his happiness.

"Spit it out. You didn't come here just to see Anastasia. What's going on? You having problems with the restaurant?"

"Do you remember Gracie's roommate, Lennon?" It's a stupid question. There's absolutely zero chance of forgetting Lennon. She's sweet and funny and sarcastic as hell. She's also the kind of beauty who can bring a man to his knees with a single look. I should know.

"The hot redheaded princess you were banging in London? Not to be confused with the hot redheaded princess you banged in Elwyn." He grins like he's so fucking smart. "Yeah, I remember."

"First, I never actually banged her in London," I admit, and Anastasia drools on my chest as she starts to fuss. "And they're cousins."

"Sway."

"What?" I ask, confused.

"Sway from side to side," Callen tells me before shoving

another forkful of chicken in his mouth like he doesn't remember what it's like to eat at a normal pace without the baby crying. "Now explain."

I sway like the grandmas with the babies always did at mass, and sure enough, Anastasia calms down and rests her head on my chest. Huh. Not so hard.

"Lennon and I weren't like that back then," I admit. "I was just a dick who let you guys think that. I mean I wanted to be, but stuff with her was always . . ."—I choose my next words carefully—"complicated. And our timing sucked."

Callen knows me better than anyone in my life.

He knows he's not getting the full story.

But he also knows me enough to know he's getting everything I can give for now.

"But man . . . this woman had me tied up in knots," I admit. "For fucking years."

"Damn . . ." He sits back in his chair and stares at me. "Tied in knots, and you weren't nailing her."

"Callen," I groan. "Seriously, man. Stop."

"Shit." He's fucking giddy. "It's like that?"

I cup the back of Anastasia's head and look down. Yup. Sound asleep.

Uncle Maddox is the favorite uncle.

Fuck my brothers.

"It's always been like that with her," I admit.

"Okay. So what's changed? Because that was what? Five . . . six years ago?"

"Five. And back then, she had stuff going on she had to deal with and asked me to walk away. And man, it was the hardest thing I ever did. But it's what she needed and what she asked for, so I did it." I hate the words even more, once they're said out loud. I sound like a whiney little bitch. "But seriously, she was the one who got away. Then a few months ago, she showed up in town during a damn snowstorm. Wrecked her car, and I found her."

Just thinking about that night pisses me off.

Not because it wasn't incredible.

But because it ended the way it did.

"So what happened?" Callen's invested now. The asshole is hanging on every word. He's not even touching what's left of his dinner.

I look at him, and he smiles, proud. "Now, that's what I call playing the long game."

"Says the ass who's been quietly in love with my sister for years," I grumble, and his grin grows.

"Yup. So that was months ago. What happened between then and now?"

I pace the floor, hoping Anastasia doesn't wake up. "My brothers showed up the next day and mentioned I'd slept with her cousin. She got pissed and left. And she showed up at il leone today and told me she's pregnant."

"Oh. My. God," Caitlin gasps from the other side of the room. "Ohmygod. Oh please, *please*, please can I be the one who tells Mom? *Please?*" she begs.

"Cait," I warn her. "This isn't funny."

"Yeah, it is," she deadpans. "You were so pissed when you found out I was pregnant."

"I was pissed you two were messing around behind my back. It had nothing—"

"Don't even, Maddox," Caitlin warns me. "Don't go there. You were pissed. Dad was pissed. Mom wasn't thrilled. And karma's a bitch you pissed off. Oh man. This is freaking fantastic," she giggles.

"Caitie," Callen tries to rein her in, but once she gets going, there's no stopping her.

"You banged two different princesses and knocked up one of them." She claps her hands excitedly. "Is there any chance they're both pregnant? *That* would be freaking amazing."

"Caitlin—" I try to stop her. "No. I haven't even . . ."

Her eyes narrow like a cat about to play with its prey. "Haven't what?" Her eyes grow wide as my words click. "No shit. Not since last spring?"

"I am not having this conversation with you." I walk over to her and give her my niece. "I'm out of here."

Cait takes Anastasia from me and pouts. "Don't go. I'm sorry. I mean, I'm not, but I'll stop. I promise." She sits down next to Callen and kicks her feet up in his lap. "So what are you going to do? Do you like this girl? Wait . . . how pregnant is she?"

"Jesus, Cait. Take a breath." Callen looks almost worried she's going to hyperventilate, she's enjoying this so much.

"I was with her early spring. Like late March. So however pregnant that makes her." I pull the sonogram from my pocket and lay it down in front of my sister.

Caitlin's entire face softens, looking at it. "Wow, Maddox. She's due on December twelfth. You're going to be a daddy," she whispers, awed. "What are you going to do?"

I think about the way we were already at each other's throats earlier.

About her fucking engagement.

About that connection between us that always sparks to life the second I see her.

"I don't know," I admit.

"Looks like you've got about three and a half months to figure it out."

Holy shit.

"That's it?" I ask, my mind blown.

"Yeah, Madman. Babies don't take that long to cook," Callen adds. "Any chance you can get her to stay in Kroydon Hills? You don't want her taking your kid back to London."

The blank stare on my face must be all the answer he needs to know I don't have a clue what I'm doing. "Oh man . . . This is basically the first time you're not the one who knows exactly what to do."

"You're enjoying this, aren't you?" I groan.

A smirk pulls at his lips. "Oh yeah. But we're gonna figure it out."

We're gonna have to. Because I'm not letting my kid grow up a world away.

Lennon
Chapter 12

**I thought my least favorite part of this pregnancy would be the fallout.
I was wrong. It's dealing with the fallout without the aid of wine. That's just unfortunate.**

—Lennon's Secret Thoughts

*B*loody Americans really don't know how to make good tea.

The water the hotel has sent up is barely lukewarm when it arrives at my door. Not to mention what they're calling English breakfast tea isn't a tea I'd be caught dead drinking in London. I stare at the small porcelain mug, attempting to decide whether it's even worth drinking before my phone buzzes.

> **MARIA**
> Do you have an itinerary for today?

> **LENNON**
> I'm planning on calling Grace, but other than that, I don't have plans yet.

> **MARIA**
> Okay. Should I have the car waiting?

> **LENNON**
> No. I'll let you know if anything changes.

> **MARIA**
> Copy that.

I pick at the blueberry muffin that came with my mediocre tea, contemplating what I want to say to Grace . . . I never ended up seeing her the last time I came to town. I had every intention of doing so, but after that night with Maddox and the shambles of the next morning, I just wanted to go home. Not Mornea home, but London home. The home I created for myself far from the glare and the weight of my family.

Not far enough, but as far as I was going to get.

I stare at my phone and wonder what I should say.

And what I *can* say.

She and Maddox are close.

Nearly as close as my brothers and I are.

I'm not sure it's fair for me to tell her about the baby.

Not yet. Not until Maddox has had more time.

And considering I didn't tell her about that night either . . . well, I guess I'm just not sure about anything. But it's Grace. The only true friend I've ever had.

Grace—one of the few people who truly never wanted anything from me.

She'll forgive me.

Even if I don't deserve it.

I pull up her number, but a knock on the door stops me, and my heart plummets.

Maria has a key and would let herself in, and no one else knows I'm here.

No one but Maddox.

Shit. I haven't even showered yet today.

I consider throwing a sweater on over the tiny camisole I slept in last night but decide against it. Let him look. "I'm coming."

He knocks again, and I have the urge to yell, *calm down*, but I don't and consider the restraint my first win of the morning. The tea might suck, and I may look like hell, but I didn't threaten to castrate my baby daddy. That's winning, right?

Good lord. *My baby daddy*. My mother is definitely rolling over in her grave.

With my hand on the knob, I take a deep cleansing breath and do a fluff of my boobs and my hair. I might not be jumping Maddox Beneventi's bones ever again, but this might be the only time in my entire life I have bigger than an A cup, and I'm going to enjoy them.

Let him see what he's missing.

That's for his reaction yesterday.

And that thought brings a momentary smile to my face as I open the door. Unfortunately, that same smile quickly falls because the persistent ass knocking isn't Maddox.

"Monty?" I ask, utterly confused by how and why he's standing in front of me instead of slogging through the woods behind his family's country home, hunting some poor animal. Confusion is quickly replaced by panic when the anger registers in the tight lines of his face.

"You don't look like you have the flu." He walks by me into the hotel suite, stinking like gin and cheap perfume that, no doubt, belonged to his latest mile-high club co-member. "Shut the door, Lennon. We need to talk."

Anxiety claws its way up my chest.

"What are you doing here, Monty?" I cross the room and throw on that discarded sweater, after all. Maddox may have been allowed to look, but I don't want Monty's eyes anywhere on me. Especially when they hold so much disgust.

"I could ask you the same thing, *darling*. Generally, you don't country hop when you're sick with the flu. But we both know you're not sick, don't we?"

The curl to his upper lip. The look of revulsion . . .

It's worse than our typical disdain for each other.

More.

He knows.

Oh God.

He knows.

How?

I wrap my arms around myself protectively. "I'm feeling better," I lie, but it falls flat. I'm not fooling anyone. I'm a lot of things. A good liar isn't one of them.

Monty shakes his head and makes an annoying clucking sound with his tongue. "Such a shitty liar. Try again, poppet —because my sources say you're not going to be feeling better for another four months."

He does know.

"I—"

"Don't bother, Lennon." The air of arrogance constantly surrounding Monty is thick with condescension today. "How can you be this stupid? Honestly . . . use a condom. Take a Plan B. Two different sources confirmed your pregnancy before drinks were served last night. Perhaps if you'd used the king's doctors, you'd have been able to keep it quiet longer, but I'll bet you don't want dear Grandpapa to know you're a lying, cheating, dirty whore."

I rock backward as if taking a physical hit, and tears fill my eyes.

Not with sadness.

With rage.

No one has ever spoken to me like this before.

"Get out," I scream and point to the door. "I refuse to speak to you right now."

But instead of leaving, he gets in my face and grabs my arms, scaring me.

We've disliked each other for years, but he's never touched me in anger before.

We barely touch unless it's in public, and even then, I attempt to avoid it as much as possible. But this . . . this isn't us putting on a show for the public.

I try to pull away, but he yanks me closer, bruising my skin and my pride. "Listen to me, princess." The word reeks of loathing. The kind of revulsion envy never fails to become. And envy is a Hasting's family trait because Monty's family has all the political pull they could ever want, but what they don't have is royal blood. That's what they'll get by marrying their prized pig to a princess. He becomes a prince, and our children become heirs to two thrones.

He hates me for that, almost as badly as he hates how much he needs me to get it even more. Monty might be a duke, but that's only because money can buy you just about anything in this world, fancy titles included. But money can't buy you class or love or a royal bloodline. Not unless you sell your soul, which is what we've done. "You are not going to humiliate me or my family like this."

For the briefest of moments, I think maybe he's calling off the wedding, and my fury turns to joy before my blood turns to ice with his next sneer.

"I'll call my mother tonight and tell her to move the wedding date up. We'll tell the world we were so blissfully in love we couldn't wait another minute. By the time the bastard comes, they'll be so feral for a royal baby, they won't even care that it was conceived before we were married. The world will never know what a filthy whore you really are, and when the kid is old enough, we'll ship it off to boarding school. Hopefully, it'll be a girl because no dirty little bastard is getting my title."

With hatred clouding my vision, I yank my arm free. "They won't need it. My children will always outrank you. Be careful who you're calling a whore, Montgomery. Only one of us has slept with the entire court, and it's not me." I yell back as fury and fear fight for control. "Oh, and don't worry, I hear they make a pill for that little . . . *problem* of yours. I've heard a few women talking about it."

A pain explodes in my cheek so quickly, I fall to the floor, shocked.

My hand flies to my face as tears fill my eyes, and my cheek throbs in time with my pulse while pain ricochets in my skull.

Monty stands over me, red-faced and furious. "You had one job, Lennon. Look pretty and shut up. That's it. That's all you needed to do. But you just had to go and spread your skinny fucking legs for some commoner. Now I'm going to have to raise a mutt as my own."

I sit up, trying to catch my breath, praying Maria will choose now to let herself in but refusing to placate this miserable shit. "Fuck you, Monty," I spit back. "He was more of a man than you could ever be."

I don't see the kick coming.

I underestimated his cruelty.

That's my mistake is the last thought I have as my head hits the corner of the coffee table, and the world around me goes black.

Maddox

Rome and I are sparring at Crucible Saturday morning when my phone starts ringing from the edge of the mat, where it's tucked inside my hat.

"What the fuck? I told you to keep your shit in the locker room."

"Funny." I duck as he throws a jab. "I don't remember caring."

We circle each other as Lucky yells, "Less talking. More hitting."

"Fuck you," we yell back at him in sync.

The ringing stops and immediately starts up again. "Unless it's Mom, you better fucking ignore that shit," Rome threatens like he scares me. Dumbass.

Lucky leans over and looks. "Not Mom."

I bring my knee up, but Rome blocks it.

The ringing stops.

"Fucking finally," he mutters right before it starts again.

"Who is it then?" I yell at Lucky as Rome and I lock arms, both breathing heavily. We've been going at it hard all morning.

"Lennon," the shit stirrer tells me like it's any other day.

"Fuck."

I make the mistake of looking at Lucky, and Rome takes the advantage and nails me with a right hook. My head swings, and I spit out blood before looking at him. "I'll give you that one," I warn and walk to the edge of the mat and squat down to grab the phone.

"Aww . . . the princess is calling. Maybe she needs a frog to kiss," Rome taunts, and Lucky laughs.

Assholes.

I miss the call and hit her name to call her back.

It rings so many times, I think she sending me to voicemail before a woman answers.

A woman who's not Lennon. "You need to come to the hospital."

"Who's this?" I ask and look at the phone, making sure I hit the right number.

"This is Maria, Princess Lennon's head of royal protection. We're at Kroydon Hills Hospital, and she's asked for you. But listen very closely to me, you little wise-guy wannabe. I'm watching you, and if you hurt her, even your father won't be able to save you," she warns, and I'm so fucking lost.

"Why is Lennon in the hospital?" I ask, and my brothers stop laughing. "Is she okay?"

"That's for her to tell you. If it were up to me, we wouldn't even be here, let alone calling you. But she's asked me to call and ordered me that it can only be you. They've taken her for an MRI. She has a private room. Come or don't. It's up to you."

The call ends, and I stare at the phone.

What the fuck?

Rome stands next to me as he rips off his gloves. "We going to the hospital, brother?"

I can't stop staring at the phone.

"Madman," Lucky mumbles, and something about the worry in his voice shakes me.

"Shit." I rip my gloves off. "Yeah. I've got to go to the hospital."

"You want me to drive?" Rome offers as he throws his shirt on.

Lucky stands and grabs his shit. "I can call Dad."

"No. I'm good. Let me see what's going on, and I'll fill you in." My head spins with all the reasons Lennon could be in the hospital, including the baby.

"Not a chance." Rome grabs my keys from my hat. "I'm driving. Let's go."

"I'm coming too," Lucky offers.

I shake my head and throw on my shirt. "No. I need you to go open West End. One of us will call you later. Until then, this stays between us."

I don't wait for anyone's response as I rush out of the gym with a million possibilities running through my mind.

And they all stop and start with Lennon.

Lennon . . . and our baby.

Maddox
Chapter 13

Most of the time, growing up in a small town is a gigantic pain in the ass. But today as I rush through the hospital, I'm grateful for it. No one stops me as I push through the doors in a blind panic. And the familiar face at the check-in doesn't blink twice when I stop. "I need Lennon Windsor's room. Where is it?" I bark at her, not caring how I sound.

Her fingers fly across her keyboard before she looks nervously up at me. "She's in room 504, Mr. Beneventi. Take the elevators to the second floor, cross the skybridge, then take the next elevator to the fifth floor."

"Thanks." I walk away without a badge or a fucking care.

I know Rome's behind me, silent.

I can feel him, but he's smart to give me space because the quick ride here felt like a goddamn lifetime.

I haven't even had twenty-four hours to process the bomb Lennon dropped, but fucking hell, whatever's between us doesn't matter. That's my woman and my baby in that room.

Even if they're not. Even if they can't be.

We don't bother with the first elevator, just taking the steps to the skybridge, then hop in the second elevator. Thankfully alone.

"Breathe, brother. You don't know that anything is wrong with her."

"She's in the hospital," I say so fucking tightly my jaw hurts. "And she's fucking pregnant with my kid."

Rome's whistle bounces off the metal box we're riding in. "Shit. When did you find that out?"

"Yesterday," I groan and drag my hands down my face. "Fuck," I give in and yell as the chaos raging in my head drags me down.

"Get it together, Madman. You're no good to her if you're a fucking mess," he warns, and he's right.

He's being the voice of reason.

He's being me.

Shit.

The doors open, and Rome grabs my shoulder. "Slow it down, man."

I shrug him off but take a breath before we move down the hall, looking for 504. It's not hard to find—because it's the only room with Maria standing guard outside the door.

She sees me coming and hardens her stance.

"Who's that?" Rome growls.

"Her bodyguard," I snap back as I see Maria's hand go to her right side, where I'm sure her holster sits on her hip under her suit coat.

"Is she in there?" I ask once we're stopped in front of the woman who's guarded Lennon for as long as I've known her.

Maria looks behind me at Rome. "Who's this?"

"My brother," I growl and grab the door, moving around the woman standing in my way.

"If I hear a single raised voice, you're gone. Do you understand?" she threatens. "I'll have her on a flight so fast, she won't have time to be furious with me." Her hard shell cracks, and I see it. See that she's concerned for Lennon. And if I'm right, upset with herself.

What the hell happened?

"Understood." I don't wait for a response, just look at Rome. "Go. I'll get a ride home."

"Not a chance, brother. I'll be right here." He looks at Maria and grins. "Right next to Robo-Barbie."

I ignore them both as I push into Lennon's room and find Dr. Mackenzie Hayes-Sinclair standing next to her with an ultrasound thing in her hand.

"Maddox?" she asks, clearly confused. "What—"

"I called him," Lennon whispers, and I get my first look at her.

Fuck... "Len... your face."

Forgetting Kenzie exists, I move next to Lennon's bed and gently cup the side of her face not currently bruised and swollen. "What happened?"

"We've got to stop meeting like this, don't we?" she laughs through red-rimmed, tear-filled eyes.

"This isn't funny, princess. Are you okay?" I wipe her tears with my thumbs, careful of the bruising.

"I'm okay. Dr. Hayes was about to check the baby though," she whispers, and I look back at Kenzie.

"Would you like him to step out, Lennon?" Kenzie asks as she rests her hand on Lennon's blanket.

"No," Lennon murmurs.

Yeah. That's not fucking happening. "I'm the father, Kenz."

If I didn't know Kenzie the way I do, I might not catch the surprise in her eyes, but she's family, and we grew up close. I know this woman as well as I know my sister, and that shock is right there.

Lennon doesn't hide hers nearly as well.

She sucks in an audible breath, and I take her hand in mine and squeeze.

Yesterday's argument forgotten.

Kenzie nods and pulls down the blanket, then pushes up Lennon's shirt, and I have to hold my fucking breath when I see the familiar purple bruising along her side and ribs.

She didn't fall. Someone kicked her.

This tiny woman who's pregnant with my child.

I see red. *Fucking murderous*. And yet somehow, I manage to keep my shit together for her sake as Kenzie keeps going. "This might be a little cold," she warns her before squirting jelly on Lennon's flat stomach.

Her abs may not be as pronounced as they were the last time we were together, but she doesn't look pregnant. Is that normal?

Lennon squirms as Kenzie runs the ultrasound thing over her belly, and immediately, a thrumming fills the room.

My eyes lock on Lennon's tear-filled ones, only these aren't sad tears.

"That's a strong heartbeat," Kenzie tells us as she continues to move the thing around.

"Heartbeat?" I ask, silently awed. "That's the baby's heartbeat?"

Lennon nods. "That's *our* baby's heartbeat."

"Everything looks great, guys," Kenzie confirms, and Lennon sags against the pillow and cries silent tears. "There aren't any issues."

Lennon covers her face. "I've felt every emotion over the past week. All of them. Fear and frustration, and anger . . . And then today . . ." she sniffs. "When I wasn't sure . . ." She wipes her cheeks and looks up at me, her lower lip trembling. "Today, when I thought I might have lost it . . ."

"Shh . . ." I whisper and kiss her forehead. "You're both okay."

Kenzie stands back and gives us a moment before interrupting, "The baby is measuring on the smaller side for your due date, but considering you mentioned dancing until recently, that could be why. It also happens to be cooperating, if you'd like to know the sex."

"I want to know." Lennon smiles up at me, like she's asking permission, and every wall I've put up comes crashing down.

Like I wouldn't move heaven and earth to give her whatever she needed.

I run my hand over her hair and watch her watching the screen.

Yesterday forgotten as we fall into new roles. "Then let's find out, *principessa*."

"Well, it looks like the world is going to be dealing with another Beneventi boy in a few months," Kenzie announces, and I stare at the screen, completely overcome.

A boy.

A baby boy.

My world tilts on its axis, and my center of gravity irrevocably changes.

I gently press my lips to Lennon's head. "We're having a boy."

Lennon

I close my eyes and soak in Maddox's silent strength.

"I'm going to leave the two of you," Dr. Hayes-Sinclair announces as she wipes the jelly off my belly and pulls my shirt back down. "A nurse will be in to go over your discharge papers, Lennon, but here's my number. Please don't hesitate to call my office with any questions." She jots something down on the back of the card before handing it to me. "Here—I added my cell phone number on the back. If you need anything, call." She holds my gaze, making sure I understand what she's saying.

This woman I've never met before but is married to my best friend's brother.

Shit. *Grace* . . . My family.

They're all going to kill me.

"Thank you, Doctor Hayes. Is there any way you could make sure this stays quiet? I'd rather not have the whole incident get out, if possible," I admit, embarrassed, then watch as she looks from me to Maddox.

"I'll do what I can, Miss Windsor."

"Thank you," I murmur as Maddox thanks her and walks her to the door.

I can't hear what's said between the two of them, but when he turns around, emotions are running rampant behind his eyes as he comes back to my bed side. "Everything was okay with your MRI?"

I nod slowly and regret the movement when my head swims.

"What happened, Lennon?"

I look away as humiliation chokes me. "I don't want to talk about it."

"Who hurt you, princess?" His words are soft but fierce, and I worry what he'll do once he knows the truth.

"It won't happen again. I appreciate you coming. . ." I babble, nervously. "I was worried something was wrong with the baby."

I run my palm over my stomach and bite down on my lip to try to control the sob ready to spill over. "We're having a boy."

Wonderment fills me.

And Maddox smiles like I've never seen before.

It's beautiful and warm and full of life.

It's everything I don't feel right now but wish I did.

"I'm not sure it felt real before now," he says in a low, hushed tone. "I mean, I knew what you said. It's not like I didn't believe you. It just didn't feel real until I heard his heartbeat. And then she said he's a boy . . ." He gently cups one side of my face, and his thumb rubs my cheekbone. "And you're both okay. We've got a lot to figure out."

"We do." I wrap my fingers around his wrist, momentarily forgetting any anger I've been clinging to when I think about this man. "But I'm not sure I've got the energy to do it now."

"You know you're going to have to tell me what happened at some point."

"I know, and I will." I squeeze his wrist and drop my hand. "But for now, I just want to get out of here."

I can tell he wants to say more. He's never been a man of inaction. This is killing him. But as usual, he's doing it because I've asked. Maddox's eyes search mine, trying to reconcile my answer with his need to control the situation. "Come home with me."

"What?" I sputter. "Why would I do that?"

"Because I can keep you safe." The certainty in his words is so strong, it almost makes me believe him. I want to, but I can't.

He can't keep me safe. No one can.

"You can't save me from my future, Maddox. Even if I wish you could." The words break what little joy I'd managed as the reality sets in. This is my future. This is what my life will look like. This is what my family forced on me.

"Monty did this?" he growls and drops his hold as I realize my mistake. "I'm going to fucking kill him."

His words leave no room for argument, but I can't not argue them.

"You can't," I force the words from my lips, even though I wish I didn't have to.

"You can't seriously still plan on marrying him." Maddox is looking at me like he doesn't know me. Like he can't believe what I'm saying. And I can't blame him. If you didn't grow up in my world, this seems insane. Contract marriages are unheard of in most circles. Lucky me, I didn't grow up in most circles.

"I don't have another option." My words are a plea for him to understand. "There's no way out of a contract like ours. Trust me. If there were, I'd have used it to end this ridiculous sham already."

My God, how I wish it were that simple. I tried. I searched for a loophole that doesn't exist. I begged my parents . . . my grandfather. I tried, to no avail.

This is it. This is my lot in life. My future.

Maddox runs his finger through his thick, dark hair.

Hair I remember touching. Pulling.

Then I remember I'm not the only one who did those things, and my heart wars with my head. Inconvenient as that may be.

He lifts his head to the ceiling, then looks down at me. "What if I came up with a way?"

"My brother's lawyer couldn't even find a way. I don't think you're going to find what you're looking for, Maddox." No matter how much I wish he could. "I promise I won't keep the baby from you. No matter what Monty says, I'll find a way."

"You wouldn't be able to legally marry him if you were already married, Lennon."

I freeze at his words.

Unable to breathe.

Unsure I heard him right over the ringing now playing a symphony in my ears.

"I don't understand . . ." I slowly sit up and swing my legs over the side of the bed, grabbing onto Maddox as his hands move to my sides to help me down. "What are you saying?"

He steadies me on my feet, and I watch his Adam's apple work as he swallows. "Marry me. Stay here with me. You can't marry Monty if you're already married to me. So marry me, *principessa*."

I work his words over in my mind.

Marry one man I don't love or another I absolutely loathe.

Is this what my life has been reduced to?

"Why would I do that?" I ask him, even though the answer is staring me in the face.

"Because I'll keep you safe. You and our baby. Because no one will ever hurt either of you as long as I breathe." He presses his lips to my forehead. "Because I don't play by their rules."

A shiver dances down my spine with his powerful words.

No one will ever hurt my son.

"Marry you and I can't legally marry someone else," I repeat slowly, trying to work it out in my mind. "That could work."

"We can make it work," he tries to convince me. Maddox has this way of saying something with such surety, you'd swear it was gospel. "We'd just have to get married before you're supposed to marry him."

That's his first mistake. "We'd have to get married as soon as possible. If not, he's going to expect me to come home and marry him in a month. He was calling his mother to move up the date this morning."

A muscle ticks in Maddox's jaw, and I realize I just confirmed it.

Confirmed without a doubt that Monty was with me this morning.

Damn it.

"Fine," he grinds. "We'll get married right away. We can go to the courthouse tomorrow—"

"No," I stop him. "That won't work. He'll try to get it annulled. I know him, and doing this will be like waving a red cape in front of a raging bull. Telling Monty he can't have something will only make him want it more." I hate Montgomery Hastings on a molecular level. I loathe him. But I also know him, and I'll never underestimate him again. "If we want this to work, it has to be big and splashy and as soon as possible. It needs to be covered by every international news outlet in the world. I need to be as badly damaged goods as possible."

Maddox's grip on my waist tightens. "You could never be damaged goods," he growls.

"They have to think I am." I pull back, not wanting to be this close. Not wanting him to cloud my judgment. "The world needs to know I'm married to another man. His pride needs to be crushed in a way that would make it impossible for him to marry me."

"And if I can make that happen?" he pushes, stepping back into my space.

I put my hand out in-between us and wait for him to take it in his. "Then I guess I'm marrying the lesser of two evils."

Maddox arches his brow in question but shakes my hand anyway. "Then let's find the nurse so we can get you out of here and get your stuff. It looks like you're marrying me, princess. Might as well move in. We've got work to do."

"Aww . . . That's the most romantic thing anyone has ever said to me," I tell him, sarcasm dripping from my tone. "But I don't need romance. This is going to be a marriage in name only. I'd say let's have a contract drawn up, but I'm not sure I ever want to sign another contract for as long as I live."

"We'll see," he murmurs as he heads for the door.

"Where are you going?" I ask, confused.

"To find the nurse and make sure Rome and Maria haven't killed each other yet. It's about time I take you home."

Home. Ha. That's a joke.

This will never be my home, but it seems I'm out of options.

Once this is done, I doubt I'll ever be welcome in Mornea again.

I'll have to give up my inheritance. My title. My right to the throne.

I'll no longer be any kind of a working royal of Mornea.

But . . . My baby boy will be safe.

He'll be raised by a man who loves him.

One who will give him a good life, far from the spotlight.

Far from the crown.

Here, I won't have to worry about Monty.

Here, I'll just have to worry about my heart.

Chapter 14

**I don't run away from my problems.
I like to sit on my sofa, play on my phone, and ignore them. Like an adult.
Wait... where's the couch?**

—*Lennon's Secret Thoughts*

I sit quietly in the back seat of a familiar dark Escalade. This time, Rome drives us back to Maddox's house. I've been promised Rome and Lucky do not live with Maddox, no matter what Rome says. Threats have been made about keys being given back, and if my head wasn't splitting with only Tylenol given to me as a pain reliever, maybe I'd think it was funny. For now, it's just loud. Far too loud.

We pull into what appears to be a private neighborhood with beautiful homes, all on what seems to be a few acres each. The SUV slows and turns down a gated circular driveway, stopping to input a code before the gates swing open, and we follow the curve until a stunning white stone home comes into view. *He did it.* He built the house he used to doodle on every small scrap of paper he could get his hands on. This man is making all those dreams we used to talk about come true, while I'm *what*? Letting everyone else control my life?

Rome pulls up in front of the house and turns off the car. "You need any help?"

I'm not sure who he's asking until Maddox shakes his head. "I'm good, man. Just try to run interference with Mom and Dad for me, if you can."

Maddox gets out and opens my door while Maria rounds the car, seemingly annoyed. "I'd like to say, again, that I don't like this."

"Me either Robo-Barbie," Rome agrees, and I can't help but wonder if he realizes just how close he is to being taken down . . . "I'm the one who crashes in the guesthouse," he grumbles.

She ignores him and turns to Maddox and me. "I don't think I should be that far away, princess."

"She'll be safe," Maddox assures her, but she doesn't even acknowledge he's spoken.

"I was in the room next to yours this morning, and it was too far, Lennon."

"I know, but no one knows I'm here, and Maddox isn't letting anyone in his home," I assure her. Apparently, this ridiculous man has only gotten as far as furnishing one bedroom and the pool house. But I'm told that was more Rome throwing a bed in there than Maddox doing anything, according to Rome. "I'll be fine. I'm just going to bed." I look over my shoulder at Maddox, who's speaking in hushed tones with his brother, then add, "Alone. I'll be fine. Get some rest and we'll figure out my plan tomorrow. I know you don't want to hear this, but I think you're going to have to go back to Mornea."

"I'm not leaving." She grabs her bag from the back seat.

"I'll stay in the guest house tonight if you keep your panic button on you."

I hold up the fob and smile. "I'll sleep with it next to the bed."

"Better hope Meatball doesn't eat it," Rome adds, and Maddox grumbles something I can't quite hear. "Whatever. I'll see you tomorrow. Text if you need anything."

Rome slides behind the wheel of a sleek sports car parked in front of the garage, and Maddox taps the top of the car like a police officer on a television show right before Rome pulls away, then he lifts both my bags and waits for me.

"Good night, Maria," I tell her and gingerly walk to the gorgeously ornate black-iron door and stare. It looks just like his old sketches. The ones he doodled on the back of every placemat and spare paper that landed in front of him back in the day. . . Back when we were friends and life was so much more simple.

He lays his palm against a sensor, then punches in a code before the door opens. "Ladies first."

"Oh, aren't you just so chivalrous?" I tease lightly, too tired for anything else.

I guess spending a day in the hospital will do that to a girl.

Tomorrow I'll go back to being mad at him . . . maybe.

Better yet, maybe today, I'll try to figure out how to move past the anger and find that friendship again.

That one is going to take a while, but considering I'm pregnant with his child and marrying him, it's probably a good start.

He steps in and locks the door behind us as I take it all in. The high, arching ceilings. The floor-to-ceiling windows. The hand-scraped hardwood floors. "You really did it," I murmur. "It's gorgeous, Maddox. Truly. You should be so proud of yourself."

"How do you even know it's my design?" he questions as

he moves in front of me and motions for me to follow, leading me through a bare house with very little furniture and up a gorgeous winding staircase.

"Because this is you. All you. It's every sketch you ever showed me," I tell him, revealing a bit more than I intended to.

"I'm surprised you remembered." His words are short and curt, and I guess in some ways, I don't blame him. In others, I most certainly do.

"I remember everything." I follow him down a long hall into the master bedroom and stand back as he places both bags on a massive bed. "I really can sleep on the couch, you know. I'm a lot smaller than you. It would be fine."

I don't tell him I've spent plenty of nights on the couch in my flat.

Nights it was easier to fall asleep watching TV than trying to go to bed, alone, with nothing but my thoughts running rampant.

"I'll be fine, Lennon. You take the bed. We'll work on furniture for one of the other rooms soon."

I narrow my gaze and cross my arms. "Why don't you have furniture?"

He shrugs. "I just moved in last month. I guess I haven't gotten around to it. Why? Are you still obsessed with decorating things?"

Little shit.

"I wouldn't say obsessed. But I do enjoy it. Both my brothers let me do their places. And Rhys let me do his office too." I always thought once I was done with ballet, maybe I'd dabble in interior design. Not that I ever told anyone that. Princesses aren't expected to work. We're expected to look pretty and serve the crown.

"Want to help me decorate the house?" he offers. "If you're going to live here, you might as well like it."

Well, that's a ringing endorsement, if ever I've heard one. But still . . . "I mean, you do need furniture and at least one more bedroom set, so you don't have to sleep on the couch."

He tilts his head, and I put my hand up. "Not a chance, Beneventi. This is a marriage in name only. We're doing this so I can get out of marrying Monty. I'll stay here long enough to give birth and make sure you're listed on the birth certificate. We can figure out everything else after that. But I can guarantee you that will not involve you and me sleeping in the same bed."

Meatball picks then to trot in and sit at my feet.

"Fucking traitor," Maddox grumbles. "Fine. But that dog is going to try to get in bed with you. Don't say I didn't warn you."

"Him, I'll take." I lean down and scratch behind the chubby bulldog's ears.

I'm fairly certain I hear him mumble, *"Lucky bastard"* under his breath.

"Do you need anything?"

"Just a shower and some sleep," I assure him, needing space and clarity and a few minutes to have the proper fucking breakdown I deserve but couldn't have while everyone has been watching. "Can we figure everything else out tomorrow?"

"Yeah. I'll call my aunts and see if they can stop by tomorrow. They run a wedding planning event company. If anyone can give us a wedding fit for a princess in just a few weeks, it's them." He turns and heads for the door.

"Thank you," I say softly as he walks through it.

So softly, I'm positive he can't hear me.

At least not until he stops without turning around.

"I would have done anything to make sure you didn't marry him. Even before today."

And with that, he walks through the door, and I'm left

standing, frozen in place, wondering not for the first time in the past week exactly when my life went sideways.

ATTICUS

Rumor around court is Monty wants to move up the wedding. He told Charlotte Cavendish he just couldn't wait to marry you any longer.

LENNON

Charlotte Cavendish is a cow who'd probably just finished polishing his knob.

ATTICUS

She is good at that.

LENNON

ATTICUS.

ATTICUS

Don't go all prude on me, preggo.

LENNON

Do you ever think before you speak?

ATTICUS

Where's the fun in that?

I contemplate the best way to answer my brother.

If it's nearing eight p.m. here, it's almost one a.m. back home, and I'm guessing he's enjoyed more than one whiskey tonight.

I think about FaceTiming, but if I do that, he'll see my face, and that's not an option. Not until I figure out how I'm handling all this. And I haven't figured that out yet.

Telling Atticus anything just puts him in the uncomfortable position of having to lie for me. Not that he wouldn't willingly do it. I'm certain both my brothers would. But that doesn't mean I want them to.

> **LENNON**
> He can try to move the wedding up if he wants to, but I've got other plans. Ones I can't talk about just yet, but I promise I'll tell you everything just as soon as I figure it all out.

> **ATTICUS**
> WTF Lennon? You can't say something like that, then leave me hanging.

My phone rings with an incoming FaceTime, which I decline.

> **LENNON**
> I'm already in my pajamas and in bed. No FaceTiming tonight. I'll call you tomorrow.

> **ATTICUS**
> Do you know me at all? You might as well have teased a socialite with a bottle of Dom. I need my hit, Lennon. Don't leave me hanging.

> **LENNON**
> Love you. Talk tomorrow.

> **ATTICUS**
> **LENNON!**

> **LENNON**
> Shutting my phone off.

ATTICUS
Don't make me get Rhys.

LENNON
Really? You're going to threaten me with Rhys?

ATTICUS
Did it work?

LENNON
Goodnight, Atticus.

Maddox
Chapter 15

CALLEN
Fair warning. My wife and your mother are heading your way.

MADDOX
Fuck. Thanks for the heads-up.

CALLEN
Good luck, brother. They're scary as shit when they're together.

MADDOX
Do they know Lennon is here?

CALLEN
Like in your house, here?

MADDOX
Like upstairs in my bed while I slept on my couch and I've got a shit ton to fill you in on, here.

CALLEN
Dude. You're screwed. No. I don't think they know that. But I'm pretty sure my wife is forcing your hand with your mom. Consider it payback.

MADDOX
Asshole. Control your wife.

> **CALLEN**
> Listen. I don't even attempt to control Caitlin. Want me to tell you why?

> **MADDOX**
> Fuck, no. Stop.

> **CALLEN**
> Yeah, that's what I thought. Good luck.

> **MADDOX**
> Yeah. Thanks for nothing.

> **CALLEN**
> I didn't have to warn you.

My doorbell rings right before the code is punched in, and the door opens.

What the fuck?

> **MADDOX**
> How long ago did they leave?

I look at the time and groan. It's barely nine a.m.

> **CALLEN**
> How should I know? Anastasia and I took a nap.

"Maddox," Caitlin calls out, and I immediately smell coffee and pastries from Mom's shop, Sweet Temptations. "Oh, Maddox," she singsongs, and I swear my mother smothers a laugh.

"I thought you said he was expecting us, Caitie," Mom questions Cait. I drag my hand over my face and sit up as I hear them getting closer. "Maddox? What on earth are you doing on the couch?"

Caitlin's grin is devious at best when it comes into view, and I know I deserve it for all the crap I gave her last year, but that doesn't mean I'm ready for it.

"Hey, Mom." I throw the blanket off and grab my jeans from the floor, then pull them up my legs. "What are you doing here?" I drop a kiss on top of her head. She and Caitlin look more like sisters than mother and daughter. Both with dark hair and pale skin. Not to mention tempers you don't want to cross. Mom's good with a gun. Cait's better with a knife. Consider yourself warned.

"We brought you coffee and donuts and that new bagel you like so much." She holds the bag up in her hand, while Cait pulls one of the coffees from the caddy and offers it to me. "Caitie said you wanted to see us."

I look between the two women and shake my head.

Might as well go with it.

"I do. I just didn't realize it was going to be this morning. I thought I'd come see you." I walk into the kitchen and pull out a stool from the island for her. I probably should make getting furniture a priority.

Caitlin opens a cabinet and pulls out a plate I'm not even sure I knew I owned and starts stacking the pastries.

"Is everything okay, Maddox?" Her eyes dart from me to Caitlin and back. "You're worrying me. Should I call your father? Did one of your brothers do something?"

Cait snorts, and I swear to God I'm going to get her back for this.

"No, Ma. Everything is fine. I just have some news to share with you guys. I'll talk to Dad later today." I don't bother telling her he probably knows already. At least part of it.

"News?" She perks up. "Good news?"

Meatball trots into the kitchen, followed by Mom and Caitlin both coughing.

Well, shit.

I turn and see Lennon, and fuck me . . . She's wearing one of my old, threadbare, green Crucible t-shirts and a short pair of soft shorts. She looks fantastic and awful all at once. Her red hair is damp around her shoulders, and her skin is pale and flushed and bruised to hell.

"Sorry." She freezes, her nervous eyes darting around the room. "I didn't realize you had company . . . I'll just go—"

"*Principessa* . . ." I reach my hand out, and she stares at it like she's looking at a python ready to strike.

Mom stops breathing like I knew she would with that single word.

One day, Lennon will understand the underlying importance in that one word.

Until then, my family will understand her importance to me.

She takes one slow step toward me, then another until her hand is in mine, and I pull her to me. "I'd like to introduce you to my mother, Amelia Beneventi."

Caitlin coughs again, and I grin but don't say anything.

"And I'm his sister, Caitlin."

Lennon's hands shake as she moves her hair forward, no doubt trying to hide her battered face, and my blood fucking boils. I'm going to kill him.

"It's . . ." Lennon's chest rises and falls before she seems to pull herself together. "It's wonderful to finally meet you. Maddox has been telling me about you both for years." She looks toward Caitlin and smiles. "Congratulations on the baby."

My mother stares at me, slack-jawed, before glaring at me. "Well, you have me at a disadvantage. My son likes to be a secretive little shit. But it's lovely to meet you . . ." She leaves the sentence hanging, and I realize I haven't given her Lennon's name.

I guess it's got to happen. "Mom, this is Princess Lennon Windsor. My fiancée."

Caitlin laughs. The little brat literally laughs. "Oh my God. This just keeps getting better . . ."

Mom looks between the three of us, less than amused. "I'd like to say congratulations, but in typical Beneventi family fashion, there is obviously more to the story than this. Care to fill me in?" She levels me with a glare that would frighten most men. Luckily, I'm not most men. "Now."

"Maybe I should leave you—" Lennon starts to say.

"Oh, I think you better get comfortable right there, dear. It sounds like you're about to become part of my family, so you better get used to this—because my children like to act like they were raised by wild animals." Her focus comes back to me. "Now explain."

"I asked Lennon to marry me, and she said yes." I pull out another stool and tug Lennon over to it. But does this woman sit? No. She stands next to me, gripping my hand but not backing down. She's stronger than she'll ever realize, but I'll make sure, one day, she knows it.

"There's more to it than that," Lennon offers, and Caitlin snickers.

"You." Mom's head spins like she's possessed in *The Exorcist*.

Scariest fucking movie I've ever seen.

Seriously. Grow up Catholic, going to mass every Sunday, then watch that shit and tell me it doesn't scare you. I fucking dare you.

"Are you part of this?" she asks my sister, apparently tired of her snark.

"No, ma'am," Caitlin answers, and it's my turn to chuckle.

Fuck. Based on the looks Mom and Lennon just threw my way, I'm going to say that wasn't the right move either.

"How much more?" Mom asks once she calms down.

"She's pregnant," I tell her.

"And kind of engaged," Lennon adds, and Mom squints like she's trying to see something that isn't there.

"To my son?" she questions.

"Yes," I answer as Lennon says, "Not exactly."

Mom tilts her head and arches a brow. "Well, which is it?"

"I was promised to a bad man. One I don't love and who doesn't love me," Lennon says softly, and Caitlin inches forward as Mom lays her hand over Lennon's.

"Is he who hurt you?" she asks her.

Lennon closes her eyes and nods while I fight for control.

My mother looks at me, and I have no doubt this won't be the last of this conversation. "The baby is yours?" she asks me.

"He is," I tell her, and a smile softens her face. "And we need to get married fast."

"Courthouse fast?" Caitlin asks.

"No. Flashy fast. It needs to be big. Like the biggest Kingston wedding we've seen," I tell them, and Lennon's body sways backward into mine, and I wrap an arm around her, hoping she takes the reassurance. "The world needs to know Lennon is married and the baby is mine."

"Have you spoken to your aunts?" Mom asks. "I'll call them now. How fast is fast?" She's looking at Lennon, not me. "I'm sure we can have big and beautiful and splashed all over the news within weeks. Are we thinking eight weeks?"

"Closer to four, Ma," I tell her and grab a bagel from the

plate Caitlin arranged earlier and offer it to Lennon. She follows my hand, sees the plate, and opts for a chocolate croissant instead.

"Okay. Let's see what we can do," Mom agrees and pulls her phone from her purse and walks out of the room, leaving me not at all surprised. Amelia Beneventi raised us to never back down from any*thing* or any*one*. She's never met a problem she couldn't handle or a situation she couldn't see her children through.

"So . . . That was my mom." I press a kiss to the top of Lennon's head, and she pulls away, glaring.

"So help me God. One day, I'm going to walk into your kitchen and not be blindsided by your family." She rips the croissant in half and points it at me. "I would've liked to have met your mother looking a little nicer than this, preferably in clothes she hasn't seen her son wear and possibly with a fucking bra on."

"Ohhhh . . . I like her," Caitlin laughs with an evil smile, and Lennon side-eyes her. "Don't worry. Everyone fears the men in our family. But really, we're the ones they should be scared of. Welcome to the family."

I should be scared of this possible friendship. My sister is a little psycho. But there's no one in the world more loyal. I forgot that once. I'll never make that mistake again. Lennon would be lucky to have her as a friend, even if Caitlin's a gigantic pain in my ass most days.

"Thanks, I think." Lennon pops the croissant in her mouth and moans. "That's delicious." Then she's glaring at me again. "Please tell me you have tea."

Lennon

*I*f I thought my family having an army of people getting things done was impressive, I was wrong. Maddox's family *is* the army of people who gets things done. And by the end of Sunday, I've met most of them. There are the aunts who own the event planning company. The senator uncle who was nominated to host the wedding in his stunning backyard. His mother's bakery will make the cakes and desserts. One of the restaurants his father owns will cater the event. And I'll be meeting with Grace's sister for my dress, just as soon as I call my best friend first. I refuse to have Grace find out what's happening before I tell her. I owe her that much.

I'll fix that today.

According to my mother-in-law-to-be, who is a force of nature, all we need to do is settle on a date. Easy-peasy. Not a term I was familiar with before today.

Not that any of this feels easy.

But what's the alternative?

All I have to do is look in the mirror or watch the way each member of the family has looked at me today to be reminded of what the alternative is capable of. And that isn't an option. Not for me or my baby.

"Hey . . . Are you okay?" Caitlin asks as she kicks off her ballet flats and sits on the edge of the pool next to me, lowering her feet into the water.

"I'm not sure," I tell her before thinking my words through. "It's just a lot."

"My family?" she asks with a beaming smile. "I mean, they can definitely be a whole lot to handle, especially all at once, but can I tell you a secret?"

"Sure."

"You'll never meet a more loyal group of people. You'll

never feel more safe or more loved than you will be when you're with the Kingstons and the Beneventis." She kicks the water with her toes, causing a current to move around our feet. "We're pretty amazing. We're all up in each other's business all the time, but sometimes, it's actually fun."

I'm not sure whether I should be relieved that this is normal or disturbed that this is what I should expect. Either way, it's so completely different from the way I was raised, I'm not sure what to do with it.

"You looked like you were having fun today," I laugh softly. "I think you'll like my brother Atticus. He's a bit of a pot stirrer too."

"Holy shit," she gasps and looks at me funny. "I know you're a princess, but it just dawned on me that Rhys and Atticus Windsor are your brothers."

I nod slowly. "They are. Not sure if they'll be able to come to the wedding. I'm not sure . . ." I trail off, not quite ready to admit all my dirty little secrets just yet. She doesn't need to know that by doing this, I'm going against my family, and by doing so, I'll be cut off. My brothers will have to go along with it or they'll be cut off as well. And as much as Rhys would have liked to have had a chance at a normal life, he'll be the most amazing king Mornea has ever had one day.

"Your brothers are so fucking hot," she laughs.

I've unfortunately heard that my whole life.

Women love my brothers. They'd die if they saw the slobs they really are.

"Yeah well, yours aren't so bad either," I admit. But really, it's just one. The one who refused to keep his hands off me all day. From the gentle brush of his hand, every time he was near, to the way his hand would rest on the small of my back each time he'd introduce me to another new family member . . . it was like he was looking for ways to get under my skin. And he did a great job if that was his goal. I'm going to have to remind him our marriage will be in name only. That's all it can ever be. But that's a problem for another day. I can only handle so much in one afternoon, and I've just about hit my limit.

I lean back on my elbows and let the late afternoon sun soak into my skin.

"Have you called Gracie yet?" Caitlin asks a few minutes later.

"No. I need to," I admit.

"You should do that soon. My husband is her uncle, and their family is as close as ours. Word travels fast in Kroydon Hills," she warns as I attempt to piece together the puzzle.

"You guys need one of those string boards to show how everyone in this town is connected. It's so confusing." I slowly push up to my feet, careful not to irritate my bruised ribs, and pull my phone from my pocket. "But thank you . . . for everything today."

She smiles a beautiful smile and looks so much like her brother in that moment, it takes my breath away. "Listen, I've been surrounded by brothers my entire life. I've always wanted a sister. And you're way better than what I was expecting."

"Thanks, I think." I hold my phone up and muster what little courage I've got left. "I'm going to call Grace."

Caitlin nods. "I'm going to go say my goodbyes to everyone. I think it's time for me to go home and thank Callen for putting up with my family."

"Bye," I whisper as she walks away. The weight of the phone is heavy in my hand because I hate the idea Grace could be mad at me . . . but I wouldn't blame her if she was. I pull up her name and stare at the picture of the two of us I set as her contact photo years ago. It was taken after opening night of our first ballet together. We were babies back then, with no idea what the world had in store for us or how many ways it would kick our asses. My thumb hovers before I finally press call.

"Lennon . . . Oh my God, I was just thinking of you," Grace answers after the very first ring, and I almost burst into tears.

"Hey, Gracie . . ."

Maddox
Chapter 16

I walk my mother to the door that night after everyone else has left. And I do mean everyone. Half my fucking family has been here today. If I had to hear one more comment about buying furniture, I was going to throw them all out. Not really, because they were all here to help. But man . . . it was tempting.

Mom turns before walking through the door and holds my face in her hands. "The boy who made me a mommy is having a baby . . . I'm not sure I was ready for that."

"That makes two of us, Ma." I smile, and her eyes fill with emotion. "Thanks for everything you did today."

"You'll see there's nothing in the world you wouldn't do for your children's happiness, Maddox. From the very first time you hear their heartbeat through the rest of their lives, they'll come first. *Always.* Every day. You're going to be an incredible father. But I'd be remiss not to mention you don't have to be a husband to be a father."

Her words land with a solid hit, as she intended. "It's complicated, Mom."

"Love always is, sweet boy. And I have no doubt that girl's life is more complicated than most. I just hope you know what you're doing." She pulls my head down to her and kisses my forehead, then lets go. "And when you're ready to deal with whoever hurt her, promise me you'll talk to your father first."

"I don't know what you're talking about," I lie, but this isn't the kind of thing we've been raised to discuss with her.

"Yes, you do. Don't ever forget I was able to handle myself long before I married your father. And you wouldn't be the man we raised you to be if you didn't know exactly what I meant. But like I said, promise me you'll speak to your father."

I nod without saying anything.

Plausible deniability.

"Love you, Mom."

"I love you, sweetheart. Don't fuck this up, okay? I like her." She waits for me to agree before leaving, and my heart squeezes because I'm pretty sure all I've done is fuck this up for years.

Once the door is locked, I expect to find Lennon and Meatball tucked into the corner of the couch, but the couch is empty, and the room is quiet. I check outside before making a loop around the first floor but come up empty-handed before taking the steps two at a time upstairs, where I hear her crying.

One day, I'm going to make it so this woman never has to cry again.

The door to my bedroom is open, and Lennon is sitting on the center of my bed, her legs crossed and Meatball in her lap with his big head nuzzled against her stomach. "Lennon . . . What's wrong?"

I cross the room as she wipes her face.

"Sorry, it's just been a lot to take in today." She pushes her hair behind her ears, and her mask slides into place. The one she uses to hide behind. The one I fucking hate because Lennon should never have to hide. "Your family is pretty great, Beneventi."

I kick off my sneakers and sit down next to her.

Does my dog come say hi to me?

No. The snoring, farting, lazy little fucker stays firmly planted in Lennon's lap.

Pretty sure he's protecting her and the baby.

Can a dog sense a pregnancy?

Good dog.

I'll have to get him some extra treats this week.

"The family can be a lot, but they mean well." I grip the back of her neck with my hands and massage her tight muscles. "They'll make this happen. Just wait and see. It'll be everything you need it to be. I promise."

"Mmmm . . ." she hums deep in her throat and drops her head foreword, giving me a better angle. "You always were good with your hands."

"You're setting me up with that one, *principessa*."

"Don't even think about it," she warns. "I'm pretty sure we make better friends than we do lovers, Maddox."

"Not sure I agree with you on that." Just hearing the word *lover* coming out of her pretty mouth sends my imagination in all sorts of depraved directions. "We were never just friends, Lennon."

"Yes, we were," she snaps. "For years, that's all we were. Then you had to mess it all up by proposing."

"Think of all the heartache you'd have saved us if you'd just said yes back then." It's the first time either of us have mentioned that night. The one where she asked me to leave. The one where I did what she asked, too young and too stupid to see what was right in front of me. Too fucked over my own hurt pride to fight for what I knew was mine.

I won't make that mistake again.

"We were always more," I remind her.

"Can we please not do this tonight?" she pleads as she

reaches for the remote and drops it in my lap. "Want to watch a movie?"

I take the hint for now, not wanting to push her after the day she's had, and pick up the remote. "Sure. What do you want to watch?"

"How do you feel about *The Avengers*?"

Lennon

Monday morning, Grace and I meet for breakfast, and I should have known better than to be worried. She sits across from me at a cute little café in town, staring in disbelief with a gigantic smile on her face as I finally finish dumping my entire story on her. "I can't believe you never told me."

I push my pancakes around the plate. "I don't know . . . I guess I didn't want anyone to know. It's all just so messy."

Gracie reaches across the table and grabs my hand. "Friends do messy. We don't run away from it. We don't run away from each other."

"You're the only friend I've ever had, Gracie." The admission should be humiliating, but somehow, it's freeing instead. "I've missed you."

"I've missed you too. But now you're here, and you're marrying Maddox. I can't believe it. Maddox Beneventi, officially off the market. The women of Kroydon Hills will be weeping in the streets."

She doesn't know how much that single statement stings, and I don't tell her either, like an insecure cow.

"And you're going to have a baby. That's insane. I'm so

excited for you both. Being a mother is the most rewarding, exhausting, frightening thing in the world. But I wouldn't change a minute of it. Especially if you're only having one. Lucky brat."

"Good grief, I can't even believe how you handle it all. You're a boss babe, Grace. I want to be you when I grow up," I tell her, meaning every word.

"You're going to be better. You're going to be you." She smiles and signals for the check. "Now let's go find you a wedding dress."

Everly Wilder is one of the premier wedding dress designers in the country, and luckily for me, she's Grace's twin sister. Maddox's sister also happens to be one of her designers, which means Everly has promised she'll do whatever it takes to get me in a dress fit for a princess in four weeks.

"Okay, these are the samples I pulled," Caitlin announces as Everly circles me in the center of the room. She looks from me to the ballroom-style gowns Caitlin pulled but shakes her head.

"I think we should go with formfitting," Everly announces, but I can tell Grace isn't sure.

"What if she pops?" Grace asks. "She's right around that twenty-week point. It's going to happen any day now."

"I looked like a cow by then," Caitlin announces. "Lucky bitch."

"Oh please. I've carried twins and triplets. Talk to me when you've basically had a hockey team skating on your bladder."

"I want her to pop," Everly announces, and I raise my hand up.

"Umm . . . could someone explain *popping* to me, please?"

All three women swing their heads my way, like I just asked the stupidest question in the world. Maybe I have.

"You know . . . popped." Grace motions with her hand in front of her stomach. "Right now, you're stomach is still flat, but soon, you're going to look like you've got a beach ball hidden under your skin."

"And it's going to feel like you're carrying the weight of a bowling ball," Caitlin agrees.

"Oh . . ." I say quietly, feeling fairly dumb.

Maybe I should get a book. I should have known that, shouldn't I?

My mom and I didn't have the closest relationship. It was nothing like Grace and her mom or Caitlin and Amelia. But it was ours, and I feel like, in this moment, I can't help but miss her more than usual.

"Listen," Everly says as she walks over to a display on the far side of the room and pulls down a gorgeous, white, silk formfitting dress with long, lace bell sleeves. "The world is going to know you're pregnant soon enough. Celebrate it. Don't try to hide it. You're beautiful. You have a stunning figure and tits and an ass I'd die to have again. Flaunt them. Drive Madman wild."

Her last statement has me blushing furiously.

It's easy to forget how close they all are with Maddox.

I can't imagine what it's like to grow up like that.

With a group of friends so close, you consider them family. But for as long as I've known Grace, that's always how she's looked at her friends. *As family.* Most of my family doesn't even feel that safe to me. But these women . . . this group of people . . . they've always been that safe place to land . . . to fall around each other.

Everly holds the dress in front of me and points me to the dressing room. "Come on, Merida. Let's try this one on."

"Merida?" I cock a brow.

"You know . . . the Disney princess with the crazy red hair."

"I never really watched Disney movies," I admit, and the ladies gasp. "I mean, if you think about it, I was already living my own version. Mine just wasn't supposed to have a happy ending." I duck my head down and let my hair fall in front of my face, covering my bruise, and walk into the dressing room.

Five minutes later, Everly has me standing on a dais, pinned to within an inch of my life. "Oh, you are stunning."

She turns me to face the mirror, and I fight the urge to cry.

It's beautiful

"Oh God. You hate it." She looks horrified.

"No." I shake my head. "It's beautiful. I just wish my mom were here. Or that my family could be here. It's just the hormones. Ignore me, please . . . I'm so sorry," I tell her as the tears fall.

Gracie takes my hand in hers. "I'm sorry, Lennon."

"Don't be. I'm just emotional. This is perfect, Everly. Thank you so much," I manage to tell her as I calm myself. "Do you think it will still fit in four weeks?"

"Just let me worry about that. We'll fit you again in three weeks, then tweak it a few days before the wedding. It will fit like a glove. Now go eat some ice cream and get me a baby bump to feature," she laughs.

"First flowers," Grace announces.

Right. We're headed to the florist next.

"Um, Everly . . . How do I get out of this without the pins ripping me to shreds?" I ask, concerned about getting blood on the beautiful white silk.

"Carefully," Caitlin deadpans, and Everly shakes her head. "Come on. I'll help you."

Grace and I did stop for ice cream before we walked down the street to the flower shop, where two beautiful blondes greet us. Wow. There must be something in the water here. "Gracie," the younger of the two excitedly calls out. "What are you doing here?"

"Hey, Lexi." She kisses the younger one's cheek, then looks confused as she turns to the woman who looks about my age. "Dillan . . . what are you doing here? I thought you were working with your sister?"

Dillan clips the stem of a beautiful white rose and adds it to a bucket. "It's definitely better for my relationship with my sister if we don't work together."

"I could see that," Grace muses. "Well, ladies, this is my friend, Lennon. Lennon, these are two of my beautiful cousins, Lexi and Dillan."

"Nice to meet you," I offer and look around as the ladies talk, until I hear Dillan choke.

"Holy shit. You're engaged to Maddox Beneventi?"

I turn slowly—because I swear to God if this woman is about to tell me she slept with him, I might use those pruning shears to cut her.

Damn. That went violent fast.

I purse my lips and smile. "I am, and Grace said this was the best place in town to come for flowers."

"It is," Grace adds. "Is Genevieve here?"

"I'll be there in a second," a woman calls out from the back room before popping out from behind the curtain.

"Sorry. I've got a big event we're prepping for tomorrow night." She wipes her hands on her apron, then offers me her hand. "Hi, I'm Genevieve. What can I help you with?"

"Umm . . ." I look around at the roomful of women, and my anxiety races. "Well, I'm getting married in four weeks, and we need to order flowers."

The beautiful brunette's smile lights up the room. "Great. How about you have a seat over here and tell me about your vision."

"Well, it's four weeks from now, so I'm not sure how picky I can be," I admit as I feel Lexi and Dillan's eyes boring holes into my head.

"Okay, let's start with your budget then," Genevieve offers patiently.

"There's no budget," I tell her, not sure what I'm doing. This is awful.

"That's not a problem. How small is no budget? I want to make sure I work within your range." She jots something down on a notepad, then looks up at me, hesitant.

"Oh . . . that's not what I meant. I meant money isn't an issue. I don't have a cap. It just needs to be over-the-top and beautiful."

"Fit for royalty," Gracie adds with a wink.

Genevieve clears her throat. "I can work with that. Do you have a color preference?"

I look at Grace and relax, confident for the first time all day. "Pinks, blues, and whites."

Finally, something in my wheelhouse. Color pallets I can do.

Lennon
Chapter 17

**There's a kind of hurt that doesn't cry or scream or cause a scene.
It just quietly changes your soul on a molecular level.**

—Lennon's Secret Thoughts

Maddox and I fall into some semblance of a routine over the next few weeks, but each morning, I wake with an ominous feeling, wondering if this will be the day. It's been too quiet. Too calm. If I know Monty like I fear I do, this calm won't last. It can't. And I'm attempting to reconcile that with this new life. The one that feels like I'm running away from my real life.

Those feelings have been haunting me since I left the hospital.

I'm just not sure what to do with any of it. The only thing I am sure of is that Maddox needs furniture. He's been on the couch for days, and that's not fair to him. Fixing that, I can handle. So, with Maria in tow and my driver on hand, we head into the city for a little interior design.

And it's not until we go to the last store that I stand there, unable to make a decision.

I've spent my day picking out beds, armoires, a beautiful bleached-wood dining table with twelve stunning chairs, a kitchen set, and new stools that don't look like they've been with the man since he probably lived in a frat house a decade ago. I've ordered rugs and drapes and found a beautiful little vintage shop with items to bring the character to his home which truly matches the man and the stunning design he created. Blues and whites and grays, with cool creams and cherrywood accents, which will all come together with clean lines and classic textures to create a beautifully serene, peaceful escape from the world when Maddox comes home.

It should be a place our child will have a happy life in.

If this all works out.

But some part of me still isn't sure it will.

A piece of me still refuses to believe it.

And now . . . Now I stand in the middle of a high-end baby boutique, staring at cribs and wanting to cry. It all just feels wrong. How am I supposed to do this—bring a baby into a lie? What if something happens?

I turn to Maria. "I need to get out of here."

She nods and calls my driver, and I'm whisked away moments later.

No sooner have we left the store than I call my brother.

Thankfully, he picks up on the first ring. "I was starting to worry about you, kid."

"Atticus," I sob. "I don't know what I'm doing."

"What's wrong, Lennon? Fuck. What happened?" I can hear the fear and desperation in his voice and hate that I put it there.

"Is that Lennon?" Rhys asks from somewhere near Atticus. "Put her on speaker."

Oh no.

"Who else is with you?" I ask, scared of the answer.

"It's just us, kid," Rhys confirms after Atticus switches to FaceTime and both my brothers' faces appear on-screen. Thanks to the magic of makeup and the time that's passed, my face is looking far less battered, but I still don't join them. They'd notice. "What the hell is going on? Monty told Dad the wedding has to be moved up to next month. I need you to come home, Lennon. Whatever it is, we'll deal with it."

"I can't come home. I'm pregnant." I drop that bomb, expecting Rhys to explode, but he doesn't say anything. He doesn't even blink. Atticus winces behind him, though, like he's not the ass who threw three pregnancy tests at my face. "Did you hear me?"

"Yeah, I heard you. Okay, you're pregnant. You're not the first pregnant princess, Lennon. We'll deal with it. I guess that makes the whole wanting to move the wedding thing up make more sense."

"Uhh . . . Think again," Atticus tells Rhys, and I wish I could crawl under a rock.

Rhys's eyes narrow, but they don't harden. He's not mad. He's worried. My family may not be the Beneventis, but my brothers are still good men, and they love me.

"Jesus Christ, Atticus. Monty isn't the father. Monty is the man who flew to Kroydon Hills, called me a whore, then beat the shit out of me." I hit the video button on the phone and let them see what's left of my fading bruises. It's faint, but makeup does little to cover the remnants.

My brothers both yell at the same time, so I can't understand either one.

"Stop," I tell them. "Yes, Monty did this. He bruised my cheek with his fist, then kicked me once I was on the floor. I went to the hospital, had an MRI and an ultrasound, and the baby is fine. *It's a boy, by the way* . . ." I murmur, wishing I could be celebrating as I tell them instead of dreading their response.

"Holy shit, poppet." Atticus sighs as his smile nearly takes over his entire face. "You're having a boy?"

I smile through my tears and nod. "We are."

"We?" Rhys asks.

"We," I confirm. "I found a way out of marrying Monty. But I can't tell you. I'd be putting you in an awful position if I do."

"My duty will always be to the crown, Lennon. But it's not on my head yet. Tell me what you're planning. Let me help you."

I look between my big brothers and make a split-second decision.

One I hope I don't come to regret.

Maddox
Chapter 18

"Lennon..." I call out when I walk in the house that evening, but I don't find her or Meatball. Instead, I find Maria in my kitchen, eating a salad at my counter. "Where's Lennon?"

"She's lying down," she tells me without looking away from whatever she's watching on her tablet.

"Is she okay?" I ask, looking at the time. It's barely seven. That's early, even by Lennon's standards.

"Monty called today. She didn't answer, but he called. It's not my place to tell you, but for her safety, you need to know, and I'm not sure whether she'll tell you." She rests her fork on her plate and turns toward me, a steely anger settled in her eyes. "I've ordered a blow-up mattress and will be sleeping in the house from now on. I need you to understand that this man is dangerous. Men who've never been told no are some of the most dangerous in the world. They're convinced they can have anything they want—and can do anything they want without consequence. I listened today to Lennon convince the future king of Mornea that she has this handled, and I'm telling you, she doesn't. If you want to be her husband, you need to be able to protect her, and I won't keep the facts from you."

I'm pretty damn sure this is the most I've ever heard Maria say, especially to me.

But now she's speaking a language I understand.

"If she wakes up, could you let her know I just ran to my parents' house, and I'll be back soon?" I ask, ready to put an end to this.

Maria stares me down for a moment. "Don't put her in danger, Beneventi. So help me God, if you do, I'll stop you myself. I failed her once. It's not going to happen again."

We're finally on the same page.

"We both failed her, and neither of us are letting it happen again. I'll put him down myself before he gets near her." A calm fury settles in my bones.

And something like respect shines in her eyes.

"You should let me be the one to get my hands dirty. I have diplomatic immunity. I can't be prosecuted."

"Noted," I tell her before leaving.

This has got to stop.

It doesn't take me long before I'm walking past a few cars in my parents' driveway and into their house. Looks like I'm about to interrupt poker night, if I had to guess. I let myself in and find Nonna in the kitchen, making a cup of tea. I still haven't gotten Lennon here to meet Nonna, and I make a mental note to fix that soon. "*Principe* . . ." she calls out and holds her shaky hands out for me to hug. "You don't come see me anymore."

"I know. I'm sorry, Nonna. I'll do better." I kiss the top of her gray hair and hug her frail body.

"You bring your *principessa* with you. Let me see her. Let me dote on the mother of your son. Your mother tells me she's too skinny. I'll make her homemade pasta. We'll get some meat on her bones."

"She'd love that. I'll make it happen soon. I promise." I step back, but she refuses to drop her hold.

"You do it before the wedding. Don't make me meet my new granddaughter that day. You hear me?"

"I do, and I will. I promise." I look around, not seeing anyone else. "Do you know where Dad is?"

"He's playing poker with your uncles in the game room."

"Thanks, Nonna," I tell her before leaving to find my father. And moments later, when I do, he's right where she said he'd be. My Uncles Bash, Becks, and Cade, along with Grace's dad, Declan, all sit with him around a poker table, cigars in hand and various drinks next to them as they hold their cards close. It's something I grew up seeing and always enjoyed, but right now, I'm too pissed to appreciate the men in this room. Right now, I'm still seeing red.

"Dad," I announce my presence, and everyone looks up.

"There's the man of the hour," Becket jokes, and I groan. "You didn't just knock up a socialite. You went for a princess. Gotta tell you, kid, you really go for the gold, don't you?"

"I will fucking gut you if you talk about her like that again," I warn him, and everyone jumps up like I'm the first person to threaten death on someone in this house.

"Fuck, Sam . . . Get your kid under control," Becket laughs, and Cade smacks the back of his head.

"You're never gonna learn, are you, Becks?" Cade groans, while Bash and Declan look between my father and uncles.

I ignore them all and approach my father. "I need to talk to you."

"Yeah . . . I'd say so." He throws his cards down and grabs his glass of bourbon. "I'm out."

I follow him through the door and outside onto the patio. "You want to try not threatening to gut your uncle like a fish the next time he says something stupid? Christ, if we killed family members every time they said something we didn't like, we'd have lost Lucky years ago."

"I need you to tell me I can't kill a duke. Because I've got to tell you, I know you never wanted your business to touch us, but if that's what it takes to make Lennon safe . . . Fuck, Dad. There's nothing I wouldn't do to make her safe." The memory of her lying beaten and broken in the hospital bed flashes in my mind. "I've kept my shit locked down. I've done what she asked. I've come up with another way. But—"

"But nothing, Maddox. You work the plan. Marry the girl. Give her your name. Our name. Protect your woman and your baby. Take it from me, son. There's nothing in the world we won't do to protect our families. And marrying her . . . loving her. That's what she needs. That's what's going to keep her safe."

"I don't—"

"Don't lie to a liar, son. You do. You have for a long fucking time. You like to point out everything else your family and friends can't see. Well, this is me pointing it out to you. That girl carrying your kid—she's been yours for a long time." He ashes his stogie on Mom's pavers like she's not going to kill him for that tomorrow, and my mind swims from his words.

"How would you know?" I finally ask, trying to figure out what exactly he knows.

"Do you really think you're the first Beneventi to know everything, Maddox?" he challenges. "Don't look for trouble, son. But don't back down from the fight either. Do you understand me?"

I think about the lengths I'm willing to go to protect Lennon and the baby.

To protect my family. "Yeah. I understand."

When I get back home, I go right to my room to check on Lennon and find her and Meatball in my bed. She's wearing another one of my shirts, and every fucking protective instinct in my body roars to life, screaming *mine*. The lights are off, and the low light of the TV is the only thing illuminating her beautiful face. I fight the urge to wake her up and jump in the shower instead.

I walk into my bathroom and am immediately surrounded by Lennon. By the minty smell of her shampoo and conditioner. Her expensive perfume. Her body lotion. She's already invaded my every waking thought, and lately, most of the ones while I'm sleeping too. But now . . . Now, jacking off in my shower to the memory of Lennon has become a regular thing.

It's like we've somehow gone back in time to when we first met.

To the way I was obsessed with her.

I've wanted this woman for what feels like a literal lifetime. Then to finally have her here in my house, in my life, but still out of reach. It's like history is repeating itself.

We talk and laugh like we used to years ago. She lets me cook for her—because some things never change, and the only thing Lennon Windsor is capable of making herself is tea and toast. But she likes to order dinner, so we can sit at the counter and talk about our days. The fantasy is right there, but it's still just out of reach because she's not ready for anything more... Not yet.

In the meantime, I'm left with a fantasy wrapped in the memory of that night.

That perfect cunt milking me . . .

Those pouty lips wrapped around me . . .

Green eyes looking up through dark lashes . . .

Do I want to fuck her again?

Of course I do.

I want to feel her from the inside. I want to touch her. I want to make her scream and writhe beneath me. I want her to ache for me. To burn for me the way I burn for her. But more than that, I want to make her remember how good we can be.

It was never about us not wanting each other.

It was being unable to choose each other.

This time is different.

She's it. She's everything. She always has been.

My obsession.

My wife.

My fucking wife.

Fuck. I groan and stroke my cock faster. *Harder.* Until I'm remembering Lennon beneath me. Above me. Her gorgeous legs wrapped around me. Her tits bouncing with each thrust of my cock. Her scream filling my room.

Her cum on my cock.

Her taste on my tongue.

Her face is the only thing I see when I finally come, groaning her name into the cascading water.

Lennon

I roll over as the bathroom door opens, and Maddox walks into his bedroom. Bare-chested with black pajama pants hanging from his lean hips. Every dip and valley of his strong body is beautifully displayed. His chest. His abs. His ridiculous muscles pointing down to the most delicious V. He's every inch my dark prince.

But he's not mine. My heart can't risk it. Not when I'm losing so much already.

My future.

My family.

My country.

My birthright.

Complicating this . . . us . . . I can't go there.

"Hey . . . you awake?" he murmurs and drops down on the edge of the bed. His hand runs over my hair and tucks a lock behind my ear. "How are you feeling?"

"Fat," I whisper on a quiet sob. "I popped."

He looks at me, confused. "What?"

"The girls called it *popping*. I popped." I push the blanket down and tug my t-shirt up, showing him the belly I seemed to have developed overnight, and Maddox's eyes grow wide.

"There's a baby in there," he whispers, then holds his hands up as if to ask for permission.

I nod silently, and he rests both hands on either side of my slightly rounded stomach.

"Fuck, Lennon . . . We're going to be parents."

I can't help my laugh. "Yeah, I guess we are. I tried to buy baby furniture today, but I couldn't do it. Maybe you could come with me next time? Maybe we could go after our next doctor's appointment next week?" I ask, scared he's going to say no.

But of course, he doesn't.

This is Maddox Beneventi.

I'm beginning to realize he's never told me no.

He presses his lips to my stomach and smiles. "Tell me where and when, *principessa*. And maybe buy us some more furniture so I can stop sleeping on the damn couch. It's not as comfortable as it looks."

"I told you I'd sleep there," I argue, stuck on the fact that he said *us*.

And what does he do but laugh at me with a beautifully possessive look in his eyes. "I'm not letting my pregnant wife sleep on the couch."

"I'm not your wife yet," I argue jokingly because I'm not sure what to do with the way I love those words.

"Technicalities don't matter." His hands frame my belly, like he's trying to memorize it, and my goodness, the feel of them on me sends my mind into overdrive.

"I bought furniture today," I whisper, and I swear a look of disappointment floats across his face before he shoves it away. "But the bedroom sets won't be in for six to eight weeks."

"Oh," he murmurs and drops his hands before he stands. "Maybe I'll get an air mattress like Maria."

"Rome stopped by earlier and moved the mattress from the guest house into the spare room for her." They thought I didn't hear them as she yelled at him to watch the walls while he was carrying it up the stairs.

Maddox nods, resignation settling in his eyes.

"Maybe you could sleep here." This is such a bad idea. "If you stay on your side of the bed, I mean. You might have to share it with Meatball though. He likes that pillow."

"You sure?" he asks softly, and I wish I could just give in.

Just give us what we both know would feel incredible.

But I can't. Because I've never just wanted this man physically.

Physically, he could give me everything I ever wanted. Hell, he already has.

It's the emotional fallout I'm not sure I can handle.

So I do what I do best. I deflect.

"Hands to yourself though. Got it?" I tease and turn off the television, while Maddox rounds the bed and climbs into the other side.

He gets in and pulls the blankets up, then presses his lips

to my temple, and I melt momentarily into his touch. And for that moment, I'm safe and cherished. For that brief moment, I forget everything else. The fear. The heartache. Everything I'm giving up for a chance at giving my baby the life he deserves. For one quick moment, it's all fine.

Until I wake up tomorrow and reality sets back in.

Lennon
Chapter 19

I don't need a happily ever after.
I don't believe in fairytales and haven't for a long time.
Prince charming doesn't exist. He's a lie.
I want someone who's going to show up for me.
Someone who will fight for us.
A prince lives his life for his country.
I want someone who lives his life for us.
I don't want a fairytale.
I want a reality.

—*Lennon's Secret Thoughts*

When I walk into the kitchen, Maddox is already standing behind the counter with a kettle beginning to whistle on the stove. He pushes my box of tea toward me, then grabs a mug from the cabinet and sets it in front of me, pulling a smile from my lips.

"Good morning," I murmur as I add my tea to the mug and pour the water over, then stare at the man who gave it to me. Maddox Beneventi in jeans is a beautiful thing. And don't get me started on this man bare-chested with pajama pants hanging from his hips. But him in a beautifully cut black suit with a gray shirt and his collar open . . . dear lord . . . he's a sight to be seen.

"Lennon?" he questions.

I'm not even sure if he said anything else, so I ignore whatever it could have been and carry on like I wasn't just caught staring at my future husband. "Are you going to il leone today?"

"Yeah," he grins, and I know I'm busted. "I'm meeting with inspectors. I think we're getting the okay to open. It's just a matter of having everything ready now."

"That's exciting." He slides a piece of toast with raspberry jam my way, and a teeny tiny piece of my heart softens, knowing he's paid attention. Some women crave salt or sweets during their last trimester. But not me. Nope. Tea and toast. It's all I've craved since the cravings hit. I take a bite, and my stomach grumbles.

"You've got to eat more, Lennon. How about you let me cook you dinner tonight?"

I take another bite of toast. "You just made me breakfast."

"You've got to eat more than one meal a day. Come on."

When a gorgeous man offers to cook for you, it's nearly impossible to say no.

When it's this man . . . there's no nearly about it.

"You don't have to do that," I tell him and sip my tea. "I'm sure you're busy."

"I'm meeting with the inspectors, then catching up with Callen and my brothers for our tux fittings. I've got nothing after that." He rounds the island and plants his arms on either side of me. Caging me in. "Let me feed you, Lennon."

Oh my . . .

When he puts it that way . . .

Says it that way, with that voice.

Well, how could I say no?

"Okay," I whisper.

I swear Maddox leans his face against my hair and inhales.

And oh my God . . . why is that so hot?

I try to ignore the way my body reacts to his, but before I get the chance to push him away—really, I was getting there—Maddox takes a step back.

He brushes his lips over my cheek, and I swallow my anxiety down.

My phone vibrates on the counter, and I grab it and toss it in my purse. "That's Caitlin. I've got my final fitting this morning."

He runs his big hand over my hair and tugs. "See you tonight, *principessa*."

I watch him leave before I take my next breath and wonder what exactly I just agreed to.

"Oh Lennon," Gracie whispers, while Amelia, Caitlin, and Everly stand off to the side of the dais, silent. "You look stunning."

Everly tugs at my train, straightening it. Judging the fit. "How does it feel?" she asks.

"It doesn't matter how it feels," Caitlin argues. "I've never seen a more beautiful bride. If you're uncomfortable, you're going to have to suck it up."

"Don't listen to her," Amelia moves next to me. "You do look beautiful, but you need to be comfortable."

"I think the cut at her bust should be lower," Caitlin offers, and Amelia glares.

"This wedding is taking place at the largest cathedral in

Philadelphia," Amelia scolds her daughter. "It's being presided over by a bishop, Caitlin. Do not tart up your sister-in-law. She looks perfect."

Caitlin and Everly both giggle, while Amelia shakes her head with a beautifully sarcastic smile that makes me more than a little envious of their relationship.

I never had that with my mother.

I turn to really look at myself in the enormous three-way mirror and run my hand over my belly . . . over my baby . . . loving that he's on display. "Everly, this is perfection. Thank you."

She beams with pride. "I never thought I'd be dressing a real-life princess. Now go let Caitlin help you out of it while I dig out a few other things I have for you."

"What other things?" Caitlin asks as we step into the dressing room.

"I said for Lennon," Everly calls back.

Very, very carefully, Caitlin helps me out of my wedding dress, then takes it away. She's waiting with the others when I step back out. A rolling rack of dresses sits next to them, and a smile is stretching across Everly's face. "I may have gone a little overboard."

"What?" I ask, utterly confused.

"You needed some new clothes, so we threw a few things together. But we definitely need to hit up Le Désir after this. You need new bras, stat, Lennon," Caitlin adds as she shakes her head.

"Where?" I ask.

Amelia links my arm through hers. "Time to do a little shopping, Lennon."

Maddox

"Dude. You're the one getting married. Why the hell do we have to wear this shit?" Lucky groans as the sales associate adjusts his silver tie.

"Because you have to look good, you fucking idiot. How else do you expect to bag a bridesmaid?" Rome argues while I hang back.

Callen's chest shakes with silent laughter. "You want to tell them the only bridesmaids are their sister and Gracie, who's married with enough kids to fill a hockey team, or should I?"

"Neither. Let them live in their delusions for a few more days. They'll find out on Saturday." I don't bother telling him I don't give a shit what they think.

I'm too worried about everything else.

The wedding.

The shitstorm that's going to rain down after.

How to keep Lennon and the baby safe through it all.

"You doing okay, Madman? You're quieter than normal, and that's saying something, you broody asshole," Callen asks as they hand him the garment bag with his tux inside.

"Yeah. I'll just feel better once we get through the weekend."

Callen doesn't call me out on the lie. He could. He knows me well enough to know I'm full of shit. But he doesn't.

"Hey. Isn't that Mom and Cait and Lennon going into the lingerie shop?" Rome asks, and all our heads turn across the street, and sure enough, there's my bride-to-be. "Damn, Madman. Maybe she's getting something sexy for your wedding night."

"Yeah," Lucky chirps. "Maybe it's something edible."

"Have you ever even had sex, you idiot?" I ask through laughter.

"Yeah, shitstain." Rome smacks the back of Lucky's head. "He doesn't need to eat her underwear. Just her."

I don't bother telling them I don't need sexy lingerie to do that.

Just permission.

Permission I haven't been given yet.

"Honey, I'm home," Lennon laughs when she walks in the house later that night. "Oh my God. What smells so good?"

"It's a family recipe." I grin once she finally steps into the kitchen. "Can't tell you or I'd have to kill you."

Her cheeks flush, and she drops her bags by the door.

"That's a lot of bags, princess," I tease and pull two cheeseburgers and truffle fries from the oven. "Hope you're hungry."

"Oh my God. You remembered . . ." She looks like she's going to cry as I set the plates on the new kitchen table that arrived earlier this week.

"Of course I did." I grab the ketchup from the fridge and two bottles of water. "I remember everything, Lennon."

"We had so much fun back then, didn't we?" she asks, and the hesitance in her voice wrecks me.

"We did," I agree and pull out a chair at the table for her to sit in. "It was a great two years."

She pops a fry in her mouth and moans. "Do you remember the first time you made these for me?"

I sit back and watch her eat. "You mean the night you burned spaghetti?"

"How was I supposed to know it wasn't enough water?" She laughs, and it tugs at places I buried a long time ago.

"I guess it was a good thing you didn't like me for my cooking skills." She adds ketchup to her burger and takes a big bite, followed by another moan. Christ. She's killing me.

"I loved you, Lennon." I tell her, refusing to allow her to downplay it to anything else. "Walking away was the hardest thing I ever did. But I did it for you. Because that was what you asked me to do."

"I know," she whispers before she winces and grabs my hand, then flattens it against her stomach.

"What— Are you okay?" Fear floods my system before her wince turns to a smile, and Lennon pushes down against my palm.

"Feel that?" she asks as she bites down on her lower lip and moves my hand the slightest bit, until something presses back against it. "That. Right there."

I look from her to her belly. "Is that . . . ?"

Words fail me.

Actually fail me.

"That's our baby," she whispers.

Lennon

Chapter 20

**Life doesn't allow do-overs.
We can fix our behavior, so we don't repeat our mistakes,
but once they're made, there's no unmaking them.**

—Lennon's Secret Thoughts

I look at myself in the mirror, blown away by just how much my body has changed since the last time I saw Dr. Hayes-Sinclair. My side profile looks like I'm hiding a somewhat deflated soccer ball under my shirt. The bruising is gone, and in its place is glowing skin, which is new for me. Redheads don't glow. We're generally either ghostly pale or covered in freckles. I fall on the ghostly pale side most days. But today, I have a glow that even I recognize.

Maddox walks into his bedroom and grins on his way to the bathroom. "I mean, not that I don't love seeing you in my clothes, *picolla principessa*, but I'm not sure that's appropriate for leaving the house."

"Tell me something I don't know," I murmur and pull out

a gorgeous maxi-dress Everly gave me yesterday, then smile when I realize I can't wear a bra with it. What a shame. "Are we still going to il leone for dinner?"

"Yeah," Maddox yells from the other side of the door. "But we've got to get moving, if we're grabbing lunch before your appointment."

"What's this new obsession with feeding me?" I call back as I slide his shirt off and my dress down. Damn. My boobs do look good. I guess there's no mistaking I'm pregnant now.

"You're eating for two," Maddox hollers as the shower turns on.

This man . . .

I grab a sweater and search for my phone as it rings somewhere under my pile of discarded clothes.

When I find it, I wish I hadn't.

With shaking hands, I slide my thumb over the screen and answer.

"Hello, Papa," I try to force the pleasantry, but my relationship with my father is strained at best, and it's rarely at its best.

"Why are you in America, Lennon? And why haven't you been returning my secretary's calls? And why is Monty telling me your wedding is next month instead of next spring? I've been summoned to your grandfather's office, and I have no answers to give him."

"Wow," I breathe out. "That's a great deal of questions."

I doubt deflection is working for me this time, but I don't know where to begin or how to answer him. There is nothing soft and forgiving about my father. He's bitter and entitled, and he rules his children with an iron fist. It's amazing any of us turned out the way we did.

"That is not an answer. Now explain."

I'm not sure which part he'd like explained, but I'm tempted to ask him to explain how his only daughter has been in another country for weeks at this point, and he's only now noticing. Rhys figured it out weeks ago. How has my father not noticed anything is amiss sooner?

Oh right . . . because unlike Rhys, he doesn't care.

I walk through the French doors and onto the small balcony overlooking the lush backyard and close my eyes as the breeze blows warm air against my skin, balancing out the chilling dread settling in my stomach.

There's little use lying now.

But I'm still going to.

I'm getting married tomorrow.

I'll tell him the truth the next day, right before he disowns me.

"I'm in America on holiday, visiting a friend. You remember my old roommate, Grace?" I'm shocked my voice doesn't shake with the blatant lie, but I somehow manage to pull it off as Maddox joins me outside. I hold a finger up to my mouth, silencing him. He's not who my father needs to hear right now. "I'll be home in a few days, and I'll make sure Grandfather is one of my first stops."

"What about Monty?" Papa demands, leaving no room to bend in his voice.

"Monty is a spoiled child, throwing a temper tantrum. I haven't agreed to move the wedding up. Grandfather's event coordinator has been busy, and we haven't even discussed it, but Monty doesn't want to hear that. He thinks because now is convenient for him, we should all drop everything." I spin the partial truth into a lie that works in my favor. "He refuses to acknowledge the intricacies of a royal wedding."

"I'll talk to his family—"

"No," I snap, then soften my voice. "I have to learn to work with him eventually. It might as well be now. I admit I've been avoiding him. I'll call him and handle it."

"You have one job, Lennon. One. Marry this man.

Strengthen relations with his family. We need them. I don't care what you have to do to make him happy. Do your fucking duty and do it with a smile." Venom coats his words, and I suddenly wish Maddox wasn't here to hear this. Not when he's grown up the way he has with such incredible parents.

He moves in behind me and pulls me back against his chest. Offering me his strength.

"Yes, Papa," I murmur, hating him in this moment and wondering where my mother would stand if she was still here. Would I tell her the truth? "He's not a good man, you know . . . He's violent and cruel."

I'm not sure why I bother telling him that.

I don't feel better, having said it.

Just empty.

"The world is violent and cruel, Lennon. Learn to live with it and avoid upsetting him. That's the best advice I can give you."

Maddox wraps a strong arm around my chest when my knees threaten to buckle.

"I'll expect you home before the end of next week." He ends the call, and I sag against Maddox until he lifts me from my feet and carries me into the room.

He sits on the edge of the bed and holds me in his lap. "You will never have to learn to live in a cruel world, Lennon. No one will ever be cruel to you again. I promise."

I close my eyes and rest my cheek against his chest, needing a minute.

"Promise me our child will always be loved. Promise he'll always come first. No matter what," I demand with more conviction than I knew I was capable of.

Maddox lifts my face to his and shows me the storm brewing behind his eyes.

One I'm all too familiar with.

One it would be so easy to get lost in.

"He will always be loved . . ." His gravelly voice is strained and intense. "You both will," he adds softly and sets me on the bed. "Come on. We don't want to miss the appointment."

I watch his back as Maddox disappears through the door, and I sit in shock.

Not by his words but by the realization that, not for the first time, I think I've fallen in love with Maddox Beneventi.

Maria moves inside the restaurant ahead of us as Maddox and I step inside il leone for what is essentially a rehearsal dinner without the rehearsal. We couldn't risk anyone getting wind of the wedding early, so there was no walk-through. No rehearsing. Just Maddox's aunts confirming everything for us while we were at my doctor's appointment, being cleared for another four weeks. Our little man is still measuring small, but he's strong and healthy.

And as of tomorrow, he'll be safe.

Tomorrow.

It's hard to believe it's nearly here.

It's even harder to believe this is really happening.

Maddox's hand on my back as we step into the marble entrance is a constant reminder that it *is* all real. And when he stops just inside the door and stares at me for a beat too long, I worry he's going to change his mind.

But that's not this man's way.

His loud, chaotic family's voices drift toward us from the

tables set up at the back of the room, and I take a chance and reach out with shaking fingers, brushing his hair off his handsome face. "You ready for this, Beneventi?"

"I've been ready for this for years, *tesoro*."

Well that's a new one.

"I'm not sure I've ever been anyone's treasure before," I admit softly.

He slips something out of his pocket and holds it up in front of me. A beautiful pale-blue diamond ring glints in the light. "I proposed to you once, Lennon. And you broke my fucking heart and asked me to walk away. Don't ask again— because you won't like my answer this time. I shouldn't have agreed then. I should have fought harder for us. But I'm fighting now. And I'll fight every day, if that's what it takes. Marry me, *principessa*."

I lick my suddenly dry lips and hold back the tears that are burning the backs of my eyes. "I wanted to say yes, you know . . . The first time." My thumb traces the stubble on his jaw as I try to force my thoughts into some kind of sense. "I wanted to run away with you and live my own happily ever after. But they never would have let us. My mother was smarter than my father. She would have found us and stopped us, and she would have destroyed you." I step closer, ignoring the ring between us, the bump between us, and all the years between us and wrap my arms around his shoulders. "I couldn't let that happen. Not then and not now."

"Don't say no, princess." He ghosts his lips over mine, and I feel that same old spark flickering back to life down to the very tips of my toes.

"I'm scared, Maddox. If you mean something to me, they can use you against me," I admit out loud for the first time ever. "I couldn't survive that."

He wraps a hand around my neck and digs his fingers

into my hair. "I'm not one of the weak little boys you're used to, Lennon. I'm not scared of your family."

My body sways toward his, as if being pulled by a magnetic force.

"Maybe you should be," I whisper, and he smiles against my lips.

"Maybe *they* should be scared of me."

I exhale a shaky breath as hope blooms in my chest. "I'm already marrying you tomorrow."

"You're taking my name tomorrow. You've already got my heart. Now I want your soul," he whispers back, and he'll never know what those words do to me.

I brush my lips over his. "You already took a piece of that with you when you left London."

"I don't want a piece. I want it all." His normally gravelly voice is smooth and confident and so incredibly sexy.

"And if I tell you it's yours?" I ask and run my fingers through his hair, unable to get close enough to quench this sudden overpowering need. The one that's drowning out the fear and the lingering anger, so all I see is him.

He takes my hand in his and holds it between us as he slides the ring down my finger, then kisses my knuckle. "Then I'd tell you you've always been mine, *principessa*. It's about time you admitted it."

When his lips find mine, it's not hard or fast.

He's slow and steady and deliciously confident, stealing my breath and my heart and my soul all in one kiss.

And when I can no longer breathe or think or fear . . . when I'm barely more than one giant hypersensitive exposed nerve, Maddox pulls back and presses his lips to my forehead. "I've loved you since the very first time I saw you, Lennon."

"You haven't always had a great way of showing that," I admit, hurt with the reminder that he may think he's loved me for years, but he had no problem using other people as placeholders when I wasn't available.

Before Maddox can answer, Lucky appears out of nowhere, smiling. "Jesus Christ. Are you seriously gonna get busy in front of a wall of windows? There's got to be an office or back room somewhere. Pick one."

"Luciano Beneventi, I will murder you," Amelia's voice calls out, and Lucky winks at us as he makes his way over to the bar.

I step aside, needing a minute, but Maddox pulls me toward him as his eyes hold me hostage. "This isn't over, Lennon."

I look around at the roomful of people before finding him again.

"It is for tonight."

He takes my hand in his and gently tugs me down the stairs and into the vault room, where I was just a few weeks ago with his father and him. He shuts the massive door. No doubt keeping us far enough away from his family, so I'm assuming we can continue this argument without being heard.

Just how I hoped to spend the night before my wedding.

Who am I kidding?

This is exactly what I envisioned. I just thought it would be with a different man.

Maddox leans back against the glass wall separating us from the temperature-controlled wine room and crosses his thick arms over his muscled chest, testing the strength of the buttons of his shirt. "Ask me."

His tone leaves no room for argument, but if he thinks that's going to stop me, he doesn't know me at all. "Ask you what?"

"Ask me how many women I've slept with since you told me you were marrying someone else five years ago . . . Since you begged me to walk away." He doesn't yell. *No*, he somehow manages to keep his voice low and steady when just those words make me murderous. "Since you lied to my fucking face and told me you didn't love me."

"Maddox—" I plead, desperate not to do this.

"No." His wild eyes blaze with anger. "You don't get to act hurt when you're the one who made the call. You ended it. Now ask."

"I don't want to know." I pace away from him, not sure how we went from the beauty of that proposal to this. "I never thought you'd be alone forever. I didn't want that for you." I spin back around as my anger wins over, my arms flung out to my side. "But my cousin? Did you have to sleep with my cousin? You could have had anyone else. My God, you probably had *everyone* else. But why her?"

Maddox's blue eyes deepen as he slowly steps forward like an apex predator stalking his prey. "Do you remember when Elwyn hosted the Kings football team last year?" he asks, not showing an ounce of emotion.

"Of course I remember," I seethe and look away. "I was forced to be there."

I remember how pissed I was to be summoned like that and wishing I wasn't in-between ballets, so I'd have an excuse to avoid it. I remember the way Monty wouldn't keep his hands off me. Or his mouth. And when I look up at Maddox . . . I know.

Damn it.

"Yeah . . . now you remember," he bites back, rage and hurt building behind his eyes and matching my own. "Imagine having to watch me kiss someone else. Imagine seeing their hands on me. Holding my face."

I close my eyes, trying to block that thought from my brain.

"He kissed me. What was I supposed to do? Push him

away with the camera in our faces?" I argue as indignation fuels me. "Are you saying he kissed me, so you fucked my cousin?"

"I've probably fucked a hundred women since you told me you were marrying him, princess. I didn't care who they were. I didn't even know most of them. I had no idea she was your cousin when I met her. And I didn't care. Because she had your face. They all did. Every time I was with a woman, I only ever saw you. Wanted you." He gets in my face, still unbelievably in control. "But I couldn't have you. You made sure I knew that."

I shake my head and push down the sob that's hurtling up my throat. "How is that supposed to make me feel? You used them because you couldn't have me?" I shove him back as pain tears through me. "Maddox . . ."

"I never said I was a saint, Lennon. But I loved you. I didn't fuck Alex because I wanted her. I didn't spend a night with her to hurt you. She reminded me of you, and when I closed my eyes, you were what I saw." He wraps a hand around my head and holds my face in front of his. "You're the only thing I ever see."

"Maddox . . ."

"You're the only woman I've ever loved, Lennon. You've got to forgive me because I was doing what you told me to. I was leaving you alone."

"I hated pushing you away," I pant and fist my fingers in his shirt. "All I wanted was you. All I ever wanted was you, and I got to have you for a little while. Pushing you away was the hardest thing I've ever done."

Anger and hurt war with love and lust until I don't know what to say or do.

"Then stop doing it, Lennon."

For a single heartbeat, I think about pushing one more time, but I can't. I've never wanted anyone or anything the way I want him. Instead, I pull him closer and lick my lips. "I hate that you were with her."

"Never again, princess. No one but you." One strong hand skims down my trembling body and drags up my thigh as his lips brush that sweet spot where my shoulder meets my neck. One finger pushes inside me, then another. "Tell me this is okay. Tell me you want me. Tell me you forgive me."

"Promise me it's just me. I'm the only woman you touch. I'm the only one you see," I pant.

"Only you, *tesoro*. Only ever you."

Maddox lifts me up and sits me on the edge of the table, careful to take my weight before he unbuckles his belt.

My hands fly to his waist as I shove his jeans down below his incredible ass, and he pushes my panties aside, then thrusts inside me in one beautiful movement.

We both hiss with the sting. My swollen body stretching to take him deep inside.

"I'll never want anyone but you," he promises as he licks into my mouth.

Swallowing my moans.

Each slow snap of his hips is a measured movement meant to drag his cock along my walls, hitting every neglected nerve ending that's been begging for attention for months.

"Do you have any idea how many times I've fucked my fist, imagining what it would feel like to be inside you again?" He pulls out and pushes back in again, even slower this time than I thought possible. One arm cradles my head while the other lifts my ass. "Just you."

"Oh God, Maddox," I breathe out on a barely audible whisper as I get lost in his touch and his taste. In us.

"Fuck, Lennon. It wasn't supposed to be like this. You deserve better," he curses against my mouth as his hips finally pick up speed. "You deserved to be worshipped."

"I don't need to be worshipped," I moan. "I need to come."

His fingers dig into my skin as he lifts me from the table and impales me, hitting something deep inside me as my toes curl and my back arches, and I lose any false sense of control and shatter around him.

Irrevocably broken, but maybe . . . just maybe, somehow finally healed.

I fit in his arms like I was meant to be there.

—*Lennon's Secret Thoughts*

When I wake up the next morning, it's with my head resting in the crook of Maddox's arm and him at my back, with his hand possessively wrapped around my stomach. I don't remember falling asleep last night, but I do know we were each on our own sides of the bed. Pregnancy has had my emotions in overdrive for weeks, but last night . . . I have no words for how confused it left me.

Should I still be angry? Hurt? Over it all?

What am I supposed to do with the information this man laid bare at my feet?

Is there a right or wrong answer? Because honestly, I'm over it all. I don't want to hold a grudge. I don't want to be mad. I want to choose happiness. I want to choose love and forgiveness. I was never given those options before. I was rarely given any options before. But now . . . Now the decision is mine to make, and I want to choose him. This. Our family.

Warmth radiates from Maddox's bare chest as he shifts his hips, and his deliciously hard dick pushes against my ass, and suddenly, I'm wide-awake and very aware of my choices.

He tugs my chest back, and his lips brush the shell of my ear. "Sleep, *principessa*. It's going to be a long day. You need your rest."

"Yes, but the rest of today is for show." I press my lips to his. "Right now, it's just us." I wiggle my ass back into his hips, needy for this man who will be my husband in just a few hours.

His lips skim over my shoulder as he pulls down my panties. "Whatever my wife wants."

I hum. "I love the sound of that."

"Getting your way?" he asks as he shoves down his boxers.

"No," I murmur and moan when his hands are back on my body. "Your wife."

Maddox growls possessively as he lifts my leg, opening me up to him from behind. "I love you, Lennon. Only you."

His words wrap around me, soothing my soul and setting it on fire.

One hand gently wraps around my neck and holds my face. "Tell me you're with me, baby."

"I think I've always been with you, even when we weren't together." I close my eyes as a tear slips from the corner. "I've always loved you."

"That's the first time you've ever said that," he murmurs against my mouth as his fingers slide over my clit, teasing me with his touch.

"It won't be the last." I keen against him. "Now please, please, please, make me come."

He takes my lips in a deliciously decadent kiss.

Pushing his tongue into my mouth as he surges up with his cock, owning me.

Body and soul.

"Jesus, *principessa*. You feel so fucking good. Like you were made to take my cock," he groans, grinding into me. Taking what's only his to take and giving me everything I ever needed.

"My fucking wife."

"Only ever yours," I whisper as the rest of the world ceases to exist. "Only ever us."

Meatball barks outside the bedroom door, yanking me back to reality the second time I wake up today. My face is plastered against Maddox's chest, and *oh God*, there's drool. Fucking pregnancy.

"Knock, knock."

I lift my head and look at my dark prince. His eyes are closed, but his face is tight with annoyance. He's not sleeping. At least, not anymore. "Why is my sister here?"

"How should I know?" I ask, realizing we should probably put clothes on.

Damn it.

"I can smell the sex out here, people. I know you're in there."

Oh. My. God. Kill me now.

"Go away," Maddox yells before he kisses my head and grabs his boxer shorts, then winks. "You know she's not giving up."

His words sound annoyed, but his smile is everything.

I hope our baby has his smile.

He crosses the room and cracks the door. "What are you doing here, Caitlin?"

"It's your wedding day, big brother. Now get pants on and get out. You're getting ready at Mom and Dad's while we beautify your bride. Grace and Everly are downstairs with a glam squad, and the photographer should be here soon."

I roll out of Maddox's side of the bed, looking like what I'd imagine a small beached whale looks like, but manage to avoid being seen. "Just let me shower, and then I'll be down."

"Just shower. We'll set up in here," she yells back before I close the door.

I turn on the water and step into the shower before Maddox joins me with a grin. "I figured we could conserve water."

"I like the way you think." I hand him my shampoo with a genuine smile.

Something I never thought I'd have on my wedding day.

"Stop fidgeting, Lennon." Grace lectures as the makeup artist applies my lip stain. "You don't want pink teeth, do you?"

"I'm pregnant, and the baby is practicing his jetés on my bladder. What would you like me to do?" I grouse, having been stuck in this chair for what feels like hours. "I have to pee."

"Have you no social graces?" a voice asks from the door, and I push away from the chair and throw it open. "Princesses do not pee. They relieve themselves of the royal piss."

I throw my arms around my brother and cry as he lifts me from the floor. "Atticus . . . You're here."

He puts me back down and runs his hands over my bump.

"We are. We just got in. We needed to make sure it was as close as possible to the wedding, so we didn't blow it in time for Dad to cause a scene."

"We?" I look behind him and absolutely destroy my makeup in one giant sob. "Rhys . . . You can't be here." I take both their hands and ignore everyone in the room as Grace and Caitlin shoo them out. "You—"

"Would never miss your wedding day." Rhys wraps an arm around me and rests the other on my belly. "You look beautiful."

"Well, she doesn't now. Stop crying, Lennon," Caitlin laughs as she hands me a tissue. "Blot. Don't wipe."

"Guys, this is my Maddox's sister, Caitlin. And you remember Grace." I listen to Cait and blot while she blushes. I'm betting she had a poster of one of them on her wall at some point, based on the look on her face. This is hilarious.

"It's nice to meet you, but now you have to calm her down. We're leaving in less than an hour, and you need touching up," she scolds. "Back in the chair."

I do as I'm told but can't stop staring at my brothers, unsure they'll ever understand just what this means to me. Just what this will show the world. "Grandfather is going to be furious with you."

"Let him be," Rhys says, unbothered. "I've done everything he's asked my entire life. I've dedicated myself to Mornea and him. But this is for you. If he has a problem with it, the crown can go to Atticus."

"The fuck it can," Atticus argues, looking horrified. "Hell no. The only thing I'd want that crown for would be a threesome on the throne."

"Haven't you already—" I start before he wraps his hand around my mouth, shutting me up while Rhys glares.

"Oh, I think I'm going to really like your family." Caitlin

smiles. "Now get off her and let her get ready, or you're going to make her late for her own wedding."

"Ohh. She's bossy." Atticus smirks, and it's my turn to glare.

"She's married," I warn. "To your future brother-in-law."

Atticus looks around, and Gracie shakes her head no.

"Got any hot bridesmaids who aren't married?"

God, I missed my brothers.

Maddox

"Stop fussing with it," Mom warns as she watches me through the reflection in the mirror before moving in front of me. "Let me."

She pulls the tie apart and fixes both ends around my neck. "You know, as a mother, they always tell you that a daughter is yours forever, but a son is only yours until they take a bride."

"Ma..."

"Shh. It's my turn." She goes about tying my tie, like she's done it a thousand times. Hell, she probably has. "People always like to say things like that. They love to say that you only have eighteen years to raise your child and to jam absolutely everything you can into those eighteen years. Basically, they like to scare you."

She adjusts the knot and the length, then runs her hand down the front of my shirt, pleased with herself. "But I've never scared easily."

"Sounds familiar."

The look she gives me has me shutting up immediately.

For a tiny woman, my mother never needed to yell to get her point across. She just needed to look at you, and you knew. Right now, I know.

"I didn't jam everything into eighteen years because, no matter where you go in your life, you'll always be my son. A parent's job is to raise their children, so they're no longer needed. Our whole job is to make sure, one day, our job is obsolete. And your father and I have tried our best to do that with all of you. You, in particular."

Dad walks in and hands me a glass of whiskey, and Mom gives him the stink eye. "It's just one, Snow. The boy's gotta take the edge off. The whole world is going to see this tomorrow." He looks back at me. "Now, ask your question."

I learned the art of reading people from my father.

Maybe one day, I'll be as good as him.

I think about not asking, just to prove him wrong, but my need to know is too strong. "Why me in particular?"

He wraps an arm around my mother's waist and pulls her into him. "Because you are the oldest, Maddox. It's a different throne, but you're still my heir."

"I never thought the family business was an option though," I admit. Not that it was something I ever wanted.

"Because we never wanted it to be. But here's the thing . . ." Mom adds. "Children rarely do what you want or expect of them."

Dad gently kisses her head. Growing up, my parents never shied away from touching each other. They still don't. "We raised you to be able to handle anything life could throw your way. And you've proven you're capable of doing that without us. You're a good man, son. Be a good husband and a good father. Whether that's here or wherever Lennon needs you to be. Because believe it or not, it appears there's a family more demanding than the Kingstons."

"Just remember to be happy, Maddox. Life goes by so

quickly. One day, you're newlyweds, with your entire lives in front of you, and the next you're grandparents, watching your babies have babies." She steps out of Dad's hold and presses a kiss to my cheek. "Choose happiness, Maddox. Make it your mantra."

"Is that what you did?" I ask, a little taken off guard by all of this.

Mom's smile is a little evil as she looks at my father. "We did. But it never hurt that your father knew I was a better shot than him either."

"Nothing wrong with a little fear." My father laughs and taps his glass against mine.

"Hey, Madman," Callen pops his head in the door. "You ready?"

I swallow my drink.

"Yeah, man. I'm ready."

Ready to make this woman my wife.

Ready to choose the happiness I'll fight the rest of my life for.

My cousin's daughter appears at the back of the aisle with Meatball at her side. His blue bowtie matches the blue sash tied around her little white dress, and I say a quick prayer that he doesn't knock her over as she drops rose petals along the pale-blue silk runner covering the aisle. Once Caitlin and Lennon had the brilliant idea to include Meatball in the wedding, I couldn't talk either of them out of it.

"Can't believe the dog is in your wedding," Callen laughs from next to me, and the bishop stares, unimpressed. Like my family hasn't basically funded this church since before my father was even born. He wanted Lennon and me to wait a year and go through classes to get married, but one big fat check later, and our date miraculously opened. Imagine that.

Once Rosie and Meatball are at the front of the aisle, she moves to sit with her father, and Lucky whisks Meatball away to sit with a friend outside, so my lazy dog can be in the pictures after the ceremony . . . if he can manage to stay awake that long.

The music changes, and Caitlin walks down the aisle with her eyes locked on Callen the whole time. Sometimes I still wonder how I missed what was happening between them. Then I feel like an ass for the part I played in the hell they went through.

But then the little brat winks at her husband before moving to the side, and I know my best friend is calculating how quickly he'll be able to get her out of that dress later, and fuck feeling bad, I kinda want to kill him all over again.

Grace Wilder walks toward us next, and I smile.

Caitlin might be my sister by blood, but Grace and the group of women sitting on my side of the aisle, together with their husbands, well, they're my family by choice. They're the people Callen and I grew up with. No other seven people in the world will know what it was like. Not their husbands or our wives. The group of us have an inseverable bond. We might not all see each other as much, now that we have kids and spouses. But somewhere deep down, there will always be a place for us in each other's hearts. And thanks to Gracie, I met my wife.

The stained-glass double doors at the back of the cathedral open again, and the packed church rises and turns as the musicians play "Cannon in D," and my beautiful bride is escorted in by both her brothers. Her smile is a work of art.

One I'll never forget. One I'll do everything in my power to make sure she wears every day.

She's breathtaking in a beautiful, curve-skimming white silk dress that clings to her bump, letting the whole world know our son is here with us today. Her hair is pulled back away from her face, and a veil that seems ten feet long trails behind her.

And it feels like a hundred lifetimes pass before she finally makes it to me.

She turns to Atticus, who lifts her veil and kisses her cheek, whispering something I can't hear that makes her laugh before she turns to Rhys, who kisses the top of her forehead and turns to me with her hand in his. He gives it to me. Gives *her* to me. Even though the look in his eye says he'd rather die than do it. "Keep her safe."

"With my life," I answer and take her hand in mine. "You are breathtaking, wife."

Her cheeks flush the prettiest pink when she smiles. "We've got about an hour before you can call me that, husband."

I gently brush my lips over hers. "Then let's do this."

"So romantic," she teases softly as we move to our places.

The bishop clears his throat, and I grin.

"We are gathered here today . . ."

Marry a man whose voice can calm you and seduce you in the same sentence.

—Lennon's Secret Thoughts

"You ready for this, *principessa*?" Maddox takes my hand in his as we stand just outside the tent that's been erected in his uncle's beautiful backyard for our reception, waiting to be announced.

"Probably not," I laugh and shove the heel of my palm into the side of my stomach. "Your son apparently really wants to join in on the party though. He's been dancing all day."

"Well, tell him to back off. He can have you soon enough. But for right now . . . you're mine." He lifts me up, cradling me in his arms, and the photographer snaps another shot.

I'm not sure I've ever had this many pictures taken of me.

Never in one day.

Possibly not even during the entirety of my life.

And considering my mother stood on the steps of the hospital hours after I was born and had pictures taken of her before she got into the car with my father, that's really saying something.

"Please welcome the new Mr. and Mrs. Maddox Beneventi" is announced over the microphone, and Maddox looks at me funny.

"Where's your title?"

I cup his face in my hands and press my lips to his. "I doubt I'll have one tomorrow. Now let's go before I get too heavy."

He carries me onto the dance floor and carefully sets me down as our first dance is announced, and the band plays the first stands of "Ordinary" by Alex Warren.

I drape my arms around my husband's neck, blown away. "Did you pick this song?"

His sexy smile comes out to play as he sings along softly and pushes me around the dance floor like a pro. "Gracie may have helped me."

Before I know it, my feet are barely touching the ground, and Maddox is hamming it up like I've never seen him do before. He looks young and free in a way that brings back so many memories.

His brothers and Callen wrap their arms around each other's shoulders and sing along, eventually joined by a few cousins and Grace and a few of her friends' husbands like a grand choir. There're hand gestures and a kick line at some point before Maddox finally puts me back down and kisses me like it's the first time we've ever kissed. Like he can't get enough and doesn't care who's watching. Until I'm certain I hear Rhys coughing and Atticus laughing. Until his hand slides down to my bump, and I rest mine on his. The song changes, and others join us, but I only see him.

He's all that matters.

Eventually, I stand off to the side of the dance floor, wiping my eyes as Maddox dances with his mom, when Sam offers me a handkerchief. "Sorry. I didn't think it was that obvious."

"They're happy tears, *principessa*." He nods toward his wife and son. "You have nothing to apologize for. You love my son. That's all a man can ask."

"I do love him," I whisper, pulling my eyes from Maddox and focusing on his father. "I think I have for a very long time."

"Ahh . . . I know that feeling. I loved his mother for years before I could convince her to marry me. Some of the best love stories start that way." He looks around with furrowed brows. "Nonna was looking for you. But I don't see her now."

"She was probably trying to get me to save her from Atticus." My heart feels so full in this moment, I'm not sure I even care that once I told my brother to stay away from Maddox's cousins, he took it upon himself to be Nonna's date for the night. I swear the two of them have danced more than Maddox and me. "He's trying to get her chicken parm recipe," I laugh.

"Didn't she give that to you last week when you were at the house?"

"She did," I gasp. "But she made me swear on my son that I'd never share it outside of the family."

"Your brothers are family, Lennon," he assures me with a kind glimmer in his eyes that reminds me so much of Maddox's.

Now it's my turn to look around the tent for Atticus and Rhys, eventually finding them by the bar, charming two of Maddox's cousins, no doubt. "They are. But I'm scared that it'll be years before I see them again. I'm afraid they risked more than they realized by coming here. My grandfather is going to be furious when word gets out."

"Sometimes we have to choose family and their happiness before everything else. Even the responsibility we hold. Take it from me, there are few things in this world an older brother wouldn't do to make sure his brother . . . or sister is happy." He steps back as the song ends. "Speaking of which . . ."

Rhys moves in next to me and offers me his arm. "Walk with me?"

I slide my hand into the crook of his arm and follow him away from the crowd. "When do you leave?"

"Tonight," he tells me as we clear the tent and make our way to a beautiful stone patio under a pergola covered with blooming roses. "The less time we're here, the less time the crown has to get in the way. By the time we're home tomorrow, the outlets will already be running this as the lead story. And the blowback will be bad enough as it is. If I weren't there to face it head-on, it would be worse."

We sit down on a white stone bench, and I take his hand in mine. "I'm sorry you'll have to face any blowback for me."

"I'd do anything to protect you, kid. I'm fairly certain your new husband would too. He's watching us." Rhys doesn't sound angry, but he doesn't seem thrilled either. "Does he treat you well? Not just better than Monty. Does he treat you the way you deserve to be treated?"

I swallow down all the emotions that have been swirling all day in hopes of answering him without crying. Thank goodness for waterproof mascara. "I'm not even sure I deserve to be loved the way he loves me."

"You deserve to be loved more than any person I've ever known, Lennon. Don't let fear stop you. And have faith that I'll do all I can to smooth things over with the king."

Rhys looks so much older than he did even a year ago, and I realize just how much I missed by not coming home for so long. "Are you okay, Rhys?"

"You're happy and safe. I've got everything I need today. Now don't cry—because your husband is coming this way, and I don't feel like having to explain myself and why you're crying to him," he teases but means every word of it. There are few people in this world my brother will ever be expected to explain himself to. But for me, he did it.

He stands and lifts my chin. "You will always be Her Royal Highness, Lennon Allison Windsor, Princess Royal of Mornea. Do not forget that—because one day you will stand next to me when I'm crowned, and I will be so proud to have you at my side, little sister." Maddox stands just outside of the pergola, close enough that he can hear every word but far enough that he's still being respectful. "And at that point, I guess I'll give him a title too."

"Not the baby," I murmur, and Maddox moves in next to me as Rhys tilts his head, confused. "I don't want him to have a title or the pressure that comes along with it. I'll do whatever I can, if and when I'm allowed to come back home. I'll serve you in any way. But I want him to have the choices we never had."

Maddox's grip on my hip tightens, like he's expecting my brother to object, but I know Rhys too well to expect that.

"Then you'll give him whatever name you want, but he'll always know he has family in both places."

Satisfied with my brother's answer, Maddox offers him his hand, and we watch as Rhys walks away. "So, no prince?"

"Pretty sure the world already has enough Beneventi princes." I trace his lips with my finger, and he catches it between his teeth.

"Are you ready to get out of here?"

"Where are we going?" I smile. He's been so secretive about our honeymoon, I haven't been able to pry a single thing out of him. "Are we leaving tonight?"

"You're really bad about surprises, you know that? They're supposed to be fun."

I look up at him, the seriousness of my earlier conversation already forgotten. "Listen, I had to trust your sister to pack for me. That's more stressful than fun."

He shrugs. "I told her you didn't need clothes because I planned to keep you naked all week."

"You didn't . . ." I gasp. " Please tell me you didn't."

His lips tip up on one side in a beautifully sexy, crooked smile, equal parts guilt and promise.

Hopefully, our destination will be warm.

Maddox smacks my ass as we board the Kingston family's private jet, then pulls me against him. "I want you naked and waiting for me in the bedroom when I'm done speaking to the pilot, wife."

"Is that safe, husband?" I tangle my fingers in his hair. "How would I put on my seatbelt?"

He shakes his head and grabs my face, licking into my mouth. "Go, Lennon."

Ohh. I love an inpatient Maddox.

I hurry back to the bedroom with a different idea, while Maddox stops in the front where Maria is sitting with the flight attendant. Maybe I should feel bad for what I have very little doubt he's saying, but I don't. Not even a little bit. We haven't had a minute of privacy since Caitlin woke us up this morning, and he's enjoyed driving me crazy all day.

Gracie warned me I'd be in a constant state of turned-on once I hit a certain point in my pregnancy, but I don't think it's the pregnancy. I think it's Maddox.

I throw a little cold water on my face and run my fingers through my hair, then adjust my boobs a bit before walking back into the main cabin. Still fully clothed.

And when the door shuts behind Maddox and the click of a lock slides into place, my skin heats as his eyes melt. "I thought I told you no clothes."

"You also said the bedroom, but I thought this could be more fun," I challenge.

Both his hands gently grab my face and hold me in place. His thumb traces my cheek, sending goosebumps dancing down my spine, and I practically purr. "Then tell me what you want, Lennon. Anything you want . . . tell me. Take it. It's yours."

I lean my face into his palm and melt into him.

My body desperate for the pleasure he's been teasing me with all day.

The tiny touches.

Lingering gazes.

The whispered words—hot and filthy little promises only I could hear.

"You don't play nice, Maddox. You've had me on edge all day," I breathe out before turning my face toward his fingers and sucking his thumb into my mouth.

Maddox sucks in a breath before he rips his hands away, and his lips capture mine.

Calloused palms slide down the short white silk dress I changed into before we left his uncle's. He drags the hem up to my hips before cupping my ass and lifting me in the air. He walks us back to the cream leather sofa and sits us down with me on his lap.

"Maddox . . ." I moan, desperate for more as he unties the bow at the back of my neck, and the most delicious sound rips from his lips at the sight of my bare breasts.

I run my fingers through his thick, dark hair and sigh as one hand slides up my bare back, resting between my shoulder blades and pulling me to him. I arch, and my breath gets caught in my throat as his tongue licks around my nipple and his teeth graze my skin.

"I've been hard all day, thinking about what it was going to be like fucking my wife," he groans, and it's so goddamned good. "You were supposed to be laid out on a bed, Lennon."

"I will be . . . later," I gasp as his hands glide up my thighs, and thick fingers trace my sex through the sheer lace covering it.

He draws his head back and stares deep into my eyes, like he can see my soul. My love. Like it's all right there, laid out for him to see. And maybe it is. I'm not sure I've ever been able to keep anything from him.

Maddox drags his hot tongue down my neck, and I drop my head back, while his other hand finally slips under my thong and skims the lips of my pussy. "You want me to fuck you now, wife?"

"I want you to fuck me all night." I try to sound strong as the words fall from my lips, but my God, it's hard when my body is already shaking with anticipation.

His tongue traces my lips, swallowing my command willingly. And when his tongue touches mine, the flickering flame that has danced all day strengthens, threatening to burn us to the ground.

Maddox drags his finger through my soaked sex, then drags it up around my clit and pushes down. "Do you want to come on my cock or my mouth, Lennon?"

"Both," I pout, and a wickedly gorgeous smile spreads across his lips. His mouth wraps around my sensitive nipple. Sucking and tugging and driving me insane as his fingers slide inside my pussy, teasing that hidden spot I could never find on my own as he circles my clit.

My orgasm crashes over me like a wildfire I could never escape and yet never want to end as Maddox swallows my screams with a scorching kiss, never slowing or stopping, knowing exactly what I need for one orgasm to roll into two. Until my body is hot and heavy and spent.

But not ready for this to end.

When I can finally lift my head, I trail my lips down his neck and my hands down his shirt, popping open one button at a time. Each flying across the cabin. Desperate to feel his skin on mine.

"My turn," I whisper and unbuckle his belt.

His eyes heat as he grabs my hands. "Baby, I need to be inside you now. You can have your turn later."

"Just a little taste." I stand and tilt my head, pouting, and Maddox reaches for me. I back up a small step, then tug his waistband with both hands and pull at his slacks and boxers until he lifts his hips, and I'm able to pull them down his thick thighs, tossing them aside. "Please . . ." I let my dress fall to the floor, then shimmy out of my thong and kick the small scrap of white lace aside.

His hands are on my hips in an instant.

Lifting me back onto his lap.

"The first time I come inside my wife, it's going to be in your tight little cunt, *principessa*. You can suck my cock later."

I'm not sure why those words turn me on the way they do, but my God, they really do.

My knees dig into the soft leather on either side of his hips as he slides his hands to my ass and squeezes.

"That's it, baby."

I lower myself onto his cock and drop my forehead to his as my body stretches around him. "Maddox . . ."

"You were made for me, Lennon . . ." His tongue licks into my mouth. "Just for me."

I slowly inch up just enough to drop back down again, refusing to give up any contact. Needing to feel his skin against mine. His breath on me.

Maddox slides one hand into my hair, anchoring me to him, and tugs.

It's possessive and protective and so deliciously Maddox, I wouldn't have it any other way. He breathes me in as I breathe him out, and I wonder how I ever lived without this. Without him.

"*Tesoro*." His voice is hoarse as my nails score his scalp.

"I'm so close," I pant, chasing my orgasm.

Lost in the moment.

Lost in him.

His head tips back, and firm lips press against my hot skin... My neck... My lips...

Until he's devouring me. Demanding more. Releasing my hair and sliding his strong hand down my body. Gripping my ass in both hands, he changes our angle, and that's it. That's all it takes. What had been just out of reach is being deliciously rubbed over and over and over again now. A torrent of emotions assaults me. Love and lust and fear and faith... in him, in us. Need and desperation and pure unadulterated want... This man. This life. It all weaves together as reality wars with memories. This is it. This is everything I've ever wanted with the only man I've ever wanted it with.

"Need you to come now, Lennon." His fingers bite into my ass as his teeth bite down on my lip, and I fall over the cliff, coming on a silent scream. My breath catches in my throat until he breathes life back into me before ripping his mouth from mine and burying it in my shoulder as he fucks me over and over again. Strong hands holding me to him. Sucking and licking... and whispering words I've longed to hear for years.

Until he loses himself in me completely, unable to hold back, and follows me off that cliff with my name on his lips.

Part Three

Lennon
Chapter 23

**No matter what happens, it was worth it.
Loving you. Being yours. Every second of it was worth it.**

—Lennon's Secret Thoughts

"You know . . ." I sip my tea and tilt my head, trying to get a glance around the corner of the man currently standing in my kitchen, drinking a cup of coffee. "I thought once Grandfather ordered Maria back to Mornea, maybe we could do without bodyguards for a while."

After all these years together, it would be hard not to miss Maria. She always made it a point to keep things professional, but she was my friend, even if she didn't want to admit it.

Maddox looks down at me as he slides on his coat. "You can look cute and pouty all you want, but it's not going to change anything. You need bodyguards, *tesoro*." He drops a kiss on my lips and another on my gigantic beach ball of a bump. "You both do."

I hate knowing he's right.

Maybe one day, people will lose interest, but since news broke of our wedding and my pregnancy, interest has only grown. Grandfather lost his mind. My father publicly disowned me. Monty has laid so low, I'm pretty sure he's hiding on a private island somewhere, drinking himself into a stupor as he tries to understand how he didn't get his way for the first time ever. And my brothers . . . I feel terrible for Atticus and Rhys because they've had to say *no comment* so often, it should be tattooed on their foreheads.

Grandfather is still deciding how to deal with me, so nothing has officially been done yet, but I expect my title to be revoked any day now. To be honest, I'm shocked it hasn't already happened. Not because he wants to, but because he has too.

"Besides, Ajax is family. He'll keep his distance, but he'll also keep you safe when I can't." He sits down next to me and lays his arm behind my neck, and even knowing he has to leave, I can't help the warmth and peace I soak in.

I know we're still in a honeymoon phase, but if it's possible, real life is even better than our honeymoon was. And we had the most incredible, relaxing, sex-filled week that I didn't even want to come home.

Screw reality.

I'd rather we'd have stayed in the fantasy for a little bit longer.

"Fine . . . What did you think of the names I left for you to look at last night?" I ask and burrow deeper under the warm, cashmere blanket I pulled from the back of our couch. The new one. Not the bachelor one that had definitely seen more than its fair share of life over the years, judging by the condition it was in. "I tried to stay up but lost the fight sometime around ten."

"I'm sorry. There have just been so many last-minute

things to get done for il leone's grand opening party tonight. I'm not even sure what time I got home."

I close my eyes and lean my head against his chest. "I know. I wasn't mad. Just curious about your thoughts. We've got a month left and no name. It's starting to stress me out," I tell him and try to get comfortable. Something that's getting harder every day.

"I liked Luke," he says, matter-of-factly as he steals a piece of the donut he'd given me earlier, and I may or may not growl in response.

Maddox lifts a brow, clearly amused.

"What?" I ask innocently. "I'm eating for two."

"I fucking love you." He kisses me again and rises. "The car will be here to pick you up at six-thirty. It's getting Callen and Caitlin, then heading here. I'll see you at il leone. Call me if you need anything."

I grab his face and pull it back down to mine. "I am so proud of you. Tonight is going to be amazing."

"Ajax," he calls out, and my new bodyguard, one of the many on the team, rounds the corner.

"Yeah, Madman?"

"Don't let her out of your sight. Not now. And not tonight." He kisses me one more time and breaks off another piece of donut. "You hear me?"

"You're crazy. I'm not even going anywhere until the car shows up tonight," I tell him and grab the rest of the donut before he can. With each week that's passed, it's like his worry has grown, and I'm not sure what I can do to give him peace of mind.

"I'll see you tonight, *principessa*."

"ennon . . ." Caitlin calls out as she and Callen let themselves into the house, and my eyes fly to the clock.

Shit. It's already six-thirty.

"I'm upstairs. But Callen can't come up. I'm not dressed," I holler down and walk into my closet, staring at the gorgeous navy-blue gown I'm supposed to wear for il leone's opening. Thank you, Everly Wilder. My new best friend. The fact she can somehow make me feel like anything less than a killer whale is amazing at this point in my pregnancy.

"Where are you hiding, Lennon?" Caitlin asks as she walks into my room, and I giggle and push the closet door wide open and stand sideways in all my huge pregnant glory.

"Pretty sure there's no hiding this." I run my hand over my stomach, and my beautiful sister-in-law smiles wide. "Listen, even nine million months pregnant, you're still hot. Now get your dress on and let's go before my big brother has a stroke, wondering why you're not there yet."

I wince as the baby kicks right up into my ribs.

I can't even take a deep breath anymore.

He's taking up all the space.

And don't even get me started on how much I pee . . .

"Fine. Can you help strap me into this thing?" I grab the gown on the hanger and give it to her while I hold the massive island in the center of my closet for balance.

"Ummm . . ." She looks at her own floor-length, tight gown and laughs before yelling, "Callen . . . Come up here, but close your eyes."

"How the fuck am I supposed to do that?" he yells back.

She scrunches up her nose and mouths *sorry*. "Carefully, sweetie. We need your help, and I can't bend down."

"Caitlin—I'm in a thong and a strapless bra. Your brother

is going to kill me, and you and I don't even want to think about what he's going to do to poor Callen."

"I second the poor Callen thing," the man in question groans from outside the closet. "My eyes are firmly closed, ladies. Now what the hell am I supposed to do?"

"Oh my God. This is ridiculous." I take the dress from Caitlin's hands and try to bend over to step into it but can't. I look at Caitlin and know if she squats down, she's going to rip her dress. Fuck me. "Callen, open your eyes."

"Nope. Not a fucking chance, princess."

"Callen," Caitlin patronizes her husband. "You won't be looking at her boobs. I promise. Just squat down and hold the dress for Lennon to step in, then pull it up."

"Why can't she put it on over her head?" he asks, but it honestly sounds more like a child whining. It's actually pretty funny until I look at the time.

"Oh, good grief. I used to change backstage in front of dozens of people. It's tits and ass and a belly the size of a gigantic beach ball. There's nothing pretty about it. Just open your eyes and man up, Sinclair," I put my foot down and wait.

"Damn, you're kinda mean," he tells me, shocked as he cracks open one eye but leaves the other closed as he takes the dress from Caitlin—who's smiling from ear to ear—and squats down.

"I know, right? Kinda hot, isn't it?" she teases him, and he groans while I laugh.

"Don't make me laugh. I'll have to pee again," I whine.

"Christ, I'm not one of the girls. I don't need to know this shit," Callen bitches as Caitlin holds my hand, and I step into the dress. "Bad enough I'm doing this. Maddox will want to kill me . . . *again*."

Caitlin's eyes sparkle with mischief as I shake my head

because he's right. Maddox will want to kill him. "Pull the dress up, honey, and I'll suck your dick later."

"Promise?" he asks with a ridiculous amount of excitement.

She nods, and he pulls the dress up with his one partially opened eye, looking at her until she moves him out of the way and takes it from him, tying the long blue silk around my neck and situating it over my shoulder and down my back. "Perfect. Now where are your shoes?"

I point to the shelf, and Caitlin laughs. "Oh, Callen . . ."

The things we do for love.

"What is with this traffic?" Caitlin grumbles as we sit at a standstill at least a ten-minute's walk from il leone, and there's no way I'm walking ten minutes in these shoes. "It's a Thursday night. What the hell is going on?"

"Relax, Cait." Callen checks his phone, then looks at his wife. "We're almost there."

I move awkwardly, trying to stretch out in the limo, and shove my hand into my side, trying to get the baby to move off whatever nerve he's sitting on. "Were you this uncomfortable a month out from your due date?"

"I had Anastasia a month before my due date. But I had all kinds of complications. So don't go by me," she drops that like it wasn't a massive bomb.

"What?" I ask as a cramp hits me hard and sharp, and I grab her arm and squeeze.

"Shit, Lennon." She gives me her hand, and I unclench my nails. "What's wrong?"

"I'm not sure," I tell her as the pain lingers for a few moments, then passes. "It didn't feel like a kick."

"You okay, princess?" Callen looks between the two of us with concern.

He's one of the few people in the world besides my husband who thinks it's fun to call me that, and from him, it's almost sweet. It's not like he's using it as my title. More like I've been accepted into an elite club. Their whole group of friends seems to have nicknames for each other. More so than any of us ever used growing up.

My chest tightens, and pain shoots straight down my back.

"Callen . . . Tell them to take us to the hospital and call Kenzie," Cait says calmly.

I'm about to tell her I don't think I have to go to the hospital when that first strike of back pain is followed by another. This one worse than the last. "Call Maddox . . ."

Maddox

"You really did it," Grace slides in next to me and throws her arms around my neck. "I'm so proud of you, Madman. This place is amazing."

Her husband, Ares, clears his throat, and she rolls her pretty eyes.

"Relax, god of war," she kisses my cheek and rests her head on my shoulder. "He's married."

Ares wraps an arm around his wife's hip and pulls her to him. "So are you, woman."

"Put your dick away, sweetie. No need to pee on me. I've

pushed five of your babies from my body. I'm pretty sure the world knows I'm yours."

That seems to make him happy enough to smile. "Yeah well, just making sure Beneventi doesn't get any ideas."

"Where's Lennon?" Grace asks, sighing like she's trying to ignore her husband. "I haven't seen her."

That's a good question . . .

"Madman," Maverick interrupts us with his fiancé, Emmie, at his side. "Fucking fantastic food." He holds up a Wagyu meatball and pops it into his mouth. "It actually melts in your mouth."

"Oh my goodness, try chewing with your mouth closed, Mav." Emmie's eyes narrow, and her face pinches as she hands him a napkin. "Thanks for having us."

"Thanks for coming." I smile, distracted as my phone vibrates in my pocket. "Excuse me."

I pull my phone from my pocket but get interrupted before I can answer. That seems to be a theme too. By the time I finally get a chance to look at my phone, I've missed eleven calls from Callen. I hit redial and walk outside as Rome grabs my shoulder. "Hey. Give me a minute—"

Rome shakes his head, clearly upset. "No can do, Madman. We gotta go. Callen has been trying to reach you. The baby is coming."

"What?" I ask, sure I misheard him. "*What?*"

"Your wife is in labor."

I stand, shocked, before my adrenaline kicks. "Shit. I need my keys."

Tires squeal as my Escalade rounds the corner.

"Nah . . . Lucky's got it. Let's go." Rome opens the front door for me, just as Lucky stops in the valet lane and waits for me to get in before he climbs in the back. "Pedal to the metal, little brother. We've got a new Beneventi prince to meet."

My heart sinks, and I call Callen's number.

"Maddox..." Lennon whimpers back. "Are you here?"

"No, baby. I just got the message. I'm on my way right now. Lucky's about to pull onto the fucking sidewalk to get around this traffic." I glare at my brother as we sit stuck behind a row of cars and cover the phone. "Fucking move, man. Get us there."

His smile is feral as he does just that and hops the curb.

I don't give a shit what kind of trouble we get in for this.

I'll get us out.

"How are you doing, *principessa*? What happened?"

"I'm so sorry. I thought it was just cramps, but it turns out, the back pain was actually labor. The baby is facing the wrong way. Kenzie's monitoring me. She's going to try to flip the baby." Emotion wraps around every word she says, and I wonder if running the thirty blocks to the hospital would be faster.

"Which hospital?" I ask, but Lucky answers.

"She's not that far."

"We were almost to you when my water broke." Her voice cracks.

"Lennon—"

"Hey, man," Callen's voice answers. "She's having a contraction..." The phone sounds like it's moved away from his face as I hear a muffled *yeah, okay*. "Hey, Kenzie says don't do anything stupid to get here. You've got time. But this kid is coming. Leave it to a Beneventi to be impatient and want to do things on their own damn schedule. Due date be damned."

I swallow down my rising fear. "Don't leave her alone, man. Is Caitlin with you?"

"She's holding Lennon's hand." He gives me a little relief. "We're not going anywhere. We've got your girl until you get here."

"I owe you." I blow out on a deep exhale.

"Callen Beneventi sounds good," he tells me dryly.

I hear my sister laugh in the background. "You can take my last name any time you want."

"Shit," Lucky yells as we swerve around an open driver's side door.

"I'll be there in ten more minutes," I tell him before I hear Lennon scream in the background.

Fuck.

Maddox

Chapter 24

By the time I'm rushed into the labor and delivery ward, I've been sanitized and thrown into scrubs. I tossed my phone at Rome and told him to handle the calls coming in from everyone and left him and Lucky somewhere between here and the front desk. Fuck if I know where.

I run down the hall to where Ajax is standing guard outside Lennon's room and push through the door without waiting when I hear her scream. My heart stops when I finally see my wife.

Caitlin is on one side of her, and Callen on the other.

Lennon's head is back against the bed, her hair pulled up. Her beautiful face is pale as tears streak down her face, while Kenzie's hand is inside her body. "Almost there, Lennon."

"I want Maddox," she cries, and I fucking snap out of it, moving to her side.

"I'm right here, baby." I press my lips against her forehead. "I'm here."

She cries as Kenzie does whatever the hell she's doing, and I want to fix it for her, but I can't, and it kills me.

"You're doing so well, Lennon. Just . . . one . . . more . . ." Kenzie blows out a breath, and I watch her look up quickly at the ceiling before smiling at Lennon. "We got him." She looks exhausted but relieved. "He flipped."

"What's happening?" I ask Kenzie as Lennon lies against me, exhausted.

"Lennon's water broke, and Caitlin and Callen rushed her here. The baby was occiput posterior—"

"Language I understand, Kenz," I interrupt dryly.

"OP is when the baby is facing forward. It's not ideal for delivery, but we do it. However, Lennon's pelvis is narrow, and she wants to avoid a c-section, so I attempted to move him. Luckily, he cooperated." She looks from me to Lennon. "How are you feeling, Lennon?"

"Like I can't do this," my girl whispers, and my heart breaks.

Caitlin holds one of Lennon's hands in both of hers. "Yes, you can. You're a badass who stood up to her entire country for this baby. You can do this, and you're going to look amazing while you do. Do you hear me?"

And I'm officially in my sister's debt for the rest of my life because I don't know whether I could have done what she just did. She drops her forehead to Lennon's, and my girl closes her eyes and nods. "Okay."

Callen claps my back. "That's my cue to go. I'll be right outside if you need me."

"Thanks," I mutter, so far out of my fucking depth, I don't even know up from down as I take Lennon's other hand.

"Okay, Lennon. Here comes a contraction. I want you to push." Kenzie gets settled between Lennon's bent knees, and I mirror the way Caitlin holds Lennon.

Lennon sits up, and Kenz looks at me. "Sit behind her, Maddox. Support her back. Give her your strength."

That I can do.

I climb on the bed behind her and take her weight. "You're doing so good, *tesoro*."

She stiffens and screams as she pushes for what feels like long minutes before finally running out of steam and falling against me again. Caitlin gives her ice chips, and Lennon lies against me until the next contraction hits.

The cycle continues on and off until Kenzie tells us this is it. "Come on, Lennon, I need one more big push. He's right there. You've got this."

"No," she cries. "I can't."

"You can, baby. You can do anything." I kiss her head, so fucking proud of her. "Let's meet our baby."

Her shoulders stiffen as she sits forward, and I inch in behind her.

Cait grabs her hand. "You ready?"

"Noooo . . ." Lennon yells as she bares down and pushes with every last ounce of her soul.

"Keep pushing, Lennon," Kenzie says. "One more . . . Harder," she yells.

And my wife does what she's told as she holds my hand so tightly, I'm surprised her fingers don't break. Kinda surprised my fingers don't break too.

"That's it," Kenzie tells her, and I look up and watch the mirror behind my friend just in time to see my son enter the world.

He's small and red and perfect.

And he's crying the most beautiful sound I've ever heard.

It's strong and fast and loud.

Our baby.

"It's a boy," Kenzie announces, and I take what feels like my first breath since I walked in the room.

"Is he okay?" Lennon asks through uncontrollable tears. She turns to me when no one answers her. "Maddox . . ."

"He's beautiful," I whisper, holding her and in absolute fucking awe of this woman.

Kenzie holds him up, and a nurse offers me scissors. "Do you want to cut the cord, Dad?"

"No. I'll leave that to the experts," I murmur, a little overwhelmed as I slide out from behind Lennon and help her lie back.

I push her damp hair away from her beautiful face, and she grabs my arm while I rest my lips against her forehead. "Love you, Maddox," she whispers.

"Love you, *principessa*."

Caitlin backs away as the nurse places the baby on Lennon's chest.

"Hello, my little prince . . ." she murmurs, and I wipe a tear from my own eye.

They called the next hour the golden hour.
We're left in the room.
Just the three of us.
My entire heart in one bed.

Our little man latched on like a little champ. Apparently, while thirty-six weeks is early, it's not always too early. His lungs are good, and his color is good. His sugar is fine, and his APGAR scores were great. He's an overachiever. Not sure where he gets that from.

I lie in bed with Lennon in my arms and our baby on her chest, scared to blink.

Scared if I close my eyes for even a second, this will all be a dream, and I won't have everything I've ever wanted.

"We need to pick a name," Lennon says softly as she runs her finger over his tiny nose. "He doesn't look like a Luke."

"He doesn't," I agree. "How about Brock?"

She shakes her head no.

"Come on, Brock Beneventi is a good name." I run my fingers over her hair. "It's strong."

"What about Brennan?" She kisses his head. "Brennan Beneventi sounds like a strong name."

"Brennan Beneventi . . . I like it. What about a middle name?" I ask her quietly as she yawns.

"I think it should be Samuel. Like you and your dad."

Well, damn.

There goes another tear.

"Brennan Samuel Beneventi," she tests it and smiles. "I like it."

"Me too, *tesoro*. Me too."

I'm fairly sure if my family were any other family, they wouldn't be allowed in the hospital after visiting hours, but our last name holds a level of clout and control few people argue with. So even though it's after eleven at night, once my parents and brothers have left, Callen and Caitlin are still allowed back in.

Lennon is asleep in the bed while Brennan lies in my arms, staring up at me, when my sister falls in love. Her eyes sparkle as she melts into a pile of goo, just looking at him. "Can I hold him?"

I carefully transfer him to her arms and listen to her have an entire whispered conversation, making him so many promises, I can't help but smile. I turn to Callen and wrap an arm around him in a tight embrace. "Thank you for everything, brother. For tonight. For everything . . . I know I've said it before, but I'm sorry for the hell I put you through last year. I get it now. I didn't then."

"Yeah . . . it's one of those things you can't understand until you find the woman who turns your world upside down," he offers as he watches his wife with my baby. "She changes everything."

I nod, silently agreeing. "Definitely brings you to your knees."

"Speaking of which . . ." Callen smiles, and Caitlin rolls her eyes. "While you're in a forgiving mood, I think it's a good time to tell you your wife and mine forced me to help your wife get her dress on tonight. I did it with my eyes closed, I swear."

"One eye was sort of open," Caitlin adds nonchalantly, and I stare at them, confused.

"It was more closed than open," Lennon whispers from the bed, and we all turn around. "And seriously, Kenzie had her entire hand in my vagina with a mirror behind her while Callen and Caitlin held my hands. He's probably seen things that are going to give him nightmares. Get over it, Madman."

"What?" Caitlin laughs so loudly, she startles Brennan.

"Hey now." I move to Lennon's side. "You don't call me Madman."

"If you can call me princess, I can call you Madman." She keeps her eyes closed and the blanket pulled up, like the exhaustion is still there, but she's fighting it.

"I told you I liked her," Caitlin announces as she slides Brennan into Callen's arms. "There. He can't hit you if you're holding the baby."

"I wasn't going to hit him," I grumble, too happy and too tired to worry about it tonight.

"Fine. Then consider Brennan an insurance policy." Cait moves to Lennon's side.

Callen smiles a shit-eating grin. "You think Anastasia and Brennan are going to get into half the trouble we did?"

"I think it's going to be his job to kick anyone's ass who even thinks about getting her into some of the trouble we got into."

"Yeah." Brennan fusses, and Callen calms him down like a pro. "I like that."

I look at my best friend holding my baby, and man, it's such a humbling thing.

"I like that too."

Lennon

In the dark of the night, I finally feel my husband lie down next to me and gather me in his arms. "I thought I told you to go home and get some sleep," I whisper as I curl into him, completely ignoring my own words.

"You did. I chose to not listen." He pulls the blanket up, and I feel his body relax against mine. "Did you really think I'd leave you alone?"

"No." I press a kiss to his chest. "I knew you wouldn't. And I didn't want you to, if we're being honest. But there isn't much you can do here in the meantime. I figured one of us should get some sleep. And somebody has to take care of Meatball."

"Rome is taking Meatball for us. And I wasn't going to get any sleep without you anyway. Besides, who's going to get up and change Brennan and bring him to you when he wants to eat? Callen told me that's my job for the foreseeable future. Change the baby and bring him to you, so you can nurse. I'm pretty sure I can handle that." His voice is scratchy but somehow lighter than I've heard it in so long. "Sleep, Lennon. I'll be here when you wake up."

The conversation we had last spring flashes in my mind, and I suddenly realize how full circle we've come.

"Thank you for saving me, Maddox..." My voice shakes, betraying my emotions. "That night in the snow and every day since I showed up last summer and blew up your entire world."

"Don't you see it, *principessa*? You are my world. Brennan was exactly what we needed to figure out a way to be together. And trust me when I say we were always supposed to be together." He sinks further into the uncomfortable hospital bed and pulls me with him. "Thank you for giving me a chance to prove it to you."

"I can't wait to get home and start our life," I admit hesitantly. "The three of us."

I close my eyes, wishing my mom was here to see this and realize I have to call my brothers. Shoot. I can't have them hear about this in the news. "Hey . . ." I wake a dozing Maddox. "Could you hand me one of our phones?"

"Umm-hmm . . ." He passes me my phone from the rolling hospital table, and I smile as he goes right back to sleep while I dial Rhys.

He picks up on the second ring, and I see his smiling face and him sitting at his desk. "Hey, big brother," I whisper. "Guess what?"

"Hey, kid. Why are you whispering? And what time is it there?"

I pan the phone over to where Brennan is sleeping soundly in his little clear hospital basinet, wrapped in a blue-and-white blanket with a matching blue beanie on his small head. "Meet your nephew."

"Lennon . . . Wow. Seriously?" He inhales. "He's beautiful, just like his mother."

"I wanted you and Atticus to hear it from me," I yawn as my body fights to stay awake. "But I'm so tired. Could you tell Atticus? And let him know I'll call in a few hours?"

"Wish I was there to meet him," he says solemnly.

"I do too. Maybe you could come back over during Christmas." I know it's a long shot, but I don't think I'm welcome at home, and I'd love for my brothers to meet Brennan.

"I'll see what I can do. FaceTime me tomorrow when you and the baby are awake. I want to meet him." I recognize the sadness in his eyes because it's reflected in my own.

"I will. Love you, Rhys."

"Love you too, little sister. Get some sleep."

I disconnect the call and steal another peek at the perfection lying in the bassinet next to me, then snuggle back into Maddox's arms. I close my eyes, knowing this is as close to perfect as a person ever gets to have in life, and I'm so lucky to be here.

Lennon

Chapter 25

**I thought I knew what beauty was,
but beauty didn't exist until I watched my husband hold
our son.**

—Lennon's Secret Thoughts

The sun drifts in through the curtains, pulling me unwillingly from my dream, and it was beautiful. Maddox and I were lying on a blanket in the rolling field with irises behind the palace with Brennan between us. It was quiet and peaceful, and somewhere in the depths of my soul, I knew my mother was there with us. So happy for me. Happy I found my way to this life. Happy I managed to get what she never had. A marriage based on love, not political or financial gain.

She whispered in my ear, *"Do not age gracefully, my love. Fight for every day. Every minute. Fight for your family and know that I tried to fight for mine."*

I roll over and reach for Maddox, but my hand brushes cold sheets instead of my husband, and I startle, now fully awake. The room is empty.

No Maddox. No Brennan. Not even Meatball, and our lazy dog loves nothing more than to climb in bed with me the second Maddox leaves it. He knows he's not supposed to be there, but he's as obstinate as Maddox.

Where is everyone?

My boobs hurt as I stand and stretch, so I know it's time for Brennan to eat. My son never misses a chance to nurse. The only issue we faced with his early delivery was that his suck wasn't quite as strong as it could have been, and my milk hadn't quite come in yet. So instead of nursing every three hours, he's been nursing every two. And instead of him being done in twenty minutes, my beautiful baby boy likes to take his time and linger. Time to find my men.

I throw a sweater over the pretty white nightgown Caitlin gave me when I got home from the hospital. According to her, it may look sweet and innocent, but something about it will drive your husband wild. A woman on some show on Netflix that was based on a romance book wore it a few times and now it has its own Reddit page. Well, she was right. Maddox loves it, and I now own three in white, two in ice-blue, and one in pale-pink.

How many more weeks before I can fuck my husband?

The alarm beeps as I make my way downstairs, and I wonder if that means someone is coming or going? What time is it, and how late did I sleep?

I smell coffee, something I still refuse to drink, even if it does smell heavenly. But better yet, it's mixing with the mouthwatering scent of muffins . . . chocolate ones. A moment later, I'm treated to the sight of Nonna in a kitchen chair, holding Brennan, while Maddox makes her a cup of coffee and Amelia lays out those muffins.

"You look beautiful, *principessa*," Sam whispers, coming out of nowhere, and I jump. "Sorry," he laughs. "I didn't mean to scare you." He holds up an armful of bags. "Where would you like these?"

Maddox looks over at us and smiles. "Ma, you've got to stop buying things."

"Nonsense," she blows him off and hands him a banana nut muffin, like that could ever be better than that double chocolate one sitting right on top. Damn. I'm hungry. "I'm a grandmother. Let me spoil my babies."

"*My* baby," Maddox jokes, and his mother pinches his ear until he tugs away. "Listen to me. The beauty of grandchildren is we get to recapture some of the magic of you being young and innocent and beautiful instead of the little shitheads you and your brothers are. Let me enjoy it."

I giggle and turn to Sam. "Is Lucky still talking about moving out?"

He shrugs. "Only on the days Amelia doesn't threaten to throw him out."

"He's not doing anything his father didn't do," Nonna tells me without looking away from Brennan, who's sleeping soundly in her arms. "Don't wish these days away. Enjoy every sleepless night and every tiny worry. This life takes so much from us, and when it gives you something beautiful, let the whole family revel in it as much as we want, *principe*." She looks up at Maddox. "Some of those presents are from me, and I will buy what I want. I'm holding my great grandson . . . something my son and my husband never got to do, and as long as I have breath left in my lungs, I'll do what I want. Because I'm old, and you wouldn't dare tell me no. Never forget, I've been feared longer than your father." Her wry smile is a little joking and a little serious, and I'm not sure whether to look away or laugh, so I do both and take a few bags from Sam and let him follow me into Brennan's room so we can leave them there.

"Do you need anything, Lennon?" my father-in-law asks

as he pulls more clothes than Brennan will ever need out of a bag.

"I don't think so, but thank you." I'm still not used to the way this family is so involved in each other's lives. It's not a bad thing, but coming from a very different family makes walking into this a little jarring and a lot intimidating.

"Maddox said you officially announced your retirement from the Royal Ballet . . ."

"I did," I answer with a sad smile. "It had been a long time coming. Dancing saved me in so many ways, but I don't need to be saved anymore. It was time to let it save someone else."

Sam takes a step toward the door but stops. "I don't think dancing saved you. I think you figured out a way to save yourself and it was dancing."

"What's the difference?" I question as I follow him out.

"The difference is you. You refused to be a victim. You found a way to get through until you could find a way. Sometimes, knowing how to survive just to fight another day is half the battle."

"I don't want Brennan to have to fight battles." Even the thought of it breaks my heart.

Sam places a hand on my back in such a fatherly move, it catches me off guard. "He'll have his own battles to fight. We all do. But you'll be there to support him. You and Maddox will make sure he has every tool he needs to succeed. Trust an old man."

"Yeah . . . trust the *old man*," Maddox laughs as he walks into the room and over to the changing table with a cranky Brennan. "He just blew out his diaper."

"You change him, and I'll feed him," I offer, and my husband smiles. "And your father is not old."

"It's okay, Lennon. Sons will always try to out-alpha their fathers. One day, he'll realize there is no out-alpha-ing me," Sam tells me before walking out of the room with a swagger.

Maddox grins as he tries to clean Brennan up. "He wishes."

I suddenly wonder if I just saw thirty years into my future.

And what a beautiful life it would be.

Maddox
Chapter 26

"I'll never understand why you all call this football," my beautiful wife bitches as every eye in the room stops and stares at her. "What? This is not football. They barely even kick the ball."

"I swear if you keep this up, I may have to find a new sister-in-law," Lucky moans from where he lies on the giant sectional Lennon bought for what she refers to as the game room. I mean, I guess it's my own fault for building such a big house where we have a living room and a game room, but it still cracks me up that she has official names for all the rooms in the house. She did a killer job decorating it, either way, so I don't complain . . . not too much. This room is a great mix of casual comfort and her airy, contemporary style. The giant couch can easily seat sixteen of us. All the furniture, including the ottoman she chose instead of a coffee table, have soft corners, so when the babies start walking, they won't get hurt, according to her. Not that we're looking at that any time soon.

Supporting her daddy in a pink Sinclair Philadelphia Kings jersey, Anastasia is sitting in the center of some kind of circular activity chair thing. I think my sister called it an exersaucer—not sure if she made that shit up or not—and Lennon loved it and ordered one when we got home that night. Cait and she have gotten really close, and I'm pretty sure I see Caitlin more now than I did when she actually lived with me.

Meanwhile, Rome is pacing around the room, trying to calm Brennan down since his screaming when the Kings missed the touchdown is what woke the baby in the first place.

You wake him, you take him.

That's my motto.

"I can't believe you've got him in Maverick's jersey," Cait bitches.

It's just my brothers, Caitlin, and Lennon and me tonight, watching Callen and the team play Dallas. Probably a good thing since Lucky is still driving our parents nuts.

"Dude, our last name is Beneventi. A cousin on the team with our last name trumps a brother-in-law without it," Rome throws back at her, and Lennon laughs.

"You . . ." Cait points at Lennon. "No input from the girl who thinks soccer is football." Anastasia throws her pink stuffed football at Lennon, probably because her mother was just pointing that way, but the way the rest of us laugh so hard scares the shit out of Brennan and has Lennon glaring at all of us.

Brennan cries gigantic crocodile tears, and Lennon pulls her feet from my lap and kicks me. "Your turn. Uncle Rome isn't cutting it."

"I didn't make him cry," I laugh but jump up to take him anyway. I spent today at il leone, and man, I hate the days that keep me away from here for too long.

I reach out for Brennan, and Rome turns away from me. "Get your own. This one's mine."

"The fuck?" I laugh in his face. "Pretty sure he's mine, shithead."

"Have we actually tested that theory?" He winks at Lennon. "I mean—"

"Finish that sentence and die, brother," I threaten, and Rome moves closer to Lennon. "Save me, princess."

Everyone has taken my nickname for my wife and started using it.

First Callen, now both my brothers.

And what does my wife do?

The little traitor smiles and pulls him down on the couch next to her.

"How is she going to protect you?" Lucky asks as he kicks Rome with the foot he just pretty much sat on. Did I say this couch holds sixteen? Maybe it would if my six-foot-four-inch brother wasn't stretched out on it.

"She can withhold sex," Rome tells him, and I growl.

"She can't have sex for six weeks," Cait corrects him, then looks at Lennon and smiles. "But I might have given it a try a little before five ... Just saying, slow and steady got it done."

"Fucking Christ, Caitlin." Lucky throws a pillow over his head, while Rome covers Brennan's ears.

I should probably be grossed-out, but I'm too busy lusting over the smile on my wife's face.

"Maybe if he agrees this isn't football, I'll let him try slow and steady," Lennon announces, and everyone groans.

Everyone but me.

I've officially become a soccer fan, and I'll call that shit whatever the hell I have to if it means I get to taste my wife tonight.

Lennon

"If you're trying to seduce me, it's working," I whisper from what's become my favorite spot, leaning against the open doorway of the nursery. I can't help it. This spot always gives me the best views. Like tonight. Maddox has showered and not bothered to get dressed. Just threw on black boxer briefs. His hair is damp, and I can smell that sexy sandalwood bodywash that mixes perfectly with his DNA and makes my mouth water more than any sweet treat ever could. Muffins be damned. He's shirtless and sitting on the rocking chair Nonna gifted us when Brennan was born, and our beautiful baby boy is sleeping soundly against his chest. His mop top of dark hair covering the Beneventi family crest inked on Maddox's heart.

Yes . . . I've seen a lot of views in my life.

I've been to the top of the Eiffel Tower.

I've seen the northern lights from an igloo on a snow-covered mountain.

I stood awed in the center of what I think was King Tut's tomb on a family vacation when I was little. Don't quote me on that, it might have been a different ancient ruler. I wasn't really paying attention.

But none of those views could hold a candle to this one.

Because this breathtaking view is mine.

Mine to cherish.

To protect with my life.

This view *is* my entire life.

Maddox's crooked smile tugs up higher on one side than the other, and a little piece of me melts. God, I love this man. "I like the sound of that, *principessa*. You think we should give slow and steady a try tonight?"

I pad into the room and carefully lift Brennan from his chest and nuzzle my nose against my baby's neck, inhaling his beautiful, sweet smell. "Let's see if he goes down without fussing."

It sounds like my husband holds his breath as I lie Brennan down and rest my hand on his back, scared to remove it. Scared the second he loses that connection, he'll cry.

Slowly and carefully, I gently pull it away and stand frozen in place when Brennan wiggles, but he doesn't cry. Doesn't open his eyes. Just finds the spot he was looking for and gets comfy.

And when I turn around, the look in Maddox's eyes is *everything*.

I walk as softly as I can and tug his hand as I pass, pulling him to follow me into our bedroom.

We walk into our bedroom, and Maddox's eyes are absolutely feral as he locks the door behind us. "You sure about this?"

I lift my shoulder and lick my lips. "I mean, I'm not sure I'm capable of doing anything too . . . exciting at this point, but I'm willing to try."

"You don't have to do anything but lie there, *tesoro*." My sexy husband lifts me from my feet and covers my mouth with his as he walks through our room. "I'll do the rest. Just not sure how slow I can be. I've needed to fuck you for weeks."

"Such a sweet talker," I tease as he lies me down, and I grab his face. "Who says romance is dead?"

"I've got much better uses for my mouth tonight." His hot breath skims my skin and sets my soul on fire as he leans down and kisses me so intensely, I forget where I end and he begins.

"Promise?" I whimper as he pulls away and nips at my lips before fingering the straps of my nightgown.

"I fucking love this thing on you, but it's got to go." He

drags the straps down my arms, and for the first time in my life, I'm self-conscious of my body. "Why'd you just freeze up, Lennon? Did I hurt you?"

"No . . . I just . . ." I lean up and brush my lips over his. "I'm not back to my pre-baby body yet."

His deep blue eyes darken, and his hand cups my face. "Do you think I care? Your body gave us our son. Your body is a goddamned miracle. And it's fucking perfect because it's yours. It's you. You're all I need."

My heart melts, and my body relaxes. "Now those were beautiful words, husband."

"Yeah well, I still have other plans for my mouth, wife." He drags his tongue down my neck as his hands tug my nightgown off, and every single nerve in my body teeters on the edge of that familiar blade, begging to be thrown off-balance.

One spectacularly rough finger runs along the tip of my sensitive nipple before his mouth is on me. Sucking and licking and biting my breasts, and I see stars.

"Maddox . . ." I whimper and grab at his skin, desperate to get him closer. "I need you."

"You've got me, wife."

That single word has a life of its own.

Hearing those four letters falling from his lips will never get old.

I drag his mouth up to mine and lick into his mouth, pouring everything from the past few weeks into this kiss. Our tongues tangle in a way so easy and natural and so exquisitely us, I think I could come just from this kiss alone. "Mine," I whisper against his lips, knowing what he wants to hear and smile. "Now fuck me. Let's try soft and slow before we're interrupted and have to give in to hard and fast."

Maddox licks down my body, tracing every new dip and flare and curve. Worshipping me. Dragging out each sensation before he drops to his knees and pulls my ass to the edge of the bed with a wicked grin that does even more wicked things to my body. He throws both my legs over his shoulders, and my breath catches as he presses a warm, wet, soft, open-mouthed kiss against my pussy, and any doubt I had about my new body and how it would react fly out the window.

This man knows what I need better than I know it myself.

He always does.

I tangle my fingers in his dark hair and lock my eyes on his, lost in the moment.

The perfection.

The reality of having everything I want.

Of having him.

The way his fingers bite my skin and tear my panties from my hips.

His tongue inside my hot core before it circles my clit.

It's too much and not nearly enough as I grind shamelessly against his sexy stubbled face.

"Fuck, Lennon. I missed your taste," he growls and locks his eyes on mine. Dark lashes frame those brilliant blue eyes I love. They watch me as he flattens his tongue and licks a leisurely line up the length of my pussy, coaxing my first orgasm slowly from my body, just like he promised.

Warmth rushes through me, and I fall back to the bed, drunk on my first orgasm as Maddox slides my legs back onto the bed and slides in behind me. "I need your words tonight. I need to know it's not too much, okay?"

I look over my shoulder and nip his lips, absolutely desperate for more. "I'm so fucking good."

"That's what I want to hear, my love." His hands are everywhere, gripping and sliding and grasping and pinching. "I fucking love you like this. Sex drunk and desperate for more." His fingers dip inside my soaked pussy, and I whimper, wanting more.

"Your pussy is perfect, *principessa*. Swollen and drenched and begging for my cock." He licks lazy circles around my racing pulse, then scrapes his teeth along my sensitive skin, and I grind my ass back against his hard cock. Solid steel wrapped in velvet. And I want every inch. "You ready for me, *amore?*"

His words . . . they're a tease wrapped in a delicious turn-on. He knows what speaking Italian does to me.

"Yes," I moan with my face buried in his arm.

My body desperate for what it hasn't had in long weeks.

He runs the thick, blunt head of his cock through my wet sex. Teasing me with just the tip inside my pussy. Never more than that. Never giving me everything I hunger for.

"Maddox . . ." I beg. *Plead*. "Please . . . I need . . ."

Before my next words can leave my mouth, he finally . . . *finally* seats himself inside my swollen, needy, pulsing pussy in a slow, soft stroke of his cock and an even slower snap of his hips.

Soft. And. Slow.

God, yes.

He takes his time and fucks me so gently, it brings a tear to my eye. Murmuring tender words of love and adoration, mixed with filthy words of decadent depravity, and I swear to everything I've ever held holy, there's never been anything hotter.

I lie tucked against his body, at his mercy.

Completely lost to him as he does all the work like he promised.

Maddox engulfs me. Fucking me. Loving me. Owning me. Saving me.

Giving me life over and over.

An eternal flame that will never burn out.

And as a white-hot heat tears through me, and flames lick at my skin, Maddox's hold on me tightens, and his movements slow, dragging the euphoria out until it threatens to burn me alive. Only then does he take what he needs and follows me into the fire.

We lie, quiet and sated in each other's arms for long moments before he climbs out of bed and comes back with a warm washcloth. "How do you feel, *principessa*? I didn't hurt you, did I?"

This man.

I'm not sure he's capable of hurting me.

"My love . . ." I run my finger along his chest. "I think I'm going to need you to put Brennan to sleep and fuck me like that every night. Think that could work?"

His still-semi-hard erection jumps, and I giggle. "Not sure I'm ready for round two just yet."

"Fuck, Lennon . . . You can't say things like that and not expect me to want more."

I lick my lips and hold back my laughter. "I love you, Maddox."

"It was always going to be you and me, Lennon. In this life. In every life. It's always going to be us."

In every lifetime.

Lennon
Chapter 27

I lived my entire life cold until the day you set my soul on fire.

—Lennon's Secret Thoughts

"Why am I the asshole carrying the tree?" Rome moans, and Lucky laughs.

"Because you two assholes practically live at my house, and I'm carrying the baby. Do you think Lennon should be carrying the tree?" Maddox barks at his brothers as they tie our first Christmas tree to the top of the Escalade.

Lucky pouts, cracking me up as Maddox opens my door for me. "You sure this is the one you wanted?"

"She's sure," Rome grumbles from the top of the SUV. "I'm not cutting down another tree."

"I'm sure," I whisper against his lips, excited to decorate for Brennan's very first Christmas. I close my eyes and lean back in the seat, soaking in the cool sun as Maddox gets Brennan situated and the guys get in the car. "Where do you feel like ordering lunch?"

Rome leans forward, popping his head between Maddox

and me. "How are you hungry again? Didn't we just have breakfast?"

"It's not my fault. Nursing burns calories." Pretty sure I just have an unnaturally fast metabolism and a love of burgers and fries. "Can we pick up something from West End?"

"I've gotta be there in like four hours. I don't want to eat there too."

Maddox turns to Lucky and grins. "Suck it up, buttercup. She wants West End."

"Fine..."

"Shit..." Rome's voice drops, and so does my heart. The way he says that single word scares me in a way I didn't know it could. "Princess..."

"What—" I fly around in my seat with my heart in my throat. "What's wrong?"

My phone rings as Rome hands me his cell phone.

The headline on his screen reads

Flags Lowered as Palace Confirms Death of King Frederic Ernest Augustus Windsor, Longest Ruling Monarch of Mornea.

My hands shake, and my throat closes as I sit, frozen in time.

The king is dead—my grandfather is dead.

My mother is dead.

Oh, Rhys...

I don't even realize my phone has stopped ringing until Maddox's hand cups my cheek, pulling me out of my state of shock. Or as far out of it as I can get. He holds the phone out for me to take, and I stare at it, unsure what to do. "It's Atticus."

Maddox's voice is so soft . . . unnaturally soft.

I don't like it.

It makes me feel broken.

Like he's scared of hurting me.

And something about that forces me out of my shock long enough to take the phone from him. "Atticus . . . Is it true?"

"Shit, Lennon . . . I'm not sure how the news got out so fast. We wanted you to hear it from us first."

I look up, and three sets of Beneventi eyes are all on me, but Maddox's are the only ones who don't shine back with pity.

"When did it happen? How?" My thoughts come out rapid-fire, bombarding me. "How is Rhys?"

"They think it was a heart attack. The butlers went to wake him this morning, and he was gone." Atticus is uncharacteristically quiet for a moment, and my heart hurts for my brother. For my country. For me. To have lost such an important man. To have lost my grandfather, and to have lost him without ever reconciling . . . it all just hurts. "You know Rhys."

I do. And that's why I'm worried about him.

"You need to come home, Lennon."

Atticus's voice carries within the confines of the car, and there's no doubt Maddox heard his order, whether he realizes that's what it was or not. I look to him for support and hope he trusts me. "How quickly can the jet get to us?"

"It's on its way there now. A full protection detail is on board."

"Maria?" I ask, concern growing.

"Yes. She's heading the team," he tells me. "And it's a full team, including officers dedicated to Maddox and Brennan for as long as you're in country."

"We'll be there soon. Take care of Rhys, Atticus. And keep Papa out of his ear." God, this is not happening. Not now.

"I'm sorry, Lennon . . ." he says quietly.

"Me too, brother. Me too."

Maddox's hand runs down the length of my back as I fold the last of Brennan's clothes and sort them into his suitcase. "Are you sure about this?"

"I'm sure *I wish* we didn't have to go." I turn in his arms and rest my head on his chest. "But I'm also sure we have to go. I need to be there for my brothers and my country. I'd feel better if we had someone with us to help with Brennan though. You have no idea how many things go into the funeral of a monarch. When my mother died, I felt like we didn't sleep for a week, and she was heir to the throne. She wasn't the king."

"My parents should be here soon. They're coming with us."

I'm not sure anything he could have said could have surprised me more.

"What? Why?" I have no words. None that make sense. None that don't sound awful. "I thought we agreed not to ask them to help."

"I didn't have to ask. They offered. They knew we'd need help with everything you're going to be dealing with, and they knew I'd want to be at your side. They also knew there isn't anyone else in the world I'd trust with our son outside of our family. This might be your world, *principessa*, but it's not mine, and I'll feel better if my parents are with Brennan when we can't be."

I wrap my arms around his waist and suck in a breath. "Your family constantly amazes me."

"They're your family now too." He rests his chin on my head, and I blow out a shaky breath, having never known what it felt like to have parents who would drop everything in their world to prioritize you. "Do we need to pack anything else?"

"I need a separate garment bag for your black suit and my black dress. We'll have to change on the flight." I step out of his hold and straighten my spine. "And I need to grab my mother's pearls."

"Won't it be the dead of night by the time we land? Who's going to care whether we're wearing fancy black clothes or not?"

His words hit me harder than he may ever know.

"The entire world, my love. The entire world will be watching. Your family may have had the eyes of this town and this state and at times, even your country, on them . . . But trust me when I say the entire world will be watching."

Maddox

My mother and Lennon are going over everything they think Brennan could possibly need when I step into my office to take the call that just came. Rhys's name flashes again with an incoming FaceTime. *Fuck*. Lennon hasn't even talked to him today.

I cross the room before answering. "Hello?"

How do you address the king of an entire fucking country?

Dad slides into my office behind me and shuts the door.

"Maddox." Rhys's face appears on my screen, and he doesn't look different, even if somehow, I expected him to. "How's my sister?"

Right to business.

This I can handle.

"She's worried about you." I sit behind my desk and switch the call to my computer. "But she's okay. We're leaving for the private airstrip in a minute."

"Do you understand what you're walking into?" He runs his hand through his hair, and I see the weariness lingering in his face. "I hope when you said for better or worse, you meant it. Because this is going to be worse."

My fists tighten at my side. "Question anything you want, but don't question my love for your sister."

"Good answer. I'm going to need you to remember that this week. No matter what anyone says . . . No matter what they try to force her to do when I'm not around. No fucking matter what happens, she's your job. Lennon is the only thing you are responsible for. Put her first because as of this morning, I can't."

Fuck . . . What the hell am I supposed to say to that?

"She'll always come first for me," I tell him with complete certainty. "Her life, her happiness . . . they matter more to me than my own."

"Good." He nods his head like that's what he needed to hear. "Remember that. I'll see you tomorrow."

He disconnects the call, and I look at my father. "Have you ever not been the scariest motherfucker in the room?"

"Nope," Dad says in all seriousness.

"Pretty sure that's about to change."

Lennon
Chapter 28

**One day your child will come home and be overwhelmed with memories.
Make sure the good ones outweigh the bad.**

—*Lennon's Secret Thoughts*

"Are you sure you're ready for this?" I check in with Maddox as I run my hands over the shoulders of his suit coat. "I mean, you're kind of screwed if you're not. But at least I asked, right?"

The joke falls flat as my husband stares back at me, all brooding seriousness wrapped in a gorgeous package. Far too serious for this early in the morning and having gotten very little sleep.

"I'm sorry. I make horrible jokes when I'm nervous, and my nerves are a mess at the moment." I drop my forehead to his chest and close my eyes as his hands cup my neck and lift my face. "You have nothing to be nervous about, Lennon. My parents will have Brennan whenever he's not with us, and I'll be by your side every step of the way."

"Promise?" I ask as someone knocks on the bedroom door of my family's jet.

"With my entire heart, love. With my entire heart." Maddox lifts my chin and ghosts his lips over mine. "Are you ready?"

My heart squeezes, making it hard to breathe. "Not even a little bit."

"Lennon, sweetheart," Amelia calls through the door. "There's a man asking for you."

Maddox moves toward the door, but I stop him and step in front, then place my hand in his, take a deep breath, roll my shoulders back the way my mother used to force me to do, and open the door. Atticus's personal secretary stands in front of us, with Maddox's parents and my security team behind him.

"Princess." The word is so formal, it sets the tone for everything yet to come. "I'm sorry for your loss. Your brother has asked that I bring your team and fill you in on everything you need to know."

"Thank you, Crowley. Do we have enough room for my mother and father-in-law as well?"

"No, ma'am. We have a separate car for them. Atticus has asked for all of you to stay with him while you're here. He's had an entire nursery brought in overnight for the prince."

"Brennan," I correct.

"Yes, ma'am. Prince Brennan." Crowley looks genuinely confused, and it genuinely annoys me more than it should.

"Just Brennan. And thank you. I'd like to get off the plane now."

Crowley steps aside, and I walk past him but stop when he steps in front of Maddox.

This is not how we're going to start this trip.

I turn and reach my hand out for my husband, who's staring daggers at Crowley, and wait until Maddox is next to me before taking Brennan from Amelia. "Are you okay with following us in a separate car?"

She runs a hand along my arm and then over Brennan's head. "We're here to help in any way we can, sweetheart. Don't worry about us."

"Thank you," I murmur, wishing everything about this trip were going to be that easy.

Maddox

She was right. The cameras flashing and reporters calling out for Lennon as we disembarked the plane were more intense than I've ever seen in one place before. Like she said, my family might be high-profile, but this is a whole other stratosphere.

Behind the official press line, which had been roped off with police guards, there was a fence with hundreds of what I'm guessing are citizens of Mornea calling out for their princess.

Until today, I'd never seen this side of Lennon.

I'd never had to share her with the world.

And I've never been more grateful she decided this isn't how she wants our son raised.

By the time we were brought to the house Atticus and Rhys share, Lennon was dead on her feet. She basically stripped out of her dress, dropped it to the floor, fell into bed, and told me to give her Brennan to nurse. The two of them were sound asleep minutes later, while I've sat here, watching them. Waiting to hear signs of life in the halls. And when I finally do, I follow it downstairs.

"Maddox," Atticus smiles a weary smile as he pours a glass of scotch. "You made it. Is Lennon awake?"

He hands the first glass to Rhys, then pours two more for him and me.

"No, she's sleeping." I hold up the glass and look at Rhys. "Am I supposed to bow to you now?"

"Do I look like I fucking care if you bow?" He swallows the amber liquid in one mouthful, then shakes his head. "Our father is going to be here any minute. Just don't be a dick in front of him."

"In front of him or *to* him?" I clarify, and the exhaustion in the lines of Rhys's eyes intensifies.

"Oh, you can handle him however you'd like. It's not going to be good. Trust me. I'm going to shower. I'll be back down in a bit." He turns to Atticus, and the two have an unspoken conversation before he heads for the stairs. "You're in charge, Atticus."

Atticus's eyes tighten, and for the first time since I met him, he looks strangely serious. "I was sorry to hear about your grandfather. Does this change things for you too?"

I may sound like an idiot, but I genuinely never gave a shit about anything royal before and have no fucking clue how any of this works.

He pours another glass and taps it to mine. "It does. Until now, I've been a partner in a law firm, but it's really been in name only. I haven't practiced in a few years. Since our mother died, our father, Rhys, and I have been carrying out business for the crown. That won't change, but I'll now be Rhys's head adviser. Can't have the brother of the king have something like a job. The crown is the job."

"You guys talk about the crown like it's a living, breathing thing," I realize.

"Because it is." He drops dramatically onto a couch that looks older than me but is probably worth more than my car.

"It's outlived us all, and if we take care of it the way we've been tasked to, it will outlive our children and yours. The crown comes first. It has to. It's why I was so goddamned grateful Lennon found you so far away from this. She was never meant for this life. She never wanted it. She's too much of a dreamer. Let her dream. Keep her far away from here."

"She shouldn't be here in the first place. My daughter made her bed with a commoner, and now, she can lie with the fleas."

My blood boils with those words, but I refuse to turn around. If this piece of shit wants my attention, let him stand in front of me and look me in the eye when he demands it.

"Hello, Papa," Atticus groans through gritted teeth as his father walks by me. "Let me guess . . . You want to see Rhys?"

"Who are you?" he fucking sneers at me like he's looking at shit on his shoe.

"I'm the man who loves your daughter more than you ever will. I'm the man who made sure she was safe, after the one you sold her to put her in the fucking hospital," I seethe. "You fucking piece of shit."

"Oh, cursing to get your point across. Such class. No wonder Lennon spread her legs for you."

I have him by the throat and pinned against the wall before Atticus can even stand. "Listen to me, you upper-crust asshole. I don't care who you are. I don't give a flying fuck what blood runs through your body. I will kill you and sleep with a clear conscience right next to your daughter like nothing happened if you ever talk about her like that again. Do you understand me?"

His face turns so red, it borders on purple, but he doesn't move.

Refuses to speak.

So I tighten my hold.

"Do you fucking understand me?"

"I'll have you arrested for this," he manages to spit past his lips.

"Do your best," I threaten with no clue whether he can or not.

"You will do no such thing," Atticus growls.

"Who's going to stop me?" he wheezes with little room to breathe as I tighten my grip.

"I outrank you, Papa. The only person I answer to is Rhys. Hell, Lennon outranks you. Who do you think she's going to choose? Better yet, which side do you think Rhys will fall on?"

Atticus gets in his father's face, while I keep him pinned to the wall. "I'm tired of this game, Papa. The one where we act like we can stand to be in your presence. None of us can. Mother never even could. So shut your mouth. Do your duty. Never say another word about Lennon again, and you can continue the life of luxury you're used to living. But so help me fucking God, if you open that mouth one more time, it won't be the king who cuts off your miserable head." He moves in closer, leaving barely an inch between them. "It will be me."

Her father gasps as I drop my hold and watch him fall to the floor.

Atticus bends down. "And in case you weren't sure, the commoner's name is Maddox Beneventi. He's Lennon's husband and your grandchild's father. And before he gets back on a plane to America, he'll outrank you too, you miserable piece of shit."

Lennon's brother stands up, brushes his slacks off, and looks at me like he didn't just impress the hell out of me. Something most people don't do. "You think Brennan's awake yet? I want to meet my nephew."

"I think it's about time we found out." I make a show of walking over my father-in-law's legs with a fucking smile and follow Atticus upstairs.

Chapter 29

**Heavy is the head that wears the crown.
Lonely is the soul that supports it.
And forever grateful are the siblings spared the same fate.**

—*Lennon's Secret Thoughts*

Tradition calls for the sons and grandsons of the monarch to walk behind the coffin of the king as it's pulled from Rosenhall Palace to St. Benedict's Abbey in a glass-enclosed carriage. My brothers, father, and even the king himself did this for my mother's funeral, but my father insisted I wasn't allowed. Today, I walk side by side with my brothers. Maddox's hand is in mine, and my father has already been driven to the abbey to greet the foreign dignitaries as they arrive, getting him out of our hair. Rhys insisted if I wanted my husband with me, then that was what we'd do. He ignored the pushback from the palace advisers and told me to let him worry about it.

So for once in my life, I did.

I let him deal with the fallout because he's the king.

The coronation may still be months away, but the crown is his.

From the moment my grandfather took his last breath until the moment Rhys does the same, that weight is his to bear. So we walk in line. Atticus, Rhys, me, and Maddox, with a row of my cousins behind us, and Sam and Amelia back at Lilihill House, keeping Brennan safe while we lay the longest reigning monarch the modern world has ever known to rest.

People have flocked to line the streets, just for the opportunity to pay their respects, and my chest tightens, knowing I'll never see him again. Even if my heart believes I will in whatever comes next. Some people are so important in your life, I truly believe you find them time and time again. I squeeze Maddox's hand, knowing this isn't the first time I've loved this man.

The procession progresses slightly longer than one mile before we stop and watch as a white-gloved military regiment silently moves into place with beautiful precision.

It's so hard to stand here, remembering the man who was heartbroken over my choice to go against my country and marry Maddox, instead of the one who used to let me sit on his lap on the throne when he and my mother were sitting for portraits. The one who would always sneak me an extra piece of cake when no one was looking. Or the one who came to see every single new ballet I danced in London.

And once the coffin has been taken down and the flag carefully folded, the soldiers stand still as we all observe a single minute of silence before they nod at my brother.

Rhys steps forward and places his palm on the casket before turning to Atticus and me.

Atticus follows Rhys's lead and does the same.

I step forward and press my lips against the casket, then step back and take Maddox's hand back in mine and wait for my brothers to walk ahead of us into the abbey, knowing when we walk out, the world will have changed.

The king may have died and passed the crown to my brother five days ago, but his burial signifies the end of one era and the beginning of another.

I avoid looking at the hundreds of people gathered, having no doubt Monty is among them, sitting somewhere with his family. He wouldn't dare miss this. I, however, would be just fine never having to set my eyes on him again, so I keep my eyes straight ahead.

We make the long walk down the aisle of the abbey. The same walk I would have made on my wedding day if I had gone through with it. And once we're in front of the archbishop, we all bow and sit down, side by side, with my father behind us.

It's a statement.

A powerful one.

The three Windsor siblings side by side.

A strategic act made by my brother to show unity between his siblings and to elevate us above our father, who is seated behind us. There is no mistaking who the power lies with, and I will forever be grateful he allowed Maddox to be next to me. I'm not sure how I would have made it through any of this without him at my side.

The world saw me marry Maddox very visibly pregnant, even if they thought I was marrying another man. I wasn't ashamed. I embraced it. Even if it meant giving up my family and my country. And I was willing to give it all up if it meant I got to have Maddox and Brennan. To be here with him beside me . . . it's almost too much.

It's more than I ever hoped could actually be.

The archbishop climbs the stairs to the pulpit, and we all sit. "It is in grief and with profound thanks we gather in this house of God to celebrate the life of a man who lived his life in service to his lord and his country..."

Choirs sing, and preachers of all denominations speak. Multiple eulogies are given, and I have to wipe my eyes several times. My heart aching for my grandfather, for Rhys, for the idea that one day the world will gather like this again, and what that could mean for us. And at the end of the ceremony, I'm reminded that nothing in this world is forever. Nothing but love.

The archbishop's voice cracks as he brings us to our feet.

"Now let us remove all symbols of power from the coffin, so that Frederic may be committed to the grave as a humble servant."

It's the only time in my life I haven't heard my grandfather's title used.

Because it no longer belongs to him.

The golden staff of the office of the king is the first to be removed from the casket, followed by his jeweled scepter, and finally the coronation crown, which is placed in Rhys's lap.

I take my brother's hand in mine and hold on for dear life.

"Life is indeed short. It is going to end. But what you do with the years you're given is the true measure of the man. Do well and live your life in service." Then the archbishop looks at Rhys, and my breath catches in my throat, knowing what is coming. "Long live the King."

Maddox

"Are you sure this needs to happen today?" I ask Rhys, most likely breaking every fucking royal protocol there's ever been, but this is my wife we're talking about, and I don't give a shit what protocol says if it means protecting Lennon. "I'm worried it's too much for her."

"It needs to be today," he confirms and looks past me at my wife and son talking with my mother. "Give me a few minutes, then meet me upstairs. Atticus will show you the way."

He moves swiftly to Lennon's side and whispers something in her ear before she passes Brennan to my mom and follows behind him.

Fuck . . . This is going to piss her off, but it has to happen. My parents cross the room, stopping in front of me, and I press a kiss to Brennan's head. "Have I said thank you?"

"More than you needed to," Mom promises. "I was thinking about taking him back to Lilihill House and putting him down for a nap. He doesn't need to be around this many people."

"That's a good idea. Make sure to take a protection officer with you," I tell them, and Dad just shakes his head like I'm an idiot. If we were back home, I wouldn't be concerned. But we're not back home. "Just humor me."

"I was just shaking my head because you act like we have a choice. Rhys's men are so far up your son's ass, this kid might not ever get to be alone." He looks at me like he gets it, though, and wraps an arm around my mother as they walk away.

Good. Less people to be worried about.

I scan the room, filled with a massive amount of people, all wanting a piece of Lennon and her brothers, until I spot Atticus. It only takes a minute to get his attention and tip my chin toward the stairs.

He does the same before he excuses himself and meets me at the bottom of the staircase, clearly uncomfortable. "Does Rhys have Lennon?"

"Yeah," I groan.

"Then let's get this done."

We climb the steps of Rosenhill Palace to the second floor, and I follow Atticus's lead down a winding hallway to a closed door with a royal protection officer stationed outside. He dips his head to the prince and moves aside immediately.

"When he's escorted up, hold him here and let us know," Atticus instructs, and the guard tips his head again before we walk by.

"Are they not allowed to speak to you?" I ask, not following what the hell that was.

"Nah, they can speak. But I screwed that one's sister a few months ago, and word got out. I'm pretty sure he'd shoot me if he could."

Fuck . . . I look around the massive room with paintings lining the walls and stop when Rhys and Lennon come into view. My wife is clearly pissed.

"Were you part of this plan?" she demands, and Atticus takes a step back. "Oh no. You stay right there. Both of you." Then she turns back to Rhys and points at him. "You too."

Lennon angles herself so she's in front of us all. "What were you thinking? If I wanted Monty dealt with, I would have done it myself. I was the one assaulted. I was the one who could have pressed charges and chose not to. What exactly do you have in mind with this little plan of yours and why do it today, of all days? Today is to celebrate Grandfather's life."

"Bullshit." Rhys levels her with a cold stare. "You were going to let him get away with what he did, so you didn't have to bring any more drama to the family. To the crown. Don't act like it was because you didn't want to see the prick strung up by his balls. And Grandfather hated most of the people here. Trust me. I was closer to him than anyone. He fucking hated them. What he would have liked most today was seeing the three of us together. He would have liked to see Brennan. I'd even go as far to say he'd liked to have met Maddox, if he could have without condoning your marriage. That one was going to take a little while. The three of us—"

Atticus coughs a fake-as-fuck cough. "Ahem . . . Four."

Rhys looks at me. His face set in hardened lines. "You're right. The four of us are here, together. And Monty is downstairs. Today's the day, princess."

"You know . . . I'm starting to truly hate that title," Lennon snaps. "It's not the worst nickname in the world under the right circumstances, but as far as titles go, I don't love it."

"Fuck, man," Atticus groans. "I hope you knew how high-maintenance she was when you married her."

"I am worth maintaining, you shitty little wanker," she snaps and looks between all of us with a fire flaming in her eyes. "Let's get this over with."

"I don't know why you're mad. You won't even be here to deal with the fallout," Atticus adds.

Lennon softens her stance, and I see the moment she gives in. "We'll come back more often, if you promise to visit me too." Rhys looks unamused and maybe frustrated. There's definitely something else there, brewing behind his eyes. Something he's not talking about. Not with us, at least.

Pretty sure a king popping over for a visit isn't exactly an easy thing logistically.

"Fine . . . I guess I'll raise a bicoastal baby," she smiles softly.

God, I fucking love this woman.

"Transcontinental, poppet," Atticus teases as an attendant dressed in a formal royal-blue uniform lets himself in the room.

"Sir, Mr. Hastings is outside."

"Please escort Mr. Hastings in." Rhys looks at us and nods as I take Lennon's hand and pull her against me.

I take her other hand in mine and brush my lips over her ear. "I love you, and this needed to happen."

"If I'd have known I'd have to see him today, I'd have brought his stupid ugly ring to throw at his stupid ugly face."

"Very mature, sister. Would you like to call him a doody head too?" Atticus jokes, and Lennon, like the proper princess she is, flips him off.

Rhys sits down on the couch while the rest of us quiet down and wait.

Chapter 30

**The true opposite of love isn't hate.
It's complete indifference.
You no longer matter to me.**

—*Lennon's Secret Thoughts*

I brace myself for the hatred I expect to seep into my bones when I see Monty for the first time since he assaulted me, but it never comes. My former fiancé is escorted into the sitting room, and the rage that rolls off my husband and brothers is strong enough to feel, and yet I no longer care.

I wouldn't wish what he did to me on anyone, but I've moved past it without even noticing. This man no longer holds any power over my life. His presence here is insignificant at best, and that brings a smile to my lips.

Watching him bow to Rhys doesn't hurt either, in reality.

Maddox pulls me against his side, blocking Monty's direct view of me.

Ever my protective dark prince.

"Have a seat, Montgomery. I believe we have some things

to discuss." Rhys pulls a folder from the end table and throws it down between him and Monty.

My former fiancé's cold eyes leer at me, seething, and I simply smile in return.

I definitely got the better end of the fallout from our engagement, and I'm not even a little bit sorry.

"What is this?" he asks as he picks up the folder before Atticus clears his throat.

"Your highness," Atticus warns. "What is this, *your highness*?"

Okay... well if we're being technical...

"Actually, it's *your grace* now," I add with a bit of satisfaction I hadn't expected to feel at the chance to correct this douchey duke.

Okay, maybe I don't *hate* him, but antagonizing him isn't so bad.

Monty bites his tongue as his nostrils flare, and he finally begins to flip through the folder, his ruddy red cheeks darkening with each new page that he skims. Once he gets to the end, the folder is slammed back on the table, and he stands, blustering, "It's nonsense. None of that is real. I never—we never. My family business isn't a criminal empire. Elections haven't been tampered with."

He takes a step forward, and Rhys clears his throat the tiniest bit, causing one of his protection officers to make a matching step forward, and Monty blanches and sits back down. After a moment, he gathers his composure and attempts to defend himself. "My family has never bought an election. This has all been fabricated. We can prove it."

"Can you though?" Atticus asks, and I'm fairly certain it's the first time Monty has ever been forced to realize he has no control over what's happening around him.

"This would ruin my father... my family."

"See, that right there..." Rhys crosses his one leg at the

knee and leans forward, like he's just getting started. "Assuming I care about you is your first mistake. Assuming I'm above hurting you when you had no problem hurting my family . . . That's your second. You see, I don't like people who hurt my family. I don't agree with preying on the weak, and while my sister may be mentally and emotionally stronger than you could ever hope to be, you are twice her size. You overpowered her and outweighed her when you hit her, bruising her face and knocking her to the floor. And then you proceeded to kick her." Rhys's words are measured and frighteningly calm. Like a venomous snake that's simply waiting for you to become frightened enough to move before he strikes. "Don't deny it. I saw the bruises. I know what you did. The question is do you know what I do to people who hurt my family?"

Monty swallows, looking like he's about to soil himself.

"You don't really expect me to believe you're going to kill me, Rhys?"

Ohh . . . Not the right answer.

"The three people behind me are the only people who will ever call me Rhys again, you ignorant little shit. I'm your fucking king. And if I wanted to kill you, you'd already be dead. Lucky for you, Maddox had other ideas."

I stare at my husband, shocked as he grins.

"I wanted to kill you at first too," Maddox admits, like he just admitted he jaywalked. "But then someone told me there's a way to make a man suffer a fate worse than death. A longer, more painful fate."

My husband's body language may be perceived as nonchalant, but the tight hold he has on me sends a shiver racing down my spine.

"And I thought . . . what would that be for someone like you, Monty? See, if I were my father, or apparently Rhys, I'd have just killed you. But that would have been too easy. Even if I made you suffer. Even if I pulled your nail beds from your fingers . . . then strung you up . . . and sliced hundreds of tiny cuts into your skin before I dipped you in gasoline just to hear you scream. I mean, I could do that for a few days before I set you on fire, but that would mean the suffering would still end, eventually. I mean . . . how long can you torture a man for?" He looks past me to Atticus. "A week? Two?"

"That's not enough, now is it?" Atticus answers, shaking his head.

"No, that's not enough. Not for hurting my wife and my son. Because that pain ends." Maddox lays it out there for Monty to absorb. "But this . . . taking away everything that matters to you. Your money. Your title. Your family land and family home. Your social standing and good name . . ." Maddox's smile is cruel and unforgiving, and I'm so glad he loves me because this man has a dark side I've never seen before now. But I can't say if someone hurt him or Brennan, I wouldn't feel the same way. "Now that's the way to break a man like you."

"But . . ." His knees start to shake. "You wouldn't just be hurting me. You'd be destroying my parents. You can't destroy them." Spittle flies from his mouth as desperation sinks in, and he realizes just how serious they are. He looks at me, petrified, and I'm completely indifferent.

I'm not enjoying this, but I'm not going to stop it either.

"Lennon . . . You can't let them do this."

"You mean the way you couldn't kick me? The way you couldn't knock me down, and leave me alone on the floor after I'd hit my head and blacked out?" Even saying the words brings bile up my throat. The fear I felt. . . The heartache as I rode to the hospital, scared I'd lost Brennan before I'd even gotten the chance to hold him. "Sorry, Monty.

I don't hate you enough to be part of this. But I love me enough to know better than to get in the middle of it too."

"My wife is far too kind to be part of this, Hastings. This part was my idea. To destroy the man, you destroy what he loves. That was me. Rhys and Atticus were the ones who found out what your parents were involved in. I was just the guy who knew the guys who could make it look like you were involved too. I mean, you were involved enough. But let's face it, you're not smart enough to be the mastermind. Though that's not what these documents say. And this way, the world will think you're the one who brought down the Hastings family. You'll be the reason your title is taken away and your accounts are seized." Maddox kisses the top of my head. "You'll be the reason you spend the rest of your life behind bars and can never hurt the people I love again."

"Lennon . . . you can't let them—"

I turn to Maddox, completely apathetic to anything Monty is saying and press my palm to my husband's chest. "I'm tired, and I want to see our son. Can we leave now?"

And because he loves me enough to know I've seen enough, he kisses my temple and calms my soul. "As you wish, *principessa*."

"You know what?" I look at Monty one last time. "It does feel pretty good to be the one leaving you while you sit here helpless." I drop a kiss on Rhys's cheek and squeeze Atticus's hand. "I'll see you at home." Then with my husband's hand on my back, we walk out of the room and away from that chapter of my life.

Chapter 31

With every smile I see from my son, I fall more in love with his father.

—Lennon's Secret Thoughts

"Come on, can't you stay for Christmas? We're going to light the tree in front of the palace next week." Atticus has been trying to push our flight off for days. This morning is his last full push while we have breakfast, just the four of us and Brennan.

Amelia and Sam left a few days ago, while Maddox and I decided to stay a few extra days, so I could introduce him to my country. But now it's time to go back to reality.

"I'm sorry to miss it, but we have to get back. Our life is in Kroydon Hills." The words hurt to say, but yet, I know they're my truth now. I look forward to bringing Brennan and Maddox back in a few months for the official coronation. But our home isn't here. "We're going to try to stay longer for the coronation. I promise."

I sit back and rest my head on Maddox's shoulder as I watch Rhys blow raspberries on Brennan's tummy. His little legs curl up toward his body as his tiny belly laughs rip through him.

Maddox tugs my hair, and I close my eyes.

I hate this.

I doubt leaving will ever get easier.

Especially now, when I finally feel like I've gotten a piece of my home back.

"We'll talk next week about housing options," Rhys adds, matter-of-factly. "There are plenty of homes on the property. You'll need a base when you come in to visit." He looks at Maddox and tucks Brennan against his chest. "Maybe you could open up a restaurant here one day."

"Maybe," Maddox agrees and stands, then pulls me to my feet. "You ready, *tesoro*?"

I nod quietly, unable to force the words out. I reach for Brennan and laugh when Rhys turns him away.

"He's going to be so much bigger by the time you come back."

"Aww . . . Do you think the people know their king is a big softy?" I steal my baby back and snuggle him against my chest. "It might help with the search for a queen."

"I'm only a softy for you and this little boy, got it?" He pulls me into his chest and kisses my head, then Brennan's. "Take care of her, Beneventi."

"With my life, your highness," Maddox answers, and I think it's the first time he's gotten that right, not that Rhys cares.

Both my brothers laugh.

"When it's the people in this room, you never need to bother with that shit, shithead." If people heard Rhys talk like this, they'd never believe it was him. Atticus maybe, but not Rhys.

"Seriously," Atticus groans dramatically. "Just don't. If you two start doing it while you're here, he'll expect me to do it when you're gone, and I really don't have the energy to kiss his royal ass in private the way I have to kiss it in public."

Smothering a laugh, I press a quick kiss to Atticus's cheek. "I love you."

"I'm proud of you, little sister."

One of Rhys's assistants walks into the room. "Ma'am. Your car is here."

I pull back and look at Maddox as tears burn the back of my lids. "Could you take him for a moment?"

Maddox takes Brennan from me, and I throw one arm around Rhys and one around Atticus. "Promise we'll do better than our prior generation."

"You already are doing better, Lennon. Now Atticus and I just need to follow your lead."

"Yeah, little sister." Atticus pulls back. "And just because this one's family owns a football team, don't feel like you need to be a convert, okay?"

"Never," I wipe a stray tear from my eye and grab my purse from the table. "I love you guys. We'll see you again soon."

As I walk into Maddox's arms, I know, unlike every other time I've left Mornea, this time I really will be coming back soon because my brothers are going to create an environment I want my son proud to be a part of.

Maddox

Once we get Brennan down for a nap, I convince Lennon to lie down on the bed in the back room of the jet and pull her in close to me. She's been quiet since we left Lilihill House, and it's not often my wife gets stuck in her own head. "You doing okay, *principessa*?"

She rests her head on my chest and wraps her arm around my waist. "I will be. But for now, I'm trying to focus on going home and enjoying our first Christmas as a family in our house. With our son and our dog, who I miss terribly, by the way. I just wish there was a way my brothers could be there too."

I bury my face in her hair and drag my hand up and down her spine. "We'll go back as much as you want. I promise. We'll make it work. And if you tell me you want us to move to Mornea, we can figure it out. I'm not saying it would be easy, but I'd make it work for you."

"I know you would, and I love you for that." She lifts her head to look at me. "But our life is in Kroydon Hills. I just want to make sure we go back a few times a year, okay?"

"You still sure you don't want to give Brennan a title? Rhys may have mentioned to me that it was still an option." I know where I stand on this particular decision, but I need her to know if she wants to change her mind, she can.

"No. No titles. I want him to have more choices than Rhys or Atticus or I did. I want him to love Mornea and his family. But I want him to never feel the pressure to live his life for his country. Everyone thinks royals are so glamorous and that it's such a fun life to lead. They don't realize we'd trade places in a heartbeat for just one tenth of the freedom."

"You still happy with your decision to marry a commoner?" I tease, just to watch her cheeks flush.

"You mean was the destruction we left in our wake worth our happily ever after?" She presses her lips to mine and hums. "One day, you'll realize you saved me, Maddox Beneventi. You saved me in the snow. You saved me from a life that would have killed me a little each day. You saved me from growing old, unloved and locked in a hell with a man I despised. Because of you, I get to live a life I never dreamed of having. So yes, it was worth all the pain and fighting and heartache. It was worth it all because I get to have you and our beautiful boy."

I cup her face in my hands and brush my lips over hers. "I will love you with my dying breath, Lennon Beneventi. Then I'll find you again and love you forever."

"Ohh . . ." She looks up at me with that smile I'll never get tired of pulling from her. "That was a good answer."

"Good enough for a little slow and steady?"

She looks over at Brennan. "Think we can be quiet?"

"I think we can try."

The first time I saw her, she took my breath away.
And every time I kiss her, she breathes life back into me.

—*Maddox's Secret Thoughts*

"I warned you my family takes Christmas Eve pretty seriously, *tesoro*." Lennon looks at me with a green tinge to her cheeks as she lies tucked into my parents' couch, as Nonna and my mother add another fish dish to their Feast of the Seven Fishes dinner. Lennon made it through one fish before she turned green. "If you didn't like calamari, you didn't have to eat it."

"I love calamari. I didn't even eat it. It was the smell. Something about the smell sent my stomach reeling," she whispers and closes her eyes. "I can't decide if I want to throw up or just lie here and pray it passes."

"Come with me," Caitlin announces as she takes Lennon's hand and pulls her from the couch.

"Cait . . . Slow down. I think I'm going to be sick."

I watch as Caitlin says something I can't hear, and the two of them head out of the room.

"Where are they going?" Callen asks as he moves next to me with a plate of calamari in his hand.

I take a crunchy bite and pop it into my mouth. "No clue. But these taste great."

"They smell fine too," Callen adds as he sniffs the plate. "I don't think it was the fish.

"Fuck. If she gets the flu, do I have to keep her away from Brennan?" I ask, hoping Callen has the answer, but he shakes his head.

"How long before we should start worrying what they're doing up there?"

I look past him at the empty stairs. "Maybe Cait's got Lennon lying down in her old room."

"Under the poster she's got up there of Lennon's brother Rhys? That's a little creepy."

Dad laughs as he joins us. "You're mother remodeled Caitlin's room last year. No more posters of princes. Lennon's safe for now. What are the girls doing?"

Callen and I shrug.

"My money's on getting Lennon something to feel better," Callen throws out, like we're betting on a horse race.

"Maybe." I think about it. "Lennon looked like she was going to puke when Cait took her upstairs."

Nonna walks in and takes the plate out of Callen's hand. "The table is set for you to eat sitting down. Not to walk around like you're in a food court."

"Sorry, Nonna." Callen still sounds the same as he did when he'd fuck up as a little kid and have to apologize to Nonna for crushing her rose bushes with a football. "We're trying to figure out what the girls are doing upstairs."

"Oh, for Pete's sake. She's green and queasy and tired and emotional. She's pregnant. The girls are probably talking about that."

"I'm sorry?" My voice rises to an octave I didn't know I could hit. "What?"

"No fucking way," Callen groans, and Nonna smacks the back of his head.

"Language, Callen."

Dad smiles skeptically. "Pretty sure that's not it, Nonna. That's just Lennon being postpartum."

Nonna doesn't look convinced and starts muttering in Italian as she walks away.

"She's wrong, right?" I grasp at straws, and I start thinking about the past few weeks.

She has been extra emotional.

And extra tired.

And her boobs have been so sensitive, but I thought that was just a nursing thing . . . And a fucking fantastic thing. God, I love her tits. But seriously . . . she can't be.

Oh, fuck me . . .

I hand Callen my beer and take the steps two at a time. No sooner have I hit the top step than I hear her crying. Or maybe it's Caitlin. Shit. Or both of them.

I turn back around and whisper-yell down the stairs, "Hey, Callen. Get your ass up here."

When he gets to the top, he stops and looks at me. "The fuck?"

Like two jackasses scared to set off a bomb, we basically tiptoe down the hall and stand outside Caitlin's childhood bedroom, staring. "Knock, man. She's *your* wife," I tell him.

"Dude, my wife wasn't green when she came up the stairs, and it's *your* parents' house. *You* fucking knock."

Lucky comes out of his bedroom across the hall and shoves open Caitlin's door without knocking. "They've been crying for ten minutes. Fucking fix it. I'm trying to concentrate in here."

I don't even want to know what the little shithead is

concentrating on because as soon as I look in the room, I find my sister and my wife both sitting with their asses on the floor and their backs against the bed. Matching red faces are covered in tears, and they're each holding a pregnancy test.

"Somebody want to explain what the hell is going on?" Callen asks, clearly not catching the tests in their hands.

And the look my sister gives him means she's unimpressed. "What's going on is that I have an eight-month-old downstairs, and you managed to knock me up again, you jackass."

I tune out whatever those two are saying as I stare down at my wife, who's refusing to look up at me. But judging by the white test strip with the giant pink plus sign, I'm guessing Caitlin's not the only one who just passed this test with flying colors. I squat down and pick her up, then carry her into my old bedroom, looking for a little privacy. Once I've sat down on the bed with Lennon in my lap, I brush her hair from her face, turning her to look at me. "Want to tell me something, *amore*?"

She looks at me with crocodile tears pouring down her face. "How come you only speak Italian words when they're romantic?"

"What?" I ask, completely caught off guard. "I do not."

"You do. You use my love for the way you sound speaking Italian to get into my pants. Admit it."

"Baby . . ." I try not to laugh at her because I'm pretty sure she's serious. "I don't know. My dad always used to do that to my mom. It just kind of seemed natural. And you never gave me shit when I'd call you *principessa* the way you would when I called you princess. Plus, *principessa* means something different in my world. It doesn't just mean that you're a princess, it means you're *my* princess. It isn't something I've ever called anyone but you."

"Are you going to be mad if I tell you I'm pregnant again?" she asks softly.

"Pretty sure you didn't get that way by yourself, Lennon. Why would I be mad?" Shocked maybe . . . but not mad. "Are you okay?"

"I don't know. It hasn't really sunk in yet." She wipes the tears from her face and blinks away the remainder from her lashes. "Brennan isn't even two months old. What are we going to do?"

"We're going to order another crib and convert one of the spare bedrooms into a nursery. And then maybe we're going to hire someone to come in and help you, but this seems like a lot on your body." My mind is going into fix-it mode, but my heart . . . my heart is fucking melting. "Maybe I shouldn't love the idea of you pregnant again, but I kinda do. I didn't get to do all those early months with you last time. This time, we know right away. And this time, we can go through it together."

"You and your super sperm had better plan on fucking me a whole lot during this pregnancy because I swear to God, I may never let you near me again after this one." She's not serious. No matter how hard she's fighting to keep a straight face. "We're going to have another baby."

I lean my forehead against hers. "We're going to have another baby."

"I want an epidural this time," she whispers.

"I'll make sure you get there on time, if it means we have to camp out in the hospital parking lot," I promise her.

"You do love me," she laughs.

"More than anything in the world, *principessa*."

"No more Italian. It makes me want to do naughty things."

I drop her down on the bed with a bounce. "It's not like you can get more pregnant."

Lennon circles her arms around my neck and presses her lips to mine. "No. No, it's not."

"Fucking gross. Shut the door," Lucky yells, and Lennon and I both laugh.

I look at the open door. Guess I should have closed that. "Maybe if we fuck up Lucky enough, we won't screw up our own kids."

"Pretty sure it doesn't work that way." Her pretty eyes dance with mischief. "Want to give it a try, *amore*?"

"Ohh... Using my own Italian against me, huh?"

Lennon's face lights up as she smiles and nods. "Is it working?"

"Yeah, baby. It's working... I love you."

"Only ever you, Maddox."

"Until my last breath, Lennon."

The End

Want more Lennon & Maddox?
Download their extended epilogue!

Download the extended epilogue here

The Philly Press

KROYDON KRONICLES

NOT READY TO SAY GOODBYE YET?

Did you think it was over?
Do you want more?

Have you been waiting patiently for Bellamy Wilder to find her Prince Charming?
What if he turned out to be a King?

Preorder Rhys & Bellamy's book, Striking, below!

WHAT COMES NEXT?

If you haven't seen my next series, Love & Legacy, will be starting this summer with Sweet Temptation.

In this series, you'll get the chance to fall in love with a different second generation character from each of the original 5 Kings Of Kroydon Hills couples:

Brady & Nattie from All In
Murphy & Sabrina from More Than A Game
Declan & Annabelle from Always Earned, Never Given
Bash & Lenny from Under Pressure
Cooper & Carys from Worth The Risk

Are you ready to see which Kroydon Hills resident falls next?

Make sure to preorder *Sweet Temptation*, book 1 in *Love & Legacy*, to see what these second generation characters are up to…

Preorder Sweet Temptation Below

#KroydonKronicles #Striking #SweetTemptation

NOTE TO THE READER

Approximately 1 in 3 women and 1 in 4 men will experience domestic violence in their lifetime.

If you or anyone you know is a victim of domestic violence, please reach out.
You are not alone.

National Domestic Violence Hotline:
1-800-799-7233

ACKNOWLEDGMENTS

Thank you so much to my family for all your support. My husband and children are my world, and my time with them often gets sacrificed for my time with these characters.

To my incredible momager, Bri. One more down and an infinite number of books still to go. Thank you for managing my business and my life.

Thank you to my amazing team. I cannot imagine doing this without each and every one of you. Dena, Hannah, Morgan, Kari, Tammy, Jen, Valentine, Val, Julie and Shannon - I have no words big enough to show my appreciation. And to my Happy Hunting girlies, thanks for cheering me on. Maddox & Lennon are better because of you.

As always, my biggest thanks goes to you, the reader, for taking a chance on Maddox & Lennon, and this fictional town I love so much. I hope you enjoyed reading *Breathtaking* as much as I've enjoyed writing it.

ABOUT THE AUTHOR

Bella Matthews is a *USA Today* & #1 Amazon Bestselling author. She is married to her very own Alpha Male and raising three little ones. You can typically find her running from one sporting event to another. When she is home, she is usually hiding in her home office with the only other female in her house, her rescue dog Tinker Bell by her side. She likes to write swoon-worthy heroes and sassy, smart heroines. Sarcasm is her love language and big family dynamics are her favorite thing to add to each story.

Stay Connected

Amazon Author Page: https://amzn.to/2UWU7Xs
Facebook Page: https://www.facebook.com/Bella.Matthews.Author
Reader Group: https://www.facebook.com/groups/bellamatthewsgamechangers
Instagram: https://www.instagram.com/bellamatthews.author/
Bookbub: https://bit.ly/BMBookbub
Goodreads: https://bit.ly/BMGoodreads
TikTok: http://tiktok.com/@bellamatthewsauthor
Newsletter: https://bit.ly/BMNLsingups
Patreon: https://www.patreon.com/BellaMatthews

ALSO BY BELLA MATTHEWS

Kings of Kroydon Hills

All In

More Than A Game

Always Earned, Never Given

Under Pressure

Restless Kings

Rise of the King

Broken King

Fallen King

The Risks We Take Duet

Worth The Risk

Worth The Fight

Defiant Kings

Caged

Shaken

Iced

Overruled

Haven

Playing To Win

The Keeper

The Wildcat

The Knockout

The Sweet Spot

Red Lips & White Lies

Tempting

Redeeming

Enticing

Captivating

Teasing

Breathtaking

Striking

Love & Legacy

Sweet Temptation

Sweet Surrender

Sweet Addiction

Sweet Salvation

Sweet Oblivion

CHECK OUT BELLA'S WEBSITE

Scan the QR code or go to http://authorbellamatthews.com to stay up to date with all things Bella Matthews

www.ingramcontent.com/pod-product-compliance
Ingram Content Group UK Ltd.
Pitfield, Milton Keynes, MK11 3LW, UK
UKHW040809020625
6187UKWH00037B/343